WINNIPEG
WITHDRAWN
D0426076

BE NOT AFRAID

ALSO BY CECILIA GALANTE

The Patron Saint of Butterflies
The Sweetness of Salt

BE NOT AFRAID

Cecilia Galante

RANDOM HOUSE NEW YORK

 Published in the United States by
Random House Children's Books, a division of Random House LLC,
a Penguin Random House Company, New York.

Visit us on the Web! randomhouseteens.com

Educators and librarians, for a variety of teaching tools,
visit us at RHTeachersLibrarians.com

Library of Congress Cataloging-in-Publication Data
Galante, Cecilia.
Be not afraid / Cecilia Galante.—First edition.
p. cm.
Summary: Since her mother's suicide, high school junior Marin
has been able to see others' pain as colors and shapes,
but what she sees in the head of classmate Cassie, who forced her to participate
in a weird conjoining rite, is much more frightening and deadly.
ISBN 978-0-385-37274-9 (trade)—ISBN 978-0-385-37277-0 (ebook)
[1. Demoniac possession—Fiction. 2. Occultism—Fiction.
3. Catholics—Fiction.
4. Family problems—Fiction.] I. Title.
PZ7.G12965Bf 2015 [Fic]—dc23 2014009301

Printed in the United States of America
10 9 8 7 6 5 4 3 2 1
First Edition

Random House Children's Books supports
the First Amendment and celebrates the right to read.

For Paul

Do not be afraid;
Our fate cannot be taken from us;
It is a gift.

DANTE ALIGHIERI, *INFERNO*

What evil can the Devil do to me,
if I am a servant of God?
Why should I not have the fortitude
to engage in combat with all of hell?

SAINT TERESA OF AVILA

One

The sinister thing about chaos is how quietly it begins. How slowly. There's no fanfare, no excitement. It trickles its way in like water through a crack, so silently that you might not even notice it's there.

Until you realize that you are wet.

Shivering.

Drowning.

The evil leaked into St. Anselm High School silently. But on a Thursday during Lent, the dam broke loose, writhing, furious, demanding to be acknowledged. We'd already been directed to head to the auditorium for Mass. I shuffled along grudgingly with the rest of the herd, tucking my copy of *One Flew Over the Cuckoo's Nest* inside the back of my skirt. There was a sudden jostling, followed by a shrill voice behind me.

"Excuse me, young lady! Young lady! The one with the book! Excuse me!"

I ducked my head as Sister Paulina's voice followed me, and I pushed my sunglasses up along the bridge of my nose. I knew she was addressing me, but I had no intention of giving her my book, even if she did outweigh me by at least seventy-five pounds, and even if she was the vice principal.

"Ex*cuse* me." The nun yanked me out of line, pulling me by the wrist. "Marin." Her prunelike face seemed to tighten even more at the recognition. "I know you heard me calling you." She reached around, snatching the book out of my waistband, and regarded the cover cryptically. "You know very well that you are not allowed to bring anything into services. Especially reading material that hasn't been cleared by the English department."

Even from behind my dark glasses, I could make out the wide orange band that ran the width of the woman's forehead. It pulsed at the ends, just above the temples, where a wiry piece of gray hair poked out beneath her wimple, and then grew lighter in the middle. A nasty headache if I'd ever seen one. Maybe even the beginnings of a migraine.

I reached for my book, momentarily sympathetic. "I'm sorry. I'll put it away."

Sister Paulina held it up, just out of reach. "Actually, I think I'll keep it."

"But it's mine."

"I know it's yours." The nun's eyes disappeared into little slits. "And you will get it back. After the service."

"I promise I won't read it." I knew that it was futile to argue with her, that it would just make things worse. But I didn't care. The truth was, I needed the book. I couldn't go inside that auditorium, even with my sunglasses on, without something to distract my eyes from the hundreds, maybe even thousands, of different shapes and colors of pain I would see once I stepped inside.

"I know you won't read it. Because it will be in my possession." Sister Paulina paused for a moment, as if deciding what to say next. "You know, Marin, we've already made quite a few concessions for you here at St. Anselm's. At the very least, you could show a little gratitude by following the basic rules of the school."

Technically, I couldn't argue. She was right. Concessions had been made since I'd started my junior year at the new school this past fall. In exchange for Nan's nightly cleaning services at the school and Dad's assistance in rebuilding the roof on the new gym, my tuition had been reduced to almost nothing. And after Nan had gone to the principal, a short, dark-haired priest named Father Nickolas, and explained the whole "light sensitivity" problem with my eyes, he gave me permission to wear my dark sunglasses all day, in each of my classes. The explanation was a lie, of course; my eyes weren't sensitive to light. But my need to wear dark glasses was very real, since they dulled the sometimes blindingly sharp colors of the pain shapes I saw. I didn't know why I saw blots and orbs inside everyone who crossed my path, or what it meant that I could. The phenomenon had started a little over a year ago, and nobody could make any sense of it, especially me. But the dark glasses did make the overwhelming sight of them more bearable. It was something.

Still, I felt a flare of anger as Sister Paulina spoke. I resented that any allowances had been brought up, as if the nun wanted to make it clear that not only was my family in her debt, but also that it was an obligation that could never be repaid. This woman had no idea about the true depth of any of our sacrifices or what they meant to me. No one did.

"The concessions that Father *Nickolas* has made for my family," I said, my voice as tight as pulled string, "are between him and us."

Sister Paulina's upper lip twitched. "Us and *him*," she corrected. "And I don't think I like your tone. In case you need reminding, I work side by side with Father Nickolas. Whatever gratuities he extends to students, I am always consulted about first. If I take issue with something, it rarely goes through." She tapped the book against the heel of her palm to emphasize her words.

I glanced down at the movement and immediately wished I hadn't. Inside the nun's hands, I could make out a string of blue shapes. They wound their way in and around the tops of her knuckles and sped along methodically, like beads on a moving necklace. Arthritis. Nan had the same ones in her hands, although they were much bigger than these, and brighter blue. At night, after she returned from washing the floors at the school, they were so large and vivid that they looked like sapphires. I sat up with her on those nights, watching as she rubbed menthol-scented liniment along the length of her fingers until they faded to a dull turquoise color. It was the only thing that helped.

"Fine," I said. "Can I go now?"

"Yes, I think we're done here," Sister Paulina said. "You may go." There was an air of satisfaction about her, an unspoken sense that she had won the argument.

I stalked off, swallowing the ugly words that knocked against the back of my teeth. I hated adults like her, people who took pains to single someone out and then grind them under their heel for good measure. The old crow. I knew perfectly well that it was inappropriate to read a book during Mass, but I was also pretty sure that God would understand, considering the circumstances. She was lucky I even came to services at all, instead of hiding out in the boiler room like Meredith Wrigley and Olivia Sanders always did. I didn't even *go* to Mass outside of school anymore. Neither did Dad. Sunday-morning services were just another piece of our old life that we had dropped after moving here last summer from Maine, the meaning behind it lost now, and unimportant.

As I entered the auditorium, the sight before me was staggering, a galaxy of colors in every size and hue. It amazed me just how much pain people carried around every day. Everyone, it seemed, had something inside. The room thrummed under the weight of a thousand different-sized orange bands; yellow eggs; pink and purple and blue dots; and green half-moons, some of them clustered tightly together like grapes, others loose and floating like specks of dust. They swam and hovered and bumped inside bodies in every direction, each one an indication of some type of discomfort: a headache or a stomach virus, a sprain, a broken bone, a cavity, anorexic starvation, tiny cuts hidden under shirt sleeves, bruises, bleeding hangnails, rotting teeth, and eye infections. I could feel the breath catch in the back of my throat as I tried to take it all in, and a vague nausea began to rise from deep within my belly. Without my book, I would have no other choice but to sit there in the middle of it all, with my eyes closed, until Mass ended and we were dismissed.

"Marin! Over here!"

Off to the right, a tiny white arm shot up through the sea of colors like a flag. Relieved, I smiled and headed toward it. Thank God for Lucy Cooper, who, since taking a seat on the bus across from me a few months ago, had attached herself to me in the oddly desperate way I had hoped someone would. We were far from best friends. I held her at arm's length the way I did everyone else, but I liked her. She didn't belong to a clique, which already put her in another league all her own. From what I could tell, flying solo in high school meant one of two things: you were ahead of your time and had already developed the good sense not to get sucked in by all the high school drama, or you had at some point closed yourself off from everyone around you. I was starting to get the feeling that Lucy was more of the second type, which was fine by me, since I always stayed on the edge of everything, never quite bringing myself to attach to anyone or anything, and Lucy seemed like that too. Plus, she was funny. And a little bit weird, in a genuinely nice way. For example, she never went anywhere without some kind of candy, and she always had a tiny dental floss dispenser in her back pocket.

"Over here!" Lucy yelled again. "I got you a seat right on the end."

"Hey." I slid in next to her, glancing at the yellow blob inside her stomach, which, if I didn't know any better, looked like a bit of scrambled egg. It was fairly new, something I'd noticed only a few weeks ago, and seemed to get the slightest bit larger every time I saw it. I still wasn't sure what it was, but it didn't look like anything to worry about. "Thanks. I was just starting to freak out."

Lucy tilted her head to one side. "Marin. I told you on the bus that I'd save you a seat at Mass. And then I reminded you again at lunch. Don't you remember?"

I shook my head, grateful and embarrassed by Lucy's fretting. She had no idea about my ability to see pain, but she had also for some reason decided that I needed regular looking after, something she did with an inordinate attention to detail. Once, after I realized I had forgotten my lunch money, she not only paid for my meal, but also created an emergency lunch fund for future occurrences, keeping the $2.40 in a small ziplock bag inside her backpack. I'd had to use it twice.

"I brought crack," she whispered, dipping a hand inside her bag and withdrawing a package of strawberry Twizzlers. Lucy called all candy crack. "I have Tootsie Rolls, too, if you're not feeling the fruity vibe. Take as much as you want. Just don't make any noise opening it. And definitely don't let anyone see it."

I selected a piece of licorice from the bag, taking pains not to crinkle the wrapper. Lucy's weight and shape made her look more like a ten-year-old than a fifteen-year-old, but as if in recompense for her size, she had been blessed with an unusually beautiful face. Her almond-shaped eyes were a deep shade of gray flecked with little bits of blue, and her skin was the color of cream. Offset with dark black hair that she wore in a different style every day, at times she looked more like a porcelain doll than an actual girl.

"Why are you so late getting here, anyway?" she asked. "I've been waiting for you for, like, ten minutes." Her hair was in two braids today, coiled into tight buns behind her ears, and I could see a small red disk in the back of her mouth. Cavity number three.

"Oh, Sister Paulina got ahold of me." I scowled. "She pulled me aside out there and read me the riot act."

"Sister Paulina?" Lucy's eyes got big. "Why? What'd you do?" Lucy had a weird fear of people in authority; people like nuns and priests practically made her hyperventilate.

Sometimes I wondered if it had something to do with the fact that everyone looked so big compared to her.

"I didn't do anything. I was just reading one of my books on the way in, and she saw it and freaked." I bit the end of the Twizzler. "She's so annoying."

Lucy sank down close to me. "Well, you know how they all are about Mass. You gotta keep your eyes fixated on the altar the whole time or they'll wig out. Which reminds me." She pushed my hand with the licorice in it down between the seats. "Keep the crack out of sight."

I stiffened as a shriek of plastic laughter sounded over my left shoulder. The falseness in that voice was unmistakable, like an alarm going off in the middle of the room. My whole body tightened as Cassie Jackson drifted down the aisle, the edge of her skirt inches away from my elbow. I didn't look up, but I could feel her eyes boring into me, two drills in the side of my face. My heart pounded in my chest, the blood rushing to my ears. I'd only been here for a couple of months when she invited me over to her house. I'd gone hesitantly, as I barely knew her, and it hadn't ended well. Now I did everything possible to keep away from her, even taking crazy detours in the cafeteria and staying late after class so that I wouldn't run into her in the hallway. Still, just her presence, even from afar, could make the hair on the back of my neck prickle.

As Cassie drifted down the rest of the aisle, Lucy nodded knowingly and patted my arm. "She's gone," she whispered. "Don't worry."

"Where's she sitting?" I spoke through clenched teeth, not raising my head.

"She's down near the front. Pretty far away, actually." Lucy didn't know the details of what had occurred between me and Cassie, but the fact that Cassie was one of the most popular girls at St. Anselm's, combined with the vicious looks she continued to shoot my way, made things pretty obvious. She'd figured out quickly that, for one reason or another, Cassie Jackson was mortal enemy number one. It was just one more thing for her to worry about when it came to me.

The strains of piano music filled the room as Ms. Mattern, the music teacher, began to bang out a hymn. On cue, the students rose as one and started to sing the opening song.

"You shall cross the barren desert, but you shall not die of thirst; You shall wander far in safety, though you do not know the way."

I took a deep breath and braced myself. Ms. Mattern played this hymn without fail at every Mass, and each time, it threw me off guard. Once, a long time ago, I had loved this song, had let it sweep me up in its strands of golden hopefulness when Mom and Dad had made me go to church. The words themselves had felt like a bridge of some kind, or an invisible barrier holding me up, blocking all the ills of the world, all the bad things I knew were out there.

"Be not afraid." Next to me, Lucy sang out in a soft voice, the words coming out of her mouth like tiny birds.

"I go before you always. Come follow Me, and I will give you rest."

For a few seconds, the words enveloped me like a salve on a burn, the way they used to. And then remembering, I steeled myself against them. It was all a lie, these pretty phrases, all just pretend. It was nothing more than a game, some ridiculous attempt to comfort people when they were drowning in sorrow, to give them the illusion that someone cared.

They weren't real.

God wasn't real.

I looked out of the corner of my eye as the Mass procession began to file past. Pairs of shoes appeared, glossy black loafers, blue leather flats, a set of black and red Saucony sneakers. My heart skipped a beat at the sight of the sneakers. I raised my eyes just a little, past the neatly pressed khaki pants and dark blue shirt, just in time to see the handsome, fleeting profile and then the back of Dominic Jackson's head. Something in my belly moved the way it always did when he came into view, and I could feel the tips of my ears getting hot. He was so good-looking and such a normal human being that it was hard to believe he was related to Cassie. But there it was. He was her older brother, a senior, last year's javelin star on the track-and-field team, and adored by legions of girls.

Lucy gave me a knowing nudge as Dominic moved past. I nudged her back, annoyed and secretly pleased that she knew I thought Dominic was cute. He held a Bible in his hands, raised up at eye level, and I could see a pale blue orb inside his wrist. A javelin injury? Maybe an old sprain. I stared at it as long as I could until he disappeared down the aisle.

Father Nickolas was next, with his odd cluster of yellow egg-shaped orbs inside his neck, followed by Father William, the parish priest at Sacred Heart, where Nan went to Mass every morning. He walked slowly, leaning on a cane, mouthing, "Hi, Marin," as he passed. I nodded back, giving him a small smile.

Since we'd moved, Nan had invited Father William over to the house for dinner a few times. He liked to stay afterward, sitting with her in the living room while they sipped glasses of warm whiskey and talked into the late hours. He was a nice man. Quiet. Easygoing. Quick to laugh, too, although I sensed a sadness about him, a heaviness that clouded his eyes and stooped his shoulders when he walked. Now, as he passed, I could make out the series of large, ruby-hued shapes beneath his heavy robes. They settled along the bottom half of his spine, glimmering like a string of fading Christmas lights as he made his way up the steps and shuffled in behind the altar.

"In the name of the Father, and the Son, and the Holy Spirit." Father William made the sign of the cross over the student body.

I closed my eyes as the priest began the opening prayers. It was Holy Week, which meant that the service would be a long one, maybe even twice the length of a usual Mass.

Around me, the sounds of familiar prayers filled the room, the lull of them creating a warm, drowsy effect. Even closed, my eyelids felt heavy. The steady cacophony of voices began to drift into the background.

Grnnnt! Sssst!

I opened my eyes with a start and tried to focus. Father William was behind the makeshift altar onstage, praying over the bread and wine. On the right, Dominic sat in a chair next to two other boys, who were acting as altar servers. His interlocked fingers hung down between his knees and he stared at the floor as if studying something between his shoes. Had they gotten this far into the Mass already? I must have fallen asleep, dreamed those weird noises. Maybe they'd even come from me. I snuck a glance at Lucy, but she was staring straight ahead, absorbed in the Mass. I exhaled and felt my muscles start to relax.

Until I heard it again, something that sounded like a low growl this time. It seemed to be coming from farther down, toward the front.

"What is that?" Lucy whispered, elbowing me. "Did you hear that noise?"

I raised myself up against the arms of my seat, ignoring the blur of colors and shapes that assaulted me, and looked in the direction the noise seemed to be coming from. For a split second, I wondered if I was imagining the sight before me. Cassie Jackson's head was thrown back against her seat. Her eyes were so wide open that they were bulging from inside her face, and her mouth was parted, as if she was struggling for air. Another hissing sound came out between her lips, and as it did, the students around her reared back and gasped.

"What is it?" Lucy whispered, tugging on my sleeve. "What's happening? I can't see anything."

"I don't know," I said. "It looks like Cassie. Is she sick, maybe?"

"Cassie Jackson?" Lucy hopped up on her seat now, folding both legs beneath her, and tried to see over my shoulder. "Why do you think she's sick? Is she throwing up?"

Up on the stage, Father William hesitated as he glanced in Cassie's direction. His voice began to intone a prayer: *"Then Jesus, taking the bread, broke it and said: 'This is my body, shed for you and all of your sins. Take and eat of it, in memory of me.'"*

At the sound of the words, Cassie began to pant. Her head lolled back and forth along the seat, and a vein in her neck bulged like rope. Father William raised the host up in the air with both hands and held it there. Suddenly, Cassie stood up. It was an abrupt, violent movement, as if someone had yanked her to her feet by an invisible string. Father William's arms dropped for an instant, and then he raised the host higher.

As he did, Cassie threw her head back. *"Nooooo!"* she screamed.

It was a horrific sound, murderous and high-pitched, and the stillness of the surroundings magnified it even more, as if a gun had just gone off in a graveyard. The auditorium seemed to gasp with one breath. Up on the altar, Dominic stared at his younger sister, his body leaning forward, both hands gripping the sides of his chair. Even Father William took a step back, the host still in his hands. The look of alarm and fear on his face was unmistakable. Two silent seconds passed as Cassie stood there, panting.

And then all hell broke loose.

"Take it away!" If Cassie's voice had been shrill before, now it was demanding and insistent. She pointed at the host on the altar and screamed a final time. "Take it away! Take it *away*!"

Mrs. Loftus, the freshman science teacher who weighed no more than a third grader and was sitting at the end of Cassie's row, had already leapt to her feet. She lunged for the girl, but Cassie swung her arms and gnashed her teeth, growling and spitting at the woman's outstretched hands. For a split second, I remembered a caged tiger I'd seen on a TV show, being trained to perform for a circus. Part of the training involved torturing the animal with electrical wires. Every time the electricity shot through it, the animal reacted like this: roaring, furious with its torturers, hell-bent on escaping. Students screamed as Cassie slapped and clawed at them, frantic to get out of the row she was in. Grim-faced teachers rushed in from all sides, trying to pick up where Mrs. Loftus, who was now standing with both hands pressed over her mouth, had left off.

"Cassandra Jackson!" Sister Paulina's voice soared above the melee with the preciseness of a bullet. She appeared from nowhere, pushing past the other teachers to get to Cassie. Her robes flapped around her like an enormous brown bird as she gestured in the girl's direction, both arms raised high over her head. "Cassandra! Cassie, look at me! Come here!"

If Cassie heard Sister Paulina, she gave no indication of it. She seemed intent instead on plowing down everyone who obstructed her path, pushing kids out of the way, even taking a flattened palm and shoving it against one boy's face so that she could get past. Dumbstruck, I watched as the nun nodded curtly at Mr. Bobeck, the gym teacher, who had sidled into the row behind Cassie. "Grab one of her arms, if you can!" she shouted. "I'll come around to the other side!"

Did they know what was wrong with her? Had something like this happened before? Did anyone know what to *do*?

Cassie gave an unnatural howl as Mr. Bobeck managed to grab one of her flailing arms and tried to drag her from the aisle. His bald head glimmered under the bright lights, and his jaw was set like a piece of flint. Just behind his rib cage, I could make out an oval-shaped yellow ball, pulsing like a miniature sun.

"Get *off* me!" Cassie screamed. She pulled backward, trying to twist her arm out of Mr. Bobeck's grasp, but he held on tight. Drawing her free arm back, she decked him hard under the chin. I flinched at the dull crack of bone meeting bone, a horrifying noise that seemed to reverberate long after it was gone. Mr. Bobeck let go of her arm and staggered backward, falling into the row of students behind him. Fresh screams rose up as he brought a hand to his face and struggled to right himself. Directly across the aisle from me, a chubby boy with red hair held up his phone and began to record the action.

"Let me out!" Cassie shrieked. She smacked at people, moving in the opposite direction of Sister Paulina, who was still edging in from the other end of the row. "Let me out! Let me out before it kills me!" She raked her nails down the sides of her cheeks as she screamed and twisted forward. "Get me out of here! Move! Move! Let me out!"

My fingers clutched the edge of my seat as Cassie stumbled up the aisle. This time, instead of reaching for her, students leaned back as she passed, not wanting to touch her, not wanting her to touch them.

Cassie was not one of the most beautiful girls in school. With her crooked teeth and slightly too-long nose, she had missed the Perfect Boat by an inch or two. Still, no one could say she was unattractive. Pretty even, in a hard sort of way. Now, though, she looked like an insane person, panting with effort, odd, guttural sounds coming out of her mouth like some kind of crazed animal. She clutched at the front of her St. Anselm's dress shirt, pulling it away from her skin as if it were hot, and bent over in half as she tried to make her way toward the door. Foot by foot, she staggered up the aisle.

And then two seats away from me, she stopped.

I drew back and held my breath. A bright purple orb glowed in the middle of her tongue, where a piercing was infected, and I could see red slash marks under her sleeves, where she had just scratched at the skin. For a few seconds, she swayed in front of me, as if trying to get her bearings. She looked disoriented, her long blond hair sticking out where she had been pulling it, the pupils in her brown eyes as large as nickels. Without warning, her whole face began to pulse and twitch, as if something behind the skin were pulling on tiny strings.

Next to me, Lucy whimpered and clutched my sleeve.

Despite my horror, I could not take my eyes off her. For a split second, everything around us fell away as we held each other's gaze. I braced myself for whatever might come next. For whatever *would* come next.

Cassie blinked rapidly, as if trying to bring my face into focus, and she fell to her knees. Raising her right arm, she pointed a finger in my direction. Her mouth contorted for a moment, like her lips were not quite sure how to work themselves, and her eyes widened. "You," she whispered. Her voice was hoarse, ragged around the edges. "It's *YOU*."

It was then that I thought I glimpsed something. Inside her head, deep behind her eyes. It was a pain shape I had never seen before, a nonshape really, an inky liquid seeping in and around the spaces of her skull. Just as quickly as it appeared, it vanished again, as if it had slipped around a corner. At the opposite end of the aisle, Mr. Bobeck held

Dominic by both arms; he was straining, twisting, pleading to get to his sister, his face stricken.

Without warning, Cassie collapsed, falling back so hard that I heard her head crack against the floor. She lay limp for several seconds, and then her body began to shake. Students screamed as her arms and legs thrashed from side to side. Her back arched and her fingers clenched into fists. A thin trickle of foam leaked out of the corner of her mouth, and her eyes, still wide open, protruded from her skull.

A horde of teachers descended around her, blocking my view, but I could hear their shouts—"She's having a seizure! Someone call nine-one-one! Where the hell is the nurse?"—until a single shriek sounded, rising above the rest of the din like a thread of smoke and winding its way up to the ceiling.

It was mine.

TWO

Someone brought me to a back room inside the main office, while Sister Paulina called Nan. Cassie had already been taken to the hospital, and I had been looked over by the school nurse, who, after determining that I was in a mild state of shock, advised that I be sent home for the rest of the day. It was cooler in the small room than it had been in the auditorium. An air conditioner hummed in one corner, and heavy red drapes covered the single window. The same portrait that hung in every classroom had been positioned on the far wall: a picture of a very good-looking Jesus, his narrow face and beautiful brown eyes framed by a cascade of thick, shoulder-length hair. *Hunky Jesus,* Lucy called him. St. Anselm's way of making Our Lord more approachable.

I felt a twinge, thinking of Lucy. She had insisted on

following me to the nurse's office and then remained there, hovering, refusing to leave.

"Luce, I'm okay," I said for what must have been the hundredth time. "Seriously. You can go."

"You're not okay," she kept insisting. "*I'm* not okay, and Cassie didn't even look at me." She pushed past the nurse, a short, fat woman named Mrs. Marcel who had a cluster of pink grapelike orbs inside her neck, and grabbed my hand. "What did that even mean, her saying 'It's you' like that? What was she talking about?"

"I don't know." Again. For the hundredth time.

"Do you think she was delirious or something?" Lucy kept talking as Mrs. Marcel put both hands on her shoulders and moved her out of the way. "I mean, it's possible that she was, right? Who knows *what* was going on in her brain? You know, I heard this rumor once about her grandmother. Cassie's grandmother. She was crazy or something. Like for real. So maybe Cassie is too. I mean, Marin, she stopped right in front of you. Like she *knew* something. The way she looked at you, and then the way she pointed . . . I'm telling you, she was—"

"Oh my God, please just *stop* it, okay?" I jumped off the small cot before I realized my legs had moved. My voice was close to a shout, and I was inches away from Lucy's face. "I told you a hundred times I have no idea what happened. Now just go away and leave me alone!"

Lucy's face seemed to crumple in on itself at my words, as if she might cry. For a moment, I thought I might too. I didn't shout at people. Ever. And I never got in their face the way I just had with her. What was wrong with me? Mrs. Marcel, who was still standing there, watching me with wary eyes, clapped her hands. "All right now, come on, Lucy. Marin needs to rest. Come on. Let's go."

I could feel Lucy looking at me over the nurse's big arm, her eyes already starting to rim with tears, but I stared at my shoes and bit the inside of my lip until the door closed. I winced now, still looking at the picture of Hunky Jesus, and then pulled out my phone. *I'm sorry I spazzed out on u,* I texted. She would reply in less than ten seconds, but that was okay. The apology had been made. I closed my eyes, my mind drifting, and tried not to think.

I'm fine. It was nothing, what I saw inside Cassie's head. Nothing at all. I'm fine. I'm totally fine.

". . . to go home and rest." Sister Paulina opened the door, still talking to Nan. "It was a very upsetting incident. For everyone." I stood up, steadying myself against the edge of the table. My fingers were trembling.

"Hello, my angel," Nan said, reaching for me with both arms. "Are you all right?"

"Yeah." I hugged my grandmother quickly, casually, not wanting her to worry any more than I knew she would. "I'm all right."

Nan was dressed in her usual uniform of baggy pants and a man's collared shirt with a red bandanna around her throat. Her white hair clouded the top of her head, and her eyes, blue as cornflowers, shone out from her wide face. The blue beads inside her fingers chugged along, just like they always did, a small train moving beneath her knuckles. But I could also make out a new, very small shape just below her left shoulder. It was pink, and no larger than a pea. I reached out and slid one of my hands into hers.

"You're sure you're feeling all right?" Sister Paulina peered at me with her dark eyes.

I struggled not to roll mine. The only thing worse than a fake was a fake in a habit. Someone whose whole life was supposed to be about *not* being fake. "Positive," I said.

"I'm so glad to hear you say that." The nun's eyes roved over me, as if looking for scars. "But I do want you to take it easy when you get home. Promise me." The wide orange band beneath her wimple was a deep tangerine color now, and it had begun to shimmer around the edges. She'd probably have to take something pretty soon, before it got too painful.

I stretched out my other arm, ignoring the command. "You said I could have my book back. After Mass."

Sister Paulina regarded my hand for a moment. It was still trembling.

"My book," I said. "*One Flew Over the Cuckoo's Nest?*"

She nodded and reached into the side of her robes, withdrawing the small paperback from a cavernous pocket. "It's wonderful that she reads so much on her own," she said, addressing Nan. "We can't *pay* kids these days to spend their free time without some kind of electronic device glued to their hands."

"Oh, Marin reads all the time," Nan said to the nun. "But why do you have her book?"

Sister Paulina glanced in my direction and raised an eyebrow.

"I was reading it on the way into services," I mumbled.

"Ah." Nan put a hand on my back as Sister Paulina nodded. She knew. I didn't have to go into any more detail. "Well, all right, then, Sister, if that's everything?"

A look of confusion flickered over the nun's face. Maybe she was hoping Nan would clap me on the back of the head or start yelling about how many times she had told me not to read during Mass. But then she caught herself. "Yes, yes, that's everything. You go home and rest now, Marin. And come back to us only when you're ready, you hear?" Her voice had adopted a clucking, falsetto quality, speaking to me now as if I were a second grader. "I mean it. You have my permission to take a full day or two. More, if you need it."

Nan nudged me when I did not answer. "Okay," I mumbled. "Thanks."

"You're very pale." Nan looked worried as we pushed through the front doors. "Do you want to go to the doctor?"

"No." I shook my head. "Absolutely not." I was through with doctors. For good. For an entire month after I'd told Dad and Nan about the things I was seeing, I'd been poked and prodded, examined up close like some sort of specimen on a microscopic slide. None of the doctors had been able to come up with any answers for my condition, and the series of tests they'd put me through—EKGs, CAT scans, MRIs—were returned with just as many blanks.

"Sister Paulina said that a girl had an epileptic seizure during Mass," Nan said, getting in the car. "Right in front of you?"

"Something like that."

"It must have been very frightening." She started the engine and turned the steering wheel, the blue beads pulsing a little under her movements. "I don't think I've ever seen someone have a seizure, not even in a movie. I can't imagine what it must have been like to see in person."

I looked out the window. Across the street, the large red dot of the Target store seemed to throb like a giant heartbeat. I was beginning to despise shapes of all kinds. Colors too. I looked away from it, steadying my gaze on the dull grain of asphalt instead.

It was nothing. What I thought I'd seen. Nothing at all.

"Marin?"

"Yeah." I adjusted my sunglasses, fiddled with a stray piece of hair just above my ear. "It was kind of scary, I guess. I just . . . I didn't really know what was happening. No one did. I didn't know what to do."

"Sister Paulina said the girl's name is Cassie Jackson?"

A knot tightened in the back of my throat. "Yeah."

"Isn't that the girl who invited you to her house at the beginning of the year?"

I nodded, picking at a tiny hole in the gray upholstery. I'd never told Nan or Dad what happened that day at Cassie's house, how she'd invited me over and then baited me into an argument. The fight had escalated until Cassie shoved me inside a dark closet and locked the door. It was a total bully move, like something a kindergartener might do after not getting her way. Still, it had been over an hour before someone heard me crying and screaming to be let out. Afterward, on my way home, I had taken the long way, even ducking inside a Barnes & Noble bathroom so I could splash cold water on my face until the swelling around my eyes went down. When Dad and Nan asked about the visit over dinner, I just shrugged. There was nothing about that visit that I was going to talk about. Not then. Not now. Not ever. "It was fine," I had said, and that was the end of it.

Now Nan glanced at me. "Are you two still friends?"

"No. We weren't ever friends."

"I didn't think so." Her forehead wrinkled, as if she was trying to sort something out. "Did something happen between you two? Lately, I mean?"

"No."

"It just seems strange that she would stop in front of you like that, don't you think?" She waited, but I didn't respond. "And Sister Paulina seemed to think she heard Cassie say something to you. Just before she had her fit?"

" 'You,' " I answered impatiently.

" 'You'?" Nan repeated.

" 'You,' " I said again. "She pointed at me and said, 'It's you.' "

"Why? What does that mean?"

"I have no idea. She freaked out on Father William too. Right up on the altar."

"Father William?" Nan braked a little too sharply at a stop sign. The car shuddered to a halt and then sagged back into place again. "While he was saying *Mass*?"

"Yeah, everything happened during Mass. She pointed at the host while he was raising it up and started screaming 'No' and 'Take it away.' Then when she was running up the aisle, she stopped and yelled at me too." The silence in the car passed with a beat. Even I could hear how insane the whole thing sounded. "Nan. The girl's totally mental. You heard Sister Paulina tell you she was epileptic. Who knows? She probably just got all confused when she ran up the aisle and then saw me and she just . . . stopped. Jesus Christ. I don't know."

"Marin." The reproach in Nan's voice was obvious. She was not big on taking the Lord's name in vain.

"Sorry. Geez, Louise, okay?"

Nan's fingers tightened around the wheel. She drove for a few moments without saying anything. Outside my window, I looked at the sudden green the trees had assumed after days of spring rain, watched a single blue jay as it swooped overhead and then settled on a branch. How could things look so normal on a day like this? How was it that everything just went on as usual, moving along in its steady, methodical beat, despite the chaos everywhere else?

"How are your eyes?" Nan asked me this question at least five or six times a day.

"The same," I answered the way I always did.

"They don't hurt?"

"Nope."

"Any blurry vision?"

"No, Nan."

"You're sure?"

"Positive."

But I wasn't positive. At least, not 100 percent. *Had* I only imagined the weird blackness inside Cassie's head? Maybe my vision had blurred. It was entirely possible. Whatever I had seen had come and gone so quickly, like a minnow darting in muddy water. There, and then not there, over in three seconds. It was hard to know.

"Well, the whole thing sounds dreadful," Nan said. "I'm so sorry you had to go through that."

I let my head fall back against the seat rest, overcome with weariness. "I'm just glad they let me go home. If I had to stay in that place for another five minutes, I don't know what I would have done."

We didn't say any more for the rest of the drive. I checked my phone, my eyes scanning Lucy's message: *It's okay. Call me when you get home.* I was relieved, and a little bit annoyed. I didn't want to talk to anyone right now. Maybe not for a good while. Thankfully, when I told Nan that I didn't want to lie down just yet, that I wanted to walk around in the backyard for a while, she didn't object. "Just not too long," she said, rubbing her thumb along the inside of my hand. The little pink shape beneath her shirt glowed an electric fuchsia. "I don't want to worry."

"You don't have to worry." I kissed her cheek. "I just need some air. Thanks for coming to get me."

Nan's farmhouse was set on three acres of lush land on the outskirts of town, prime real estate in dinky Fairfield, Connecticut, where most houses had been built over collapsed coal mines. To the right of the house, a small pond was edged with cattails, pussy willows, and giant swaths of honeysuckle vines. A single, enormous oak on the north end dangled its limbs over the water like a wide umbrella. Beyond the pond was a tangle of woods, through which Nan had long ago cut a path, leading to an empty greenhouse she was trying to restore. Sometimes, if I was really bored, I wandered back there, poking around at the empty terra-cotta pots and barren shelves, as if I might find some kind of hidden secret Nan kept from the rest of us. Now, though, I went around to the back of the farmhouse and sat down next to the garden.

The garden was not really a garden. Or rather, it was the beginnings of one, a ten-foot by fourteen-foot plot of dirt Dad had dug out last fall for the sole purpose of transplanting all of Mom's flower bulbs. He'd gotten as far as creating a border around the edge and removing a few of the really deep rocks along the right-hand side before putting the shovel and pickax away for good. It didn't take me long to realize that the whole thing had been just another one of his "grieving ideas," something he had momentarily gotten into his head to remember Mom by, only to abandon without explanation a few weeks later. The cardboard box filled with her bulbs was still sitting on the other side like an afterthought, collecting dust.

I walked over to examine the contents of the box. It was more than half full, most of the bulbs withered and frayed around the edges. They made a dry rustling sound when I picked them up, and chunks of dried dirt fell off the bottoms. The majority of them were the size and shape of small onions, but there were some rhizomes in there, too, a type of iris root, which were shaped like thin, lopsided carrots. They were rotted at the bottom, the wet, fibrous material emanating a kind of mushroom smell, and I wrinkled my nose. It would have been nice if Dad had actually gone and planted them, even just a few, but he didn't know anything at all about these bulbs; he had never even been able to differentiate between the types of flowers they produced.

I was the one Mom had given her flower knowledge to, pointing out the bearded iris in her garden with their telltale whiskery strands inside the petals, the colors ranging from a soft, watery lavender to a buttery yellow. She'd planted allium, too, purple and pink puffballs perched like little globes on the ends of stiff stems, and dinner plate dahlias, their cranberry-colored faces adorned with rows of circular petals. To the right of the dahlias had been rows of *Nerine*, long, curly petals flush with pink and orange hues; next to them had been the begonia and the hyacinth, the gladiolas and the lilies, and finally, the endless rows of red and orange and white tulips.

Mom loved each of the flower species with an intensity that sometimes aggravated me, and she'd tended to them as dutifully as she might other children in the family. And as much as I sometimes resented the time she spent in the garden, when the tiny buds finally opened and the flowers bloomed, even I found it hard to feel anything but awe. Once, all the crested irises on the right-hand side of Mom's garden bloomed at the same time as the allium and the tulips, so that every morning for an entire week, as the light began to creep up into the sky, the tips of the flowers would gleam, creating such a swath of multihued brilliance that it looked as if a rainbow had caught fire.

I sat there for a minute, fingering a mangled rhizome root, and then pushed it into the soil. It was a pointless gesture; none of them were any good. The rotting fungus would prevent them from ever reaching their full bloom potential. But it belonged there, in the dirt instead of inside an old, dusty box. In the soil at least, it could die a dignified death. I stood back up, regarding the remaining bulbs that I knew would never grow. And then I reached down and grabbed a handful. One by one I hurled them into the wooded thicket beyond, listening to the soft plunk they made as they hit the ground.

Over and over and over again, until every last one was gone.

Three

A little over a year ago, back in Maine, I had run home from my friend Janine's house, something gnawing at me inside, tapping me on the shoulder: *Go, go faster, move, MOVE.* My pace had increased with each step until I was running so hard that I couldn't breathe without feeling pain. Dad's earlier instructions echoed in my head, his simple request keeping time with the smack of my sneakers against the pavement: *Just stick around with Mom for the afternoon, okay, honey? I'll be home early.* Except that I hadn't stuck around. When Janine had called at two o'clock, squealing about the new CD she'd just bought, the one I absolutely had to come over and listen to, I'd gone. Janine and I were good friends, but I probably spent more time at her house than I needed to. For as much fun as we had together, the real truth was that I jumped at any excuse to get out of the house, especially when Mom started spending whole afternoons in bed or not getting out of bed at all. Janine's mother was having an affair with her boss, so Janine understood the whole concept of crazy moms. Sort of.

I'd knocked on Mom's door first, pressing my lips against the cool wood in case she couldn't hear me. I hadn't seen her since the night before, when I'd poked my head in to say good night. "Mom?" No answer. "Mom?" I'd said again, louder that time.

"Hmmm?" The sleepiness in her voice was unmistakable. But that was because all she did those days was sleep; it was all she ever seemed to do anymore. A flare of annoyance had risen inside me. She'd done this exact thing last year, just after Christmas, and then snapped out of it a few months later when it came time to plant her bulbs. It was so unfair. Why did *I* have to be forced to hang around the house doing nothing all day, just because *she* wanted to waste her time sleeping? I had friends to see, places to go, music to hear!

"Mom," I said again. "Janine called. I'm gonna go over and hang out for a little bit. I'll be back soon."

Through the door, I heard the rustle of sheets, the sound of a body shifting. "Where are you going?" Her voice was hoarse, as if she'd been crying. Or screaming.

"Janine's!" I said again, impatient this time. "Dad's at work, and I'm going to Janine's house. But I'll be back soon." I paused. "Okay?"

"Okay, honey." She sounded frightened. Or had I imagined that?

I headed for the stairs. But a muffled sound coming from behind the door stopped me. I went back. "Mom? Did you say something?"

There was a pause. Then: "I love you, Marin." The frightened tone was gone, replaced with something I did not recognize.

"I love you, too, Mom." I rolled my eyes. She was always so dramatic. Everything was always so end-of-the-world-like. Even leaving for school every morning was an ordeal; she'd always rush over just as I stepped through the door, grab me around the wrist, and say, "Goodbye, sweetheart," as if she'd never see me again. It was weird. And annoying. I was going a little more than a quarter mile down the road now; it was hardly anything to start getting theatrical about. "Okay, bye!"

Janine and I were on the sixth song when the gnawing sensation in my belly reached a fever pitch. I sat up as the hairs on the back of my neck began to prickle. "I'm sorry," I said. "But I have to go. I'll call you later." I made it home in less than five minutes, a record. My eyes raced over the inside of the house as I burst through the front door. The chair in front of the wide bay window—where Mom sometimes sat reading a book, or arranging a vase of irises, or more and more these days, just staring out at the ocean view behind the glass—was empty. *Okay,* I told myself.

When I left, she was in her room. And that's where she probably still is.

I raced up the steps, two at a time. Her room was empty, the blue cotton sheets still wrinkled and mussed. A cry escaped my lips, and I bit down on the back of my wrist to quell it. I was jumping to conclusions, already thinking the worst, which was what I always did when I was unsure of something. I had to relax. Try not to panic. There was still any number of places where she could be.

I raced out to the garden, half expecting to see the brim of Mom's straw hat bobbing in and among the green, but there was no sign of it. Still, I tore through the swaths of irises, pushing them aside as if she might be hidden among them, the white and yellow and purple petals fluttering behind me like pieces of candy-colored velvet. Nothing. She wasn't in the tool shed or in the garage, either. Maybe we were out of the cranberry juice she liked to drink and she'd gone to the store. I flew into the kitchen, looking for an envelope, a scrap of anything that Mom always found to write on whenever she had to leave. Once, she'd even scribbled a note on the side of a sneaker, BACK IN TEN MINUTES, and left it on the kitchen counter for me to find. But there was no note.

I went outside and cupped my hands around my moth. "Mom!" I shouted. "Mom, please! Where are you?" My voice cracked on the last word, a glass shattering in the distance.

There was nothing else to do except call Dad. My heart hammered like a snare drum in my ears, and the faint taste of bile pooled along my gums. "Dad, it's me. Do you know where Mom is?"

"What do you mean, 'where Mom is'?" His voice was tinged with alarm. "She's home. With you."

"She's not home. I looked everywhere."

"She left? Without telling you?"

"I left." I closed my eyes at the weight of my words. "I know you told me not to, but Janine called and . . ." My voice wobbled. "Mom said I could go, and I did."

"*Mom* said you could go?" He sounded incredulous. "What did *I* tell you?" There was a pause on the other end of the line as he waited for me to answer. But the only thing that came out of my mouth was a tiny sob, which escaped my throat so suddenly that it startled me. I pressed my fist against my lips, but not fast enough.

"All right." Dad's voice was tight. I could hear the fear behind it. "Don't move. I'll be right home."

I did as he said, sitting in Mom's chair with my knees together, my feet pressed tiptoe against the floor. And I did not move. Not when Dad came through the door, his dark hair askew, his blue eyes shifting back and forth as he took the stairs two by two, shouting Mom's name, and then down again, faster this time, when she did not answer. I did not move when Alice, Mom's best friend, came over a little while later, having been summoned by Dad, and joined him on the beach, hollering Mom's name. And I did not move when they found her, in the one place I had not been able to make myself go look, her neck broken, the police said, against the enormous boulders by the sea, the waves licking her bare feet and calves in vague consolation. In fact, I did not move for the rest of the night, not when the ambulance came, and then the police, who asked me at least ten times what Mom had said behind the closed door before I left, not when Janine materialized suddenly, her face white and peaked as she stared at me across the kitchen before disappearing again without a word, not even when Dad came over and put his arms around me and carried me upstairs.

Neither of us said anything as he put me in bed and pulled up the covers. For a moment, he just stood there looking down at me, and I remember thinking that because of me, he was never going to be the same. The thought frightened me even more than the dead look in his eyes. I wondered if he wanted to scream at me. Or hit me. Maybe it would have been better if he had. Maybe it would have let something out, dislodged the small, dark thing that he still kept buried deep inside, a stone locked in cement. But he did nothing. I did nothing. And after a while, I felt nothing, either. I wondered if this was what Mom had felt, just before taking that last step.

After a few seconds, I closed my eyes and I did not open them again until the sound of Dad's footsteps trailed down the hallway. Staring into the darkness, I let the absence of light fill my pores, enveloping me like a physical thing, until morning.

Two weeks later, I saw pain for the first time.

I didn't know it was a pain shape, of course, but by then I didn't know much of anything anymore, having hibernated in my room since the day Mom jumped. I was sleeping, ironically, in much the same way she had those last days. No one could convince me to go to the funeral, and the urge to use the bathroom was the only thing that dragged me once or twice a day from my bed. I smelled gross, an odor that either came from my mouth or my armpits; I didn't know or care. The bedsheets were ripe with stink, the air in my room stale from a lack of oxygen. Nan, who had driven down from Connecticut the day after it happened, knocked incessantly on the door at first, and then left plastic-wrapped plates of food in the hallway, which I ate at night when I knew everyone was asleep and my hunger got the best of me. I did not see or hear a word from Dad.

Until the day I was roused by a strange noise coming from one end of my door. I sat up groggily, my vision obscured by sleep crust, and peered at the flakes of sawdust fluttering down along the copper hinges. The screws seemed to be moving, too, and every few seconds the bottom of the door slid to one side, as if it might topple over altogether.

"Hello?" My voice was stiff from having been silent for so long, and I cleared my throat. "Hello? Who is that?"

I watched in amazement as the screws began to drop to the floor, each one making a small, pinging sound as it hit the wood, and then the door swung open. Dad stepped through the opening. I turned over before his eyes met mine and pulled the blankets over my head. "You took my *door* down?"

I could hear him talking, his voice muffled through the material.

"It was either that or the wall," he said. "You gotta get up now, Rinny. Enough's enough."

"No, thanks."

"Yes, thanks." He strode across the room, pulled back my blankets. I covered my face with my hands. "We're leaving."

I didn't move. "Leaving?"

"Maine," he said. "We're leaving Maine. We're going to Connecticut, to live with Nan. I just got word about a job today."

Something inside clutched at me—fear? anger? dread?—until I realized that it didn't matter. Nothing mattered anymore.

"School year's over," Dad went on. "You're lucky you only had a week or two left, or I would have knocked down this door a lot sooner. We're heading out day after tomorrow, and then you'll have the whole summer to settle in before you start eleventh grade." He paused then and cleared his throat. Maybe he realized how gruff he sounded. Or maybe he was afraid *I* would go and kill myself if he didn't start being a little nicer. Whatever it was, he sat down on the edge of my bed and folded his hands. A silent moment passed. He breathed in. Out. "Rinny."

I didn't answer.

He put a hand on my shoulder, left it there. "Talk to me," he said. "How are you?"

I'm nothing, I thought. *Which is actually worse than anything I can think of. Worse than being dead, even. I'm dead-nothing.* His hand felt like a weight on my shoulder, something pushing me down. I shrugged it off, most of my face still hidden by the pillow.

"Rinny." I could hear the pleading in his voice, and I turned over, an inch at a time. His face was pale with deep shadows under his eyes. The deadness was still there, a fossil embedded in his pupils, and he was thinner, too, as if he had been subsisting on coffee and air. But something else caught my attention: a small red dot against the flat of his cheek. It was so faint that at first I thought something had flown into my eye, but then I blinked and looked again. It was still there, even brighter this time, as if a raspberry had exploded against his face.

"What's on your face?" I asked. "You have paint or something, right on your cheek there."

He reached up with two fingers and drew them along the spot I had indicated. "Where?"

"Right there." I pointed as Dad moved his fingers again. "Lower. A little lower. There. Right there." He looked at the tips of his fingers and then back up at me, perplexed. There was nothing on them. I sat up and squinted. The shape was still there, but now it was glowing, as if a light had been turned on behind it. It pulsed around the edges. "That's weird." I leaned in even closer. Dad stood still, staring over my shoulder like an obedient patient as I examined his cheek.

"Is it pollen?" he asked, looking up at the ceiling. "There's a ton of it this year. My allergies are going crazy."

"No." I frowned, rubbing at it. "But whatever it is, it's not coming off." I blinked again, as if my eyes were playing tricks on me. I didn't know how it was possible, but up close, I could tell that the little spot was *beneath* my father's skin. Stranger still, with every second that passed, the color, which seconds ago had brightened, now seemed to be draining again, as if it were fading right before my eyes. I pressed on it with one finger. "There's a little red spot right there. I can *see* it." I pressed on it again. "Can you feel that? Does it hurt?"

"Marin." He jerked his head out from under my fingers and strode into the bathroom across the hall. I waited, my head buzzing with hunger, until his voice barreled out into the hall. "What are you even talking about? There's nothing there!" He appeared in the doorway again, looking aggravated. "You need to get up. Seriously. You've been in bed too long. You're starting to see things."

It was still there. I could see it, plain as anything, dark as a cherry now. "I am not! Let me look just one more time." I threw back the sheets and moved toward him. Rolling up on my tiptoes, I scanned the broad planes of his face, settling my fingers along the red dot. "It's there! Right under . . ." My words faded as I realized the spot was diminishing, right before my eyes. Three more seconds, and it was gone.

Completely. There wasn't even a hint of it on the surface of—or beneath—his skin anymore. "Wait," I said. "It's gone now."

"I don't have time for this," Dad said, shaking his head. "We have a lot of work to do before we leave. Go take a shower, get cleaned up, and find Nan. She'll tell you what to do."

I stood there for a moment after he left, feeling dazed. I was sure I had seen the red shape on his cheek. But maybe I hadn't. Maybe Dad was right. It had been so long since I'd maintained any sort of regular schedule, much less gotten any exercise, and I'd lost so much weight that my pajama bottoms hung off me. My brain was foggy; maybe I was seeing things.

"Is that my angel?" Nan entered my room, wiping her hands with a white dishtowel. "Are you up, sweetheart?"

I turned to go back to bed, angry at Dad's dismissal, not wanting to deal with Nan's coddling and then her orders, which were sure to include packing and cleaning instructions to the nth degree. But as I did, I caught sight of the blue shapes inside her hands. Dots, maybe, or tiny beads, some the color of blueberries, others a paler shade, like lilac buds. They flowed fluidly, in tandem with her movements, almost as if sitting atop a wave.

"Marin?"

I looked up, stricken. "What happened to your hands?"

"My hands?" Nan paused, drawing the dishcloth a final time over her fingers, which were thick and chapped at the tips. "Well, I have arthritis, honey. And liver spots. Maybe even a little bit of that carpal tunnel thingie from all those years typing letters at the post office. But that's what happens when you get old."

"Nan." I took her hand in mine and stared down at the blue beads, which were already starting to fade, even as they continued their swift headway beneath her skin. "Please. Look at your hands." I traced a fingertip over the tops of her knuckles. "Tell me you can't see those."

"See what?" Wisps of her cottony hair trailed along her shoulders, and the red neckerchief, combined with her old denim overalls, made her look like a farmer. She flexed her fingers and then straightened them again. The blue beads kept moving, never once losing their gait. "What am I looking for?"

"Those," I whispered. "In your knuckles. The blue . . ."

Nan turned her hand over and then righted it again. She peered closely at me. "Sweetheart." There was an edge of sorrow to her voice, a you're-in-mourning-so-you-can't-help-acting-crazy look on her face. "What in the world are you talking about? What's blue?"

"Nothing." I turned away, pulling my hands through my hair. "I don't know what's wrong. I don't feel good, I guess. I need to take a shower." I ran my tongue over my slimy teeth. "Use a toothbrush."

"Well, go slowly." Nan put her hand on my arm. The blue beads persisted. I looked away, desperate now for them to be gone, seriously starting to freak out. "There's no rush. How about some tea? Would you like some tea?"

I drank two cups of tea and ate a bowl of Nan's chicken stew with biscuits before standing under the running hot water until the mirror fogged over and a thick cloud of steam engulfed the bathroom. I flossed and brushed my teeth and then flossed them again, just for good measure. After braiding my wet hair, I secured the ends with matching white rubber bands and put Vaseline on my chapped lips. My limbs felt rubbery and heavy, but I put on my favorite pair of jeans and an old T-shirt and slid my feet into a pair of flip-flops. Then I walked out into the kitchen. Dad and Nan were sitting at the table, drinking coffee.

"Good," Dad said, turning to look at me. Another red dot glowed from his cheek, this one on the opposite side of his face, bright as a sticker.

"Atta girl." Nan's voice was soft. "Now we can start packing." The blue beads in her hands raced along, as if trying to overtake something I could not see.

I sat down hard in my chair and tried not to look at either of them.

It got worse after the move, the colors and shapes I saw in people increasing in number and intensity. When I went to the grocery store for Nan, I saw a pink, grapefruit-sized ball curled up beneath the ribs of the cashier and a lime-sized red oval staring out from behind the kneecap of the boy who bagged the groceries. Celeste, who was Nan's hairdresser at Kut-n-Kurl and who shaped my hair into the short pixie style I wore now, had a lavender, pea-shaped blob inside the back of her mouth. One night I went to the movies with Nan and became so overwhelmed that I had to close my eyes and keep them closed. Everywhere I looked inside the theater, shapes and colors bloomed. It was like sitting in a garden of mythical lights, their hues bleeding into the darkness like small, exploding stars. When Nan asked what was wrong, I told her I had a headache. We left early.

After another month, I told Nan, who convinced Dad that I had to see a doctor. July passed by in a flurry of medical tests, most of which, despite their deceptively brief names—EKG, EMG, MRI, AFP, ABEP—were so long in length that I fell asleep during most of them. I spent whole days lying inside long, smooth machines, holding my arm out for another blood sample, and sitting in blue chairs, answering questions. Dad and Nan held their breath along with me, only to exhale every time another test came back negative. There was simply no indication that anything was wrong. Nothing was askew inside my brain, my head, my eyes, my blood, even my heart. Nothing. Anywhere.

At the doctor's insistence, two psychiatric visits were next, their questions ranging from the idiotic—"Do you experience any kind of scent awareness along with the colors?" and "Would you say that you have an overactive imagination?"—to the painfully personal—"Do you think you might be trying to get attention, since your mother just died?" or "Is it possible that you might be acting out now that you are becoming sexually mature?" They used words like *psychosomatic* and *latent juvenile depression,* both of which I realized after a while were just big words, none of them rooted in anything tangible. Sure, I was depressed about the fact that my mother had committed suicide, but what did that have to do with the things I was seeing? What did that have to do with anything at all?

And what exactly, the psychiatrists wanted to know, are you seeing?

By then, I had a pretty good idea of what I was seeing. It had to be pain. I kept this information to myself, of course, because I knew it sounded crazy, and maybe I was going a little bit crazy, but I also knew that there was nothing else it could be. Whether the color and shape were simply an indication that the pain was there or whether it was the actual physical pain itself, I could not be sure. But it was not a coincidence that Nan's arthritic hands flared in exactly the same spot where I glimpsed the blue beads. Or that on the day of my haircut, Celeste had confided that she didn't know how she was standing upright since she'd just had root canal surgery that morning. The red blob inside Dad's cheek (which returned again and again) had to be connected to his repeated sinus infections, and when I overheard the bagger at the grocery store telling the cashier that he'd been off for so long because he'd just sprained his knee, my suspicions were confirmed.

I began to notice patterns, too, in the shapes and the colors. Blue, for example, seemed to indicate muscular pain, while red only appeared inside cartilage or bones. Yellow ran the gamut from heartburn to hunger, and orange only seemed to surface inside people's heads. I assumed the size indicated the severity of the pain, but there was no way of knowing that for sure. Not really.

I didn't know why I was seeing pain in people—or more disconcertingly, what I was supposed to do about it—but the whole thing was so bizarre that after a few weeks, I just stopped talking about it altogether. I found a pair of dark sunglasses and wore them whenever I was in public. Unless it was absolutely necessary, I also stopped looking at people, ducking my head when someone walked by or leaving the room when someone came to the house. Still, I couldn't help but wonder if this was the way it would always be. Was I going to spend the rest of my life seeing colors and shapes inside other people's bodies? Or was it just a temporary thing, a fleeting affliction that I would only understand later?

There was no way of knowing.

And the one thing I did know—that the person whose pain I would have given anything in the world to see—was lost to me now.

Forever.

Four

It was almost dusk by the time I came back in from the garden, the blue draining from the sky like water through a sieve. The kitchen was infused with the smell of Nan's cooking, onions and apples and butter. I went to the sink and washed my hands before she noticed how dirty they were. She was the last one who needed to know anything about the bulbs I'd just thrown into the woods. Irrational acts like that (which was what she called any unexplained action of mine these days) would lead to an entire night of prolonged questions, and maybe even another visit to a psychiatrist. There was no way I wanted to risk either one.

"Mmmm," I said, turning from the sink to survey the table. "Looks good, Nan." A platter of fried pork chops was nestled beside a bowl of buttered peas and carrots. The wicker basket was filled with pieces of Nan's homemade sourdough bread, and there was a bowl of white beans and bacon too. Nan always cooked as though an army were coming to dinner. There were always leftovers.

"I hope you're hungry." She withdrew a pie from the oven and placed it on a wire rack arranged on the counter. "It's apple-rhubarb. Your favorite." She grinned, wiping the sweat from her upper lip with the back of her wrist. I leaned over and kissed her cheek.

The doorbell rang just as I started to fill the water glasses.

"Get that, will you, angel?" Nan did not turn from the stove, where she was whipping up a milk gravy for the pork chops.

"Father William," I said, opening the front door. "How are you?"

"I'm just fine," he answered. "I think the more appropriate question is how are *you*?" He was still dressed in his clerical shirt and collar, although he had donned a gray V-neck sweater over it, which bagged in the front. A black fedora sat on his head, framing his bushy eyebrows, and he leaned on his cane with both hands. Even through his clothes, I could make out the knobby red shapes along his spine again. They looked darker than they had earlier, as if the day's events had taken their toll.

"I'm all right." A beat. "Are you staying for dinner?"

"No, no." Father William waved me off as Nan's footsteps sounded in the hallway. "I just came to see how—"

"Bill?" I stepped to one side as Nan appeared, tossing a dishtowel over one shoulder. "Oh, come in, please. We're just starting dinner. There's plenty."

"I can't, thank you," Father William said. "I'm actually on my way to visit a friend. But I was in the neighborhood and I thought I'd swing by and see how Marin was feeling."

"You mean after all the craziness today." Nan put an arm around me. "I was going to call you later. You witnessed the whole thing too?"

Father William nodded. "I did."

They both looked at me, waiting, I guess, for me to say something—anything—that might shed some more light on the situation. An awkward moment passed as I stared at the floor. It reminded me of the time a few months ago when Nan had asked Father William to come over so that he could "give his take on things" regarding my pain sightings. She had started calling it a blessing then, and so I hadn't really been surprised that she had asked him to look at me. For someone who never missed Sunday Mass and kept a rosary in the front pocket of her apron at all times, it made perfect sense for Nan to explore a possible spiritual explanation after the physical and emotional diagnoses had been eliminated. Father William had been polite, but it was obvious that he was skeptical of my explanation, asking me the same questions over and over again, as if waiting for me to change my answers, to catch me in some kind of lie. The entire night had been full of awkward pauses and curious stares, and after he'd given his final verdict—"Honestly, I don't know what to make of it"—I'd said good night and gone to bed, mortified.

"Sister Paulina said the girl has epilepsy," Nan said. "That it was some kind of seizure she had today."

"That's what I was told too." Father William nodded. "Terrifying to think about. Let's hope she gets the help she needs now." He took out a white handkerchief and blew his nose. I looked away while he wiped at his nostrils and then stuck the kerchief back inside his pocket. "May I ask you something, Marin?"

I looked up.

"Did you *see* anything?" The priest looked embarrassed, as if he did not quite believe he was allowing himself to ask such a thing. "I mean, inside that girl today? Were you able to see any sign of the epilepsy?"

My chest tightened. "No. Everything happened so fast, and then she just fainted." I cringed inwardly at the lie and then dismissed it. Admitting anything right now to Father William would mean admitting it to myself, a thought that frightened me even more than lying.

"Yes, yes." Something drained out of his face at my answer. "I just wondered, I guess, since, at least from my vantage point, it seemed as if she stopped right in front of you." He paused, studying me again with that inquisitive stare of his. "But nothing? You didn't see anything inside her?"

"No."

"All right." He nodded a few times, resigned. "You

know, from where I was sitting up on the altar, I couldn't really tell what was happening. There was so much commotion around you that it was difficult to make anything out." He lifted his cane and then set the tip of it back down again hard, as if squashing a bug. "Well, as long as you're all right. That's what counts. I went looking for you in the main office afterward, but they said you had gone home."

"They called me right away." Nan patted his shoulder. "I drove over and got her. Thank you, Bill. For stopping by. I appreciate it." She nudged me.

"Yes," I said. "Thank you, Father."

We watched him leave, waving as he beeped his car horn and disappeared down the street.

Dad's first response after hearing the details was not quite as concern-filled as Father William's. He turned on me as Nan finished relaying the events, his dark eyes snapping. "Do you know this girl?"

I shrugged, chasing a wayward pea around my plate. "Not really."

"Marin was invited to her house earlier in the year," Nan volunteered. "Remember? They live near the Woodruff family, over in Liberty Hills."

Dad grunted. Liberty Hills was a wealthy enclave a few miles outside of Fairfield. He'd even been on a team that had built some of the houses there. But Dad wasn't impressed with things like that. Working hard and earning your living was his big motto in life, not the number of big houses and television sets you owned. "She invited you to her house, but you're not friends?"

"No."

"Why not? What happened?"

"Nothing happened." I caught the pea, smashing it flat beneath the tines of my fork. All Dad needed to hear was that Cassie and I had argued and he'd be on the phone with her parents. If I told him what really happened, he'd be on their front porch. With a gun. "We're just . . . different. I don't know. We didn't have anything in common, so we just . . . didn't end up becoming friends. It happens. No biggie."

He snatched at a forkful of food, gesturing with it as he spoke. "Okay, then, here's what I don't get. There's got to be eight or nine hundred kids in that school, right? So why'd this girl stop in front of you? And if you're not even friends, what the hell does her saying 'It's you' mean?"

"John," Nan chided. "Please. Your language." The pink shape in her chest was pinker now, and the size of a small cherry.

A muscle pulsed in Dad's jaw. "Answer me, Marin."

This was the way we talked to one another now, about everything, each of us having settled into a new, suspicious place with hard edges and harder words. I was starting to hate him for it. "Maybe because she's crazy?" I said. "Or confused?"

He waited, still looking at me.

"I have no idea why she stopped in front of me. It was totally random. She could have done that to anyone."

"But she didn't," Dad pointed out. "She stopped in front of you."

I bit the tip of my tongue. Hard. "Well, whatever. I don't know what to tell you. And I don't know what she was talking about either. I already told you, the girl's nuts or something." I paused, tasting blood. "Why are you looking at me like that?"

Dad stayed quiet, staring at me. His jaw was moving up and down so hard I could hear his teeth clicking.

"What?" I said.

"There's something you're not telling us." He clenched his fork. "I can feel it."

"What, do you think I'm secretly friends with Cassie Jackson?" I tried to laugh, but the sound got trapped in my throat. "Do you think we talk in code or something, just the two of us? Oh, I get it. *That's* what we were doing today! We were talking in code, in front of the whole school, right in the middle of Mass."

"There's no need to be sarcastic, Marin."

"I don't know what you want me to tell you!"

"I want you to tell me the truth."

"I *am* telling you the truth!" My voice quavered. "Why won't you believe me?"

He held my gaze until I couldn't look at him anymore. "I don't know, Marin." He dropped his fork, letting it clatter against the plate. "I just don't know what to believe anymore."

Anymore. As if I'd been some sort of poster child before, an obedient, perfect little girl. He was still frustrated by the whole thing with my eyes, acting as if I was purposely keeping myself afflicted or stuck, playing some weird game that had to do with Mom dying. He thought that was the thing that had changed me. But the truth was, I'd become someone else long before it had arrived. He just didn't remember anymore.

"I can't even believe you." I stood up, balling my fists. "You're being such a *jerk*."

"Marin!" Nan pleaded. "Sit down, sweetheart."

I ignored her. "Why are you acting like any of this is *my* fault? I didn't *do* anything. I was just sitting there, minding my own business. She's the one who flipped out, okay? Not me!"

He studied me for a moment, his jaws still grinding his food. A new S-shaped glob glowed bright yellow under both cheeks, getting darker behind his nose. The original sinus infection had cleared up somewhat, but his allergies, which flared up in the spring, were a source of constant annoyance.

"Okay," he said. "Fine. If you're telling me you're not involved in something with this girl, then I don't have any choice but to believe you."

"But you don't believe me." I stared at him.

"No, I do." There was a catch in his throat, and he

cleared it. "I just . . . I don't want anyone pushing you around, okay? I mean it."

It was this kind of seesawing, this up and down between hate and love, that threw me the most. It was hard to hold on to either one, harder still to know which one to trust.

"Yeah, well guess what?" I shoved my chair against the table. "That includes you, too, Dad."

I braced myself for his comeback as I stalked out of the room, a flying barb that would hit me in the neck, but there was nothing.

Behind me, the silence screamed.

I went out back, fastened my helmet under my chin, and unlocked my bike, a silver Aggressor that Dad bought me last year for Christmas. My fingers were shaking, and my legs felt like jelly. I stomped hard on the ground—once, twice, three times—and shook out my arms.

Nan appeared on the back porch, rubbing the space between her knuckles. "You're going for a bike ride now? It's almost dark."

"It won't be dark for at least another two hours." I swung my leg over the seat. "I'm just going to Lucy's. I'll be back."

She sighed. It was a heavy, weighted sound that made something twist inside my stomach. I knew how hard it was for her to watch Dad and me fight. But I didn't know what to do about it. "You have your phone?" she asked.

I patted my back pocket. "Don't worry, Nan. I'll be fine."

I rode off, feeling her eyes on me. She would stand there the way she always did whenever I left on my bike, one hand inside her apron pocket, her lips moving silently, until I crested over the first big hill and she couldn't see me any longer. The familiar pop and snap of gravel sounded beneath my tires, and my thighs burned as I pedaled harder, not stopping to coast even as I went downhill, squeezing the handlebars with a grip that turned my knuckles white. The pain felt good, directly proportional to the buzzing ache inside my head, and I pushed down harder, as if to squeeze it out of my pores. The dirt road went for a mile past the farmhouse, and I rode it almost to the end without pausing, relishing the feel of dust and wind against my face, the explosion of freedom that always accompanied such treks.

A green Jeep Cherokee appeared around the bend. It seemed to brake as it saw me, and I moved over, giving it room to pass.

"Marin?" I heard my name float out behind me. I braked hard and glanced over my shoulder.

The Jeep was backing up; a thin arm with a chambray shirtsleeve settled along the window ledge. A little farther up, I could see a blue shape inside the wrist, smooth along the edges, darker in the middle. I froze.

"Marin?" Dominic Jackson said again. The Jeep was stopped right alongside me now. If I reached out and stretched a little, I could touch his arm. "Holy shit, I can't believe I caught you. Where are you going?"

I opened my mouth, but nothing came out. He remembered my name? "Oh, I'm just out for a ride."

"I can see that." He grinned, his eyes taking in my bike for the first time. "Nice bike."

"Thanks." How much of a dork did I look like right now with my helmet and my sunglasses on? I didn't want to think about it.

"I was just on my way to your house," he said. "Like, right this second. To talk to you."

"Oh." For a single, preposterous second, I imagined that he had come to ask me out, that the two of us would walk over the bridge to Kirby Park and sit under the two willow trees next to the tennis courts. He would sit close enough that I could feel the soft material of his shirt against my hand, the heat of his breath against my cheek. "Marin," he'd say. "If you only knew . . ."

Except that he wouldn't say that. This boy was here to ask me something else entirely.

"About Cassie?" I asked.

He nodded once, a solemn look on his face. "She's in the hospital. They took her to Fairfield General this afternoon, and she had another fit there. It was actually worse than what happened at school."

I bit my lip, tried not to imagine it.

"She got hold of some kind of scalpel or something nearby and carved a number into her face." Dominic's face paled as he spoke, and his lips twisted, as if he had just tasted something rotten. "It was really bad. It took a long time to stop the bleeding."

"She carved a *number* into her face?" I repeated.

"Yeah. An eight." He stared at me for a moment, as if I might tell him something, or explain the significance of such a horrific action. His upper body, framed inside the window of the Jeep, could have been a photograph. The light illuminated his smooth skin and turned the green in his wide, expectant eyes a pale emerald color.

"God. That's awful." I looked away from him, stared at the black triangle of another farmhouse roof peeking out in the distance. It looked like a toy, a picture in a book. "So you just . . . I mean, you drove over here to tell me that?"

"No. I'm here because I want you to come with me to the hospital. To see Cassie. She keeps begging to see you, Marin."

I jerked my gaze away from the farmhouse, fastened my eyes on Dominic's face. "To see *me*?"

"Yeah, you. She's been begging us almost constantly, since this afternoon."

"Why?"

"We don't know. She won't tell us. She won't say anything except that she wants to see you." He paused, studying me, waiting. "Do *you* know why?"

"No." The answer came out like a bullet. "I have no idea."

"Marin, listen." He opened his door and stepped out of the car. "We don't know what else to do here, okay?

Even the doctor suggested it. Bringing you to the hospital, I mean. She's at Quiet Gardens now. They transferred her there after they finished stitching her up at General."

"Quiet Gardens?" I repeated. "Isn't that a mental hospital?"

"Yeah." Dominic nodded. "And her doctor really . . . I mean, he said it might calm her down if you came. You know, since she keeps asking for you." He hesitated, realizing the weight of his request, and shoved a hand inside the pocket of his cargo pants. "Will you come with me? I mean, can you? You can ride with me if you want. In my car."

"Right now?"

"Yeah. I told you, that's why I'm here. That's why I drove out."

"But *I* don't know what she wants." I squeezed the rubber grips on the handlebars, felt the stiff ribbing twist against my skin. "I mean, I don't know what I could do."

"Maybe she just has to tell you something." His fingers clutched the edge of the windowsill. "I don't know. But she's hysterical. She's been hysterical for hours. They gave her something to calm her down a little while ago, so it's not quite as bad right now, but I'm telling you, as soon as it wears off, she's going to start asking for you again."

I looked down at my Keds, squeezed my eyes tight behind my sunglasses. This could not actually be happening.

"Marin." He took a step toward me. The movement brought him less than a foot closer to me, but I understood.

He was here to make a point, and he wanted to make sure I knew it. "I know you're probably still a little freaked out after everything that happened between you two at our house, and you have every right to be, but you won't be alone with her. She's in a private room. There's doctors and nurses and stuff, and my parents and I are right there too. Nothing will happen. I promise. I'm pretty sure all she wants to do is talk to you."

A long, silent moment passed as I stared at the ground. My cheeks burned, remembering. Aside from Cassie and me, Dominic was the only other person who knew about the closet incident. He was the one who had heard my screams that day, the one who had flung open the door, only to stare down at me, horrified, as I cowered inside.

"Maybe she wants to apologize," he said. "You know, for what she did that day."

The ribbon of heat moved up my face, flushing out across my forehead. Cassie Jackson was the sort of girl who might apologize . . . if someone held a gun to her head. I chewed on the inside of my lip, tried not to think about what might happen if I went.

Or if I didn't.

"Five minutes." Dominic's eyes were pleading. "I promise. Just so she can see you. And hopefully calm down a little. Please, Marin. I told my parents I'd drive over and try to get you to come. I'm on a mission here." He laughed, waiting maybe for me to laugh, too, or at least smile. I did neither. “We don’t know what else to do,” he said. “We’re desperate here. Please.”

I didn’t look up for at least another twenty seconds. And when I did, I could see the sun starting to set just behind Dominic’s shoulder. It hovered like a gold dinner plate in the horizon, watering the clouds beneath it in a milky hue. It was getting late. If I was gone too long, Nan or Dad would call my phone. Or worse, come looking for me.

“Okay,” I heard myself say. “Five minutes. But then I have to go.”

Five

Dominic put my bike in the back of his Jeep and tossed at least fourteen empty Gatorade bottles onto the backseat to make room for me on the passenger side. I crawled in tentatively, trying not to touch anything, and held my helmet on my lap. The smell of deodorant, melting chocolate, and salty traces of sweat drifted up from the seat and then faded again. Crumpled peanut M&M wrappers littered the floor, and half an uneaten bag of Smartfood Popcorn was wedged into the driver's-side pocket. A gold medal stamped with the imprint of a runner dangled from a green and yellow ribbon behind his rearview mirror, and between the seats was an opened CD case filled with rap music. Eminem. Run-DMC. Jay-Z. I wondered if his iPod was filled with tracks like these, if he had certain ones that he listened to when he trained for track season.

He got in and turned the car around with desperate, jerky movements, as if I might try to jump out if he didn't move fast enough. I braced myself against the seat, buckled up, and reached out to grab hold of the leather armrest. It would be just my luck to get carsick and puke all over the inside of Dominic Jackson's car. I steadied my gaze on a point in the distance, tried to focus behind my sunglasses. Between us, the track medal swung back and forth beneath the mirror, throwing small shadows across the dashboard, and the empty candy wrappers skittered along the floor. Dominic didn't talk until we were on the street again, a safe distance from the dirt road and the farmhouse. Then he sighed once, heavily.

"Damn, Marin." He turned his head to look at me. "I honestly didn't know if I was going to be able to get you to come. Thanks. I mean, thank you, really. You have no idea. Maybe my sister will be able to get some sleep now." He left the sentence hanging between us.

"She hasn't been sleeping?" I asked.

"No." He moved his eyes between the road and me. "Not for months."

"Maybe because of the epilepsy."

"Maybe."

"That's what they said she has, right?"

"That's what they think so far."

I looked out the window. The light was fading quickly, pale fingers of it draining behind the trees. A wedge of birds streamed in front of a slip of clouds. We were almost in town, which meant that in less than five minutes we'd be at Quiet Gardens, which as far as I knew, was the only mental hospital in Fairfield. Behind my glasses, I closed my eyes again.

He'd been so kind that day after finding me in Cassie's closet, trying to get me to calm down, asking question after question to find out what had happened—*What's your name? How did you get in here? Did Cassie do this? On purpose? Where is she?*—and finally letting me go when I shrieked at him to just give me my clothes, that I had to get out of there, that I just wanted to *leave*. We'd never spoken another word since, had never even exchanged a wayward glance. Still, it would have been a lie to say that I didn't look up when he swept by in the hall, engulfed by the other seniors, preoccupied with any number of things that had nothing to do with me, and wonder if he remembered.

I would never forget.

"I really like your bike," he said. "It's an Aggressor?"

"Yeah. A three-point-oh."

"I've heard good things about them. They're fast. You like it?"

"It's okay. I could go faster."

He smiled a little. "You like to ride?"

"Sometimes."

"Me too." He draped the inside of his wrist along the top of the steering wheel. The blue disk inside faded a bit as I looked at it.

"Do you ride?" I asked.

He nodded. "I have an Epic Twenty-Nine. I take it out every chance I get. I think it's probably my favorite way to spend time."

"An Epic Twenty-Nine?" I looked at him out of the corner of one eye. "Isn't that what last year's winner of the World Cup rode?"

Now it was his turn to look at me again. "Yeah, actually," he said. "It was. You know your bikes, don't you?"

I looked back out the window, flustered by the compliment. He would never know how the bottom of my stomach plummeted, like an elevator in free fall, whenever he came into my presence. Right now, I wasn't sure my stomach even *had* a bottom anymore. "What about running?" I asked, struggling to sound nonchalant. "I thought running and track were more your thing."

He shrugged. "Running's cool. But it's sort of my second speed. Like you said, I could go faster. Being on top of that bike sometimes can make me feel like I'm flying." He paused. "I like that feeling, you know?"

"Yeah." My heart pounded. "I know."

The car slowed as he eased it along the curb in front of a low gray building. Thick hedges flanked the entrance, and small windows stared out at the night like empty eyes. He turned off the engine, ran his fingers through his hair. "All right. You ready?"

No. I nodded.

He pointed to the hospital. "This way."

Maybe I was still in *One Flew Over the Cuckoo's Nest*

mode, expecting to see patients slumped over in chairs muttering to themselves or tight-lipped nurses in starched uniforms handing out pink and blue pills. Still, even with my sunglasses on, I hadn't expected things to look like this. Except for the woman sitting behind a wide desk at one end of the hallway, the entire first floor looked like someone's living room. A *wealthy* someone's living room. Plush red chairs with fat pillows were pressed up neatly against the walls. Two gigantic area rugs pictured flying cranes and gold-roofed pagodas. The windows were dressed with heavy brocade drapes that fastened in the middle with silk braided ties. The sound of classical music drifted down from somewhere by the ceiling, and I could smell wood polish in the air.

"This place is unreal," I whispered, trotting to keep up with Dominic.

"This place has a lot of money," he murmured back. "Treating mental illness is frigging expensive."

He stopped in front of the desk, which, besides the pane of glass surrounding it like a moat, could have been any front desk. In any hospital.

"I'm back to see my sister, Cassie Jackson," Dominic said to the receptionist. "She's in special observance on the third floor? I have another visitor too." He reached out and touched my arm lightly. "Right here."

"Your names?" The woman, young, pretty, glanced at me and then back at Dominic. Beneath her hands, which were poised over the computer keyboard, I could see a copy of *Twilight: New Moon* overturned in her lap. And except for a pale blue mark on the outside of her neck, her flawless skin had an alabaster quality to it. I looked at the blue spot on the woman's neck again; at this distance, even with my dark glasses on, I could see the navy, cylindrical shape beneath it, one side of it darker than the other.

"I'm Dominic Jackson." He stepped back, making room for me. "And this is Marin Winters."

I slid a glance at him. He remembered my last name too?

"Have a seat, please." The woman looked at the screen as she spoke, her fingers racing along the keys. "Someone will be with you in a moment."

We sat down in the beautiful, silk-backed chairs. A trembling had started in my fingertips, and I slid my hands under my legs. I could feel the muscles in my arms quavering; the middle of my stomach felt light and dense at the same time. Across the room, the blue mass in the receptionist's neck throbbed like a traffic light. *Please,* I thought. *Please let the inside of that hickey be the only thing I see in this place today.*

Several silent moments passed. I stared at my red Keds, pressing the insoles together over and over again, as if the movement might realign everything else inside that felt off. When an attendant appeared and said, "Marin and Dominic?" I stood up too quickly.

The attendant, who was dressed all in white besides his black shoes, led us into an elevator that smelled like

Windex. I looked around, but there were no buttons to push, no panel to direct us where to go. Instead, the attendant inserted a small silver key into a keyhole near the doors and turned it to the right. The elevator jolted awake and began to move. I stared at the floor, then over at the attendant's shoes, which were tied with big, loopy laces. I wondered what kinds of things he saw in a place like this, if he'd ever gotten hurt, wrestling someone to the ground. Had anyone ever spit on him or charged at him with some kind of sharp object? What made someone want to go into this line of work? What made someone keep coming *back* to work like this?

The doors opened again, and the attendant stepped out into a bare hallway. "She's at the end of the hall," he said, looking at Dominic. "You know where to go."

By now my armpits were sweating, the tips of my fingers ice cold. I stared at the series of van Gogh prints on the wall—*Starry Night, Sunflowers, Sidewalk Café at Arles*—and wondered if the people who decorated this place knew that van Gogh had been out of his mind, too, or if it was just a sad coincidence. The hallway was nothing like the waiting room downstairs. Except for the paintings, it was almost bare. Vivid white walls, no greenery or plants. The linoleum, a smudged creamy color, was littered with footprints, and the absence of windows cast a gray tint over everything.

"Who's with her?" I asked, my nerves getting the best of me. "I mean right now. Who's back there with Cassie?"

Dominic slowed, falling back into step alongside me. "Just my parents."

I nodded. I had never met Mr. or Mrs. Jackson. They had been out of the country in October when everything happened at their house, and I still wasn't sure if they knew about any of it.

"They just got here this afternoon," Dominic said. "They were in Florida at our time-share." He lowered his voice. "They're not very happy."

I looked over at him curiously. They weren't very happy about what, exactly? That their daughter was in a mental hospital? Or that they'd had to cut their vacation short? I kept my mouth shut. It wasn't any of my business what kind of parents they were. Although maybe, just maybe, it explained a few other things.

Cassie's room was at the very end, a wing all its own, complete with a small waiting area in the front and a private bathroom. One of the pale blue walls had been decorated with a poster of a small kitten hanging from a rope. Beneath the kitten's dangling feet was the adage, *When you come to the end of your rope, tie a knot and hang on!* Two adults stood up from a couch against the other wall as Dominic and I approached. I could feel the suggestion of Dominic's first two fingers against the small of my back as he moved me toward them, and I tried to breathe normally.

"Mom, Dad, this is Marin."

"You're Marin?" Mrs. Jackson spoke first, looking me

up and down with a sweep of her eyes. She was expensively dressed: a yellow silk blouse, close-fitting black pants cinched with a leather belt, high black heels. She had beautiful auburn hair, which had been twisted up and anchored in the back, and her ears were adorned with large pearl studs.

"Yes. Nice to meet you." I tried not to stare at the orange ball beneath her blouse, which appeared to be moving up and down inside her stomach. I'd seen one like this before in a student at school, but it was nowhere near as big. This one was enormous, and the center was almost brown, as if it was starting to rot from the inside out. I was pretty sure it was an ulcer.

"You as well." Mrs. Jackson shook my hand stiffly. "Are you a new friend of Cassandra's? I don't know if I've ever heard your name before."

"Not really." I shook my head. "I mean, we know each other from school. A little."

"Oh." Mrs. Jackson looked even more puzzled.

"Thank you so much for coming." Mr. Jackson stepped forward, his hand extended. "It means a lot." I shook it, marveling at the enormity of his fingers, the width of his palm. Like his wife, Mr. Jackson was dressed well—navy blue pants, a white-and-blue-checkered dress shirt, and jacket. He looked like Dominic but older, with gray hair around his ears and deep lines in his cheeks. Handsome to a fault. "Ever since we got here, all she's been saying is that she wants to talk to you."

"Yes." Mrs. Jackson tilted her head to one side. "What in the world is all that about?"

"I don't know." I glanced away from the orange ball in her stomach. "I really don't."

"Well, maybe it's just part of everything else that no one seems able to make sense of today." She crossed her thin arms over her chest and gazed around the room. "Although, they are ninety-nine percent sure it's epilepsy, what she has. And that she had a grand mal seizure today. So that's something at least. A diagnosis. And it's an entirely treatable condition, too, thank God. With the right medication, she's going to be just fine." She pressed the fingers of one hand against her breastbone and winced. "They're saying she might even be able to go home tomorrow."

"Tomorrow?" Dominic repeated. "Really?"

"That's what they're saying," Mrs. Jackson replied. "There's no reason to keep her in a mental hospital if she has epilepsy. It doesn't make any sense."

"I know, but—"

"I don't want her here." Mrs. Jackson caught herself, glancing at her husband. "We don't want her here. She doesn't belong in a place like this. I'd rather have a nurse come to the house and help me take care of her there." She nodded once, the discussion finished.

A pregnant pause filled the room. I bit my lip, stared down at my shoes.

"They just gave her a little something to calm her down." Mr. Jackson gestured toward a closed door behind him. "She's in there resting now. I think it might be a good time, if you want to go in."

I could feel something sour pooling in the back of my throat as I looked at the door.

"You want me to go in with you?" Dominic asked.

Yes. I hesitated. "No. It'll be all right." I tried to smile. "I'll yell if I need you."

"Yell?" Mrs. Jackson inquired. "Why would you need to yell?"

Dominic and I exchanged a look. "She won't," he said. "Go ahead, Marin. Take your time."

The room was tinier than I expected, smaller even than my bedroom at home, with tan padded walls, a dark-green-carpeted floor, and a panel with three different colored buttons close to the door. Cassie was in the middle of the room, stretched flat on her back in a hospital bed. Both her eyes were closed and white blankets had been pulled up to her waist and then folded over again. A single pillow beneath her head looked as if it had just been fluffed, and someone had combed her long blond hair. Heavy straps secured both of her wrists, and her hands were positioned carefully on either side of her, as if someone had arranged them after she had gone to sleep.

Her body told a different story. The purple orb inside her tongue had gotten darker. Beneath the lower half of her bare arms, I could see little blue and pink glimmers under the skin, darting this way and that way, like bright fish.

And on the right side of her face, beneath the soft gauze taped to her cheek, was a deep, cavernous carving of the number eight. I stared at it for a moment, repulsed and horrified at the same time; the damaged nerves and severed vessels quivered with pink ribbons of pain, and the edges of it dripped blue.

Would that be the worst of it? I flicked my eyes over her face, scanned the top of her head. I dropped them lower beneath her eyes and then over the top of her head one more time, just in case, but there was no sign of anything else. No dark suggestion of what I thought I'd seen before.

Okay.

Deep breath.

Okay, then.

I walked closer to the bed and rested my hands on the metal railings. "Cassie?" My voice was a whisper.

Beneath the lids, I could see her eyeballs moving, first to one side, and then to the other. She blinked once and again and then stared up at the ceiling.

"Cassie." I said her name again, a little louder.

She turned her head, looked at me, her eyes coming into focus. "Marin?" Her voice was hoarse; her lips quivered.

I nodded.

She tried to sit up, but the restraints around her wrists made it impossible. She yanked on them, an impatient grunt coming out of her mouth.

"No, no, don't." I reached out and touched one of them. "Just stay still." I paused as she searched my face, looking for something. Her gaze felt like an insect of some kind, crawling over my skin, getting ready to burrow under the topmost layer. "Your brother came to get me." I swallowed. "He said you wanted to see me? To talk to me?"

She nodded, her eyes glued to my face. "My head," she whispered. "I think it's in my head."

I stared at her, confused. "What's in your head?"

There was a long pause, as if she was trying to retrieve the answer from somewhere very far away. "She is," she said finally. "Don't you remember?"

Her answer made me take a step back, as if she had swung at me.

Cassie blinked at the movement, raised her head an inch or so off the pillow. "Marin? You remember, don't you?"

I took another step back as a small moan drifted out between her lips, and then another, until I was within arm's reach of the door.

"It hurts." She turned her eyes away from me, moving her head from side to side. "Oh my God, it hurts so much, Marin. You have no idea."

"It's 'cause you're sick," I said. "You had a seizure at school this morning, and you hit your head on the floor. The doctors think you have epilepsy. But there's medicine you can take, and—"

I stopped talking as Cassie's hands curled into balls and then released. For a moment they seemed to freeze just above the metal frame of her bed, and then they curled up again. Her knuckles bulged beneath the skin, knobs of bone smooth as shells, and then her fingers relaxed once more. Slowly, she began to scratch the sides of the bed. *Scritch scritch scritch*. She dragged them across the thin metal, her nails making a low, rasping sound. The veins on the backs of her hands stood out as she scraped harder, and the edges of her nostrils turned white. The movements became more frenetic the harder she clawed, as if she were trying to flay a layer of skin with the top of the metal bar. A fingernail split and then broke, followed by another one on the other hand, but she didn't seem to notice, did not even break her stride. The back of my throat tightened. Was this the beginning of another fit? Should I call for help? The horrific scraping sound continued, but now as I watched, the tips of her fingers began to turn a strange gray color. The color deepened and swelled, the gray morphing into a faded purple and then a violet, until, impossibly, all ten of her fingers were black. I squinted, as if my eyes were playing tricks on me. But these were not pain shapes inside her fingers. It was as though ink had leaked through her skin, staining her fingertips from the inside out. They looked dead, lifeless, as if she had suddenly gotten gangrene.

By now, I had flattened myself against the door. My hands were over my ears, in a desperate attempt to block out the horrifying scraping sound. Without warning, Cassie turned her head and stared at me with the same awful intensity that she had in the auditorium, pleading, furious, demanding. The movement made me jump so spastically that my sunglasses fell to the floor, but I made no move to pick them up. Instead, I glimpsed the sudden swish of black again, a ribbon caressing the inner hollows of her head, slipping in among the wide space behind her eyes like a dark, fluid stream of water. There was no room for hesitation this time, no possibility of doubt. The blackness was as real as anything I'd ever seen; it moved slowly, deliberately through her head, as if on display this time, wanting to be seen.

I opened my mouth to scream for Dominic, but nothing came out. It was like something clutched at my vocal cords, was squeezing them into paralysis. My hand scrabbled for the doorknob behind me, even as I felt my legs giving way.

Cassie struggled to sit up. Her long hair fell around the front of her shoulders, and a vein bulged along the side of her neck as she wrenched at the restraints around her wrists. A horrible tearing sound came from one of them as the Velcro began to give, but they stayed. Impossibly, they stayed.

I became aware of a faint rattling sound. It was coming from my teeth, which had started chattering, clicking against each other like some kind of windup toy. Cassie strained against the cuffs again, leaning forward, grunting with increased deliberation. Her dead fingertips curled at the tips like black hooks, and the inky stream inside her head continued to flow in an endless, steady current.

Runrunrun! my brain commanded. *Runrunrun!* But I could not make myself move. It was as if the blackness inside her head had somehow riveted me to the floor, some weird energy putting nails in my feet, stakes in my legs. The color was so dark that I could not see her pupils anymore—they had been swallowed into a mass of tar. Finally, I pounded on the door behind me with the sides of my fists, kicked at it with my heels.

"Let me out!" My voice choked over the words. "Let me out!"

I could hear the sound of someone pressed up behind it, the knob rattling in its slot. "Marin!" It was Dominic. "Marin, get away from the door!" Without taking my eyes off Cassie, I moved myself to the right. The door flew open, throwing me to the floor, and the attendant with the black shoes rushed in, followed by Dominic and Mr. and Mrs. Jackson. The attendant lunged for Cassie, grabbing at her flailing arms, his face tight with exertion, and shoved her back down against the bed.

Cassie threw her head back and shrieked as he leaned over her, pinning her to the mattress with the weight of his body, and secured the loosened straps back around her arms.

"Don't hurt her!" Mrs. Jackson screamed. "Don't you hurt her! She's sick!"

Dominic got down on one knee and helped me up. "Marin. Are you all right?"

I was about to answer him when I heard a sob. It was coming from behind the attendant, who was standing up straight again, securing Cassie's leg straps around her ankles; it was mingled with words, a plea of some kind, with my name in it. "Marin. Oh God, Marin, help me. Please."

I moved out from behind Dominic. Cassie's hands were stretched inside the wrist straps, straining toward me. Her fingertips were white again, and she was weeping, her face freezing in horror and then giving way, over and over. There was no sign of the gangrene in her fingers, none of the serpentine blackness in her head. Both of them had vanished. She stared straight at me now with watery eyes, the ocean after a storm.

"Please." She began to lower her arms, as if exhausted. Her voice followed, just as weary. "Please help me, Marin. Please."

"What happened?" Mrs. Jackson's voice was like a razor blade going through paper. "What's going on? Will somebody please get the *doctor*?"

"Marin." Dominic's head whipped back and forth like a metronome, staring first at Cassie and then back at me. "Marin, what just happened? Talk to me."

But I was not going to talk to him. I was not going to talk to anyone. I knew that if I didn't get out of this space, away from whatever was in this room right this minute, this second, everything inside me was going to disintegrate. And I wasn't talking about passing out the way I sometimes felt I might do in school when the colors got too overwhelming.

I was talking about disappearing. For good.

With a surge of adrenaline, I pushed past Dominic and Mr. and Mrs. Jackson, almost knocking them over.

And then I ran like hell.

Six

Air. I needed air. I needed to breathe. Oxygen. In and out of my lungs, as fast as possible, so that it could fill everything inside that had been touched by whatever I'd just seen back there, and then erase it. I ran harder than I had ever run before, forgetting about my bike in the back of Dominic's Jeep, weaving in and around stop signs, trees, bushes, garbage cans with a terrified agility I didn't know I possessed.

"Marin, wait!" The sound of Dominic's voice filled me with fresh panic. He wasn't far behind. And he could outrun me. I had to lose him. "Marin! Please!" I darted off the sidewalk and into the empty street. For a moment, all I could hear was the slap of my sneakers against the asphalt, the pull and release of my staggered breathing, and the faint pounding of Dominic's footsteps, which were getting closer with every second. I swerved back onto the sidewalk as a car veered toward me, beeping frantically. Darting through someone's back lawn and into an alley, I hot-stepped through a maze of puddles, trying not to get my feet wet, and yelped when I did. No matter. The narrow brick buildings loomed up like castle walls on either side of me, and an opening beckoned at the end of the alley. There were no sounds behind me anymore; Dominic's racing steps and measured breathing had vanished into the night.

"Marin!" Dominic burst out at the end of the alley, both arms raised high in surrender.

I screamed at the sudden sight of him, jerking to a halt and almost falling over.

"Just hold on a second!" He reached out and grabbed me, holding me around the waist.

"Let me go!" I yelled, pushing at his arms. "Get your hands off me! I mean it! Get *off*!"

His hands gripped me harder. I twisted and kicked, but it was impossible to wrench free. His arms were like a vise, the grip of his hands like a lock. I stopped struggling, pretending to give up. "Okay, fine. *Fine*. I won't run, all right? Just let go." I pushed at his arms one last time. "Just get *off*."

He released me slowly, cautiously, his arms still hovering a few inches nearby, ready if I tried to bolt again. I thought about it and then changed my mind. I could just as easily talk my way out of this too. He wasn't going to get any answers, because I didn't *have* any answers, but that was his problem, not mine. I leaned over, still panting, and settled my palms against my knees, trying to catch my breath.

Turning my head, I looked down the length of the alley. The puddles shimmered in the dark, their smooth, opaque surfaces like a collection of gigantic pool balls. Across from me, about twenty feet down the other side, a small garbage bag had been tossed against a wall, the ends tied in a knot.

"Marin." Dominic's voice was soft.

"What?"

"What happened?" His voice sounded incredulous. "Why were you screaming inside Cassie's room?"

Something by the garbage bag caught my eye. A movement of some kind, a flutter. I straightened up. "I don't know. Seeing her like that, I guess. It freaked me out. I just wanted to get out of there." I pushed myself off the wall and headed toward the bag.

"Seeing her like what?" Dominic grabbed my wrist.

I looked down at his hand until he released it. "Don't grab me again," I said. "I mean it."

"Where are you going?" If he was embarrassed, he didn't show it. "What are you doing? All I want to do is talk, Marin."

I moved toward the garbage bag without answering and stooped down beside it. The faint scuttling movement had disappeared into a space between the bag and the brick wall; now it was still again. Had I imagined it? I reached out and pulled the bag back a little until my eyes fell on a tiny bird with brown feathers. It was no bigger than an aspirin bottle, its beak the size of an aspirin itself. Huddled into a ball, its tiny head was bent beneath one of its wings.

It startled at the sight of me, struggling to scurry farther into the tiny corner. The patch of red I could see gleaming inside its wing suggested that it was broken in several parts, but the terrible, awkward angle it hung from its body confirmed it. "Oh, it's just a poor little baby," I whispered. "He can't fly. His wing is broken."

Dominic leaned over me to look. "It won't be much longer, probably."

"Till what?" I didn't take my eyes off the bird, which had stopped moving. Now it just sat there, its chest heaving in and out.

"Until it dies." Dominic straightened as I turned to look at him. "Marin, it's half dead already. And it can't fly. It probably fell out of a nest somewhere and hobbled into the alley to find a quiet place to die. Animals do that, you know. When they know there's no hope left."

I looked down at the bird again and then at the garbage bag. It was too far gone to bring to a vet. And Nan would kill me if I brought a half-dead animal into the house. There was a reason she didn't have any pets of her own. She was big on germs, half-crazed about the number of diseases they could carry. Dad would just think I was nuts. But then, what else was new? Still, I didn't want to touch him, couldn't bear the thought of handling something so tiny. So fragile. "Can you get him out of there for me?"

Dominic drew back. "Why would you want to get him *out* of there?"

"I just do." I stood up, unable to look at the bird any

longer. It was dying right in front of us, its tiny eyes half-lidded and glazed, breathing its last breaths. "Please."

"You're not planning on taking it home?"

"No."

"Well, why do you want me to get it, then?"

I didn't answer.

"It's dying, Marin."

"I *know* it's dying." I bit my lip. "That's why I want you to get it."

"Why?"

"So that it can die *with* someone, okay?" I shook my head. "With us. And not all alone out here."

Dominic's eyes met mine for a moment and then moved back over to the bird. He pulled the garbage bag to one side, making room to center his feet, and then he reached over and slid a hand under the bird. I watched fearfully as it fluttered under his touch, little brown feathers quivering on the tips of its wings, and then settled down again. Its breathing was labored, and up close, inside its chest, I could see a green dot fading.

"Oh, Marin, it's dying now." Dominic lifted the bird close to his face, examining it. "Watch it breathing. I'm going to put it down and just let it die."

"Don't put it down." I put my hand on his arm. "Please. I know it sounds weird, but please just hold it and wait. Come on. We'll sit over there where it's drier."

The alley was not quite dark; pockets of deep blue still lingered along the horizon, as if resisting bedtime, and the moon hovered like a shy child behind a clot of clouds. The mouth of the alley opened up into a dirt lot, which segued into a paved parking space filled with cars. In front of the cars, the raised deck of Elmer Sudds, one of the popular downtown bars, was filled with customers. I paused as we made our way toward the lot and stared at the people on the deck. They were too far away to hear much, but I could see them laughing and talking, bottles of beer in their hands. A multitude of colored shapes—a blue orb here, an orange band there—dotted their dark silhouettes. I sat down next to the wall at the end of the lot and stared straight ahead.

Dominic slid down against the wall next to me, his arms resting along the tops of his knees, the tiny bird pocketed inside his hands. For a moment, neither of us said anything. The sounds of laughter drifted across the parking lot.

"Is it still breathing?" I asked.

"I can't feel anything." Dominic opened his hands a little and peeked in. He winced, as if tasting something sour. "Hard to tell. Maybe just barely."

I nodded, turning my attention back to the people on the deck. The majority of them were huddled around a pretty woman with blond hair who seemed to be telling them some kind of story. Every twenty seconds or so she would stop and take a drink from her beer, wipe her mouth with the back of her hand, and then continue on again. *Maybe we should go somewhere else,* I thought. Somewhere quieter. More respectful. Or at least a place that didn't have beer around.

"I'm pretty sure it's dead," Dominic said. He peered at the space between his hands and then reached in and nudged the baby animal with his fingertip. "Yeah. It's gone."

I sucked in air, hard, and then let it out again.

"You okay?" Dominic asked after a few more minutes.

"Yeah," I lied. "I'm fine."

He sighed and turned his head, tipping it back a little against the brick wall so that he could stare up at the sky. I waited for him to say "I told you so," or something like that, but it didn't come. Instead, he reached out and touched my arm. "You want to bury it?"

We moved to the other side of the lot, opposite a row of Dumpsters, beneath the only tree in sight, a large maple with thick branches and new leaves. I stood behind him as he got down on his knees and dug a hole, clawing and scraping at the dry soil with both hands. It was hard not to notice the way his shoulders rolled under his shirt as he moved, or how, from this angle, the backs of his ears looked like small seashells. Even in situations like this, things like that were hard to miss.

"That should be deep enough," he said. He cupped the dead bird in his dirty hands again and then paused, scooting over a little to make room for me. If I'd been braver, I would have leaned over and kissed him for doing such a thing. Instead, I knelt down next to him, watching as he placed the little bird in the hole. It looked ridiculously out of place, lying on its side there in a pocket of dirt, two tiny feet curled up under it like fern fronds. The small triangle of beak was parted just the tiniest bit, and a section of breast feathers was damp and matted. I had never looked at a dead person before—even if I had gone to Mom's funeral, it had been a closed casket—but I wasn't surprised to see the absence of colors or shapes inside this bird. No more pain. It would never hurt again.

Dominic waited, looking first at the bird and then at me. "You . . . um . . . want to say something?"

I stood up, brushed the front of my jeans. "No."

He stayed put, scooping the unearthed dirt back into the hole. Slowly, the bird faded from view. I waited as Dominic tamped down the little mound and then placed a tiny rock on top of it. Finally, he stood up, swatting at the dirt on his jeans, and wiped his hands on his back pockets.

"Thank you," I said, readjusting my glasses. "I mean, for doing all that."

"You're welcome." He paused. "I'm actually kind of glad we did."

Behind him, another shriek of laughter curled out over the rest of the voices from the bar like a strand of light. For a split second, I remembered how I used to feel when Mom laughed, how everything in the world seemed possible after hearing such a sound.

"I have to go," I said, turning around. "My dad's going to kill me if I don't get home."

"I can take you." Dominic fell into step beside me. "I mean, you're not going to walk, are you?"

"It's fine." I brushed him off. "Seriously. I'll be home in less than thirty minutes. It's only a mile or so."

"Marin." Out of the corner of my eye, I could see him pull his hand back. "Come on. I have a car and your bike. Don't be crazy."

"I'm not being crazy." I kept my voice steady. "I just want to be alone."

"Could you just please—"

"NO!" I turned, whirling on him. "Listen, I'm sorry your sister's sick, and thank you for helping me bury the bird, but I went to the hospital with you like you asked, and I really have nothing else to say to you, okay? I just want to be alone right now. I need to be alone. Now, *please*. I mean it."

I kept walking, my shoulders hunched up tight around my ears as if to block his voice as he called my name one final time, but there was only silence.

And when I finally turned and peeked over my shoulder to see if he was following me, there was no one there.

I moved through the dark neighborhoods on autopilot, one foot in front of the other. This part of town was foreign to me, and my disorientation created a new, faint anxiety inside my chest. I turned down a street flanked with a series of bright orange mailboxes, toward what I thought was the sound of traffic ahead, and tried to think. But my thoughts were jumbled, like random pieces of a puzzle thrown into a box. It was impossible to know where to start. And even if I did, none of it would make any sense. None of the pieces would fit. The tips of my fingers were numb and my lips tasted like rubber. There was nowhere to go. No one I could tell. No one, anywhere, who would understand. Or believe me. About any of it.

It was that simple.

That terrible.

After what seemed like a very long time, I found myself on Main Street. My panic began to dissipate and I could feel my fingers unclench. Lucy lived three blocks from here. I'd go see her, hang out at her place for a little while. It was where I was supposed to have been all along anyway. Without my bike, it would take a little longer to get home again, but that was okay. I needed normalcy right now, even just a semblance of it. Something quiet, regular, the complete and total opposite of drama.

Mrs. Cooper opened the door, one finger pressed against the middle of her ear. The grimace on her face did not hide her beautiful features, all dark hair and milky skin with widely spaced eyes and a tiny mouth. She was one of those cool mothers, funny, attractive, and kind to a fault. In other words, the bane of Lucy's existence.

"Hi, honey!" she said, letting me in. "Are you okay? You look all worn out."

"Yeah, I'm okay. I was just running a little." I glanced at the pale orange shape inside her ear; it throbbed in and out, like a small jellyfish hovering in shallow water. A bad ear infection. "Would you mind if I got a glass of water?"

"Of course not! Let me get it for you."

I followed her into the kitchen and stood by the sink as she filled a glass from the faucet. She kept her middle finger against her ear, tapping at the center of it as I tipped the glass and guzzled it down. "Thanks," I gasped, putting the glass back on the counter.

"You want another one?"

"No thanks." I paused as she tipped her head to the side again and fiddled with her ear. "Are you okay?"

"Just waiting for the ear drops to kick in." Mrs. Cooper winced. "I've had the most terrible pain in there for almost two days now. I should probably go to the doctor, but I know he'll charge me an arm and a leg for some kind of antibiotic, and I'd just as soon slide glass under my fingernails than give him another dime after the number he did on our new health insurance plan. So I'm just going to suck it up."

There was an awkward beat as I tried to figure out what to say. It had taken a while for me to get used to Mrs. Cooper's casual, easygoing nature, something Lucy seemed to think she had adopted in overdrive after her father had filed for divorce. Mom would have never made small talk like this with Janine. She wasn't aloof or rude, but there was a definitive, unspoken line between adults and kids when it came to her. Talking to one of my friends as if she were a peer would have been unfathomable to her.

"So, Lucy's upstairs hanging out in her room," Mrs. Cooper said at last. "Go on up."

I took the steps two at a time and stopped outside Lucy's bedroom door, which was partially ajar. I could see her flopped faceup on her four-poster bed, the glob inside her stomach thrumming an electric yellow color. Her eyes were shut tight, and both arms pounded the air to a soundless beat streaming through a set of headphones. Aside from candy, Lucy also had a serious addiction to Led Zeppelin. She knew every song from every album, forward and backward, and she thought Jimmy Page, who played the guitar, was a god.

I pushed the door open and went in, wondering how long it would take her to notice I was there. The eight pillows sprawled across her purple bedspread matched the plush rug, and the curtains on both windows were cinched with elaborate velvet ties. Opposite the bed, an entertainment center held a small flat-screen TV, a DVD player, and a stereo system with surround-sound speakers. On the wall next to the entertainment center was a handmade poster of a quote by Robert Plant, Led Zeppelin's lead vocalist, which read: *"I'm just looking for an angel with a broken wing."* My mind flitted back to the bird, but the truth was, there was no real reason why I found myself drawn to the quote every time I came over, except for the way it had been rendered, drawn in elegant calligraphic writing that Lucy had done herself. It was beautiful.

Lucy's arms were still pummeling the air, a sure sign

that the song was nowhere near finished. I took off my glasses and settled them on top of my head. Besides home, Lucy's house was the only other place I ever took off my sunglasses. I'd gotten used to her shapes and colors, as well as the occasional ones inside Mrs. Cooper. I could handle it.

I reached out and poked Lucy in the leg. Her eyes flew open and when she saw me, she gave a shriek and sat up. The tinny sound of music drifted out of the headphones as she snatched them off her head and tossed them aside. "Marin!" Her blue eyes were huge; the cavity in the back of her mouth glowed a faded rose color. "God, you scared me! How long have you been standing there?"

I laughed a little, which I didn't mean to do, not really, but things were still kind of off inside. "Sorry. I didn't mean to freak you out. I just got here. Your mom said I could come up."

"Did you call?" She reached out and grabbed her phone, scrolling through the screen. "I've been listening to music for over an hour, I think. I didn't hear my phone."

"No, I didn't call."

"Oh." She lowered her phone and patted a space on the bed. "Well, sit down. What's up? How are you?" She looked at me carefully, as if seeing something for the first time. "You look kind of beat up. Are you all right?"

I sat on the edge of the bed, letting my hands hang down between my legs. "I *feel* kind of beat up." I hadn't planned on saying that either, but there it was. "Just tired, I guess."

"You need some crack?" Without waiting for an answer,

Lucy leaned over the side of the bed and withdrew an American Eagle shoebox. We both peered inside as she lifted the lid off her stash. There was a treasure trove of sugar. Every kind you could think of, from gourmet chocolates individually wrapped in gold foil to packages of Jelly Bellies to full-size Kit Kat and Almond Joy bars. I selected two miniature Sweet Tarts and a strawberry Tootsie Roll.

"That's it?" She was already tearing off one end of a full-size Snickers bar. "You're not hungry?"

"I'm good." I put a pink Sweet Tart on my tongue, letting the small disk dissolve into a puddle of sweetness. Without warning, I could feel the tears coming. They rushed up inside me, a volcano about to spew, and I pushed my fingers hard against my eyes. My whole body shuddered with the effort, and a squeaking sound came out of my mouth.

Lucy paused, mid-chew. She moved toward me, scuttling along the bed like a small crab. "Hey," she said softly. "It's okay, Marin. You can cry if you need to."

I shook my head, furious at being seen in such a way.

Her hand began to move in little circles along my back. "Can you try to talk to me?"

I pushed my fingers deeper into my eye sockets. The truth was, a few times I had come close to talking to Lucy, even telling her about my eyes, but I'd always pulled back. After the incident with Cassie at her house, it had taken me months to even consider the suggestion of opening myself up again to a possible friend. The fact that Lucy was somewhat of an outsider like me had made me less wary, but still. I wasn't about to risk something this big. Not with anyone.

"I guess the whole thing in school today just freaked me out more than I thought," I said. "It was just so . . . I don't know. Crazy."

She nodded, her face as somber as I'd ever seen it. "That's what I was telling you in the nurse's office. I don't know how you didn't totally lose it right then when Cassie just stopped in front of you like that. I was about to have a freaking heart attack, and I was like, a foot behind you."

"They put her in a mental hospital."

"Quiet Gardens?" Lucy looked frightened.

"Yeah. Apparently, she had another seizure at the hospital and carved up her cheek."

Lucy gasped and pressed both of her palms against her face. "Oh my God."

"They're pretty sure it's epilepsy, that she had a grand mal seizure or something at school and then another one at the hospital. I guess things can get pretty bad before they put you on the right kind of meds."

"Who told you all this?" Lucy's voice was a whisper.

"Oh." I looked down, picking at the bedspread. "Father William stopped by to see how I was doing. You know he's friends with Nan? They were talking. I was right there."

Lucy nodded. She peeled back a little more of her Snickers wrapper but made no move to take a bite. "You know, everyone was talking about it on the way home from school. And you know how I told you that Cassie's grandmother was crazy? Well, I heard Bobby Mason telling someone on the bus that she was schizophrenic or something. For real. He said she used to walk around downtown in her bathrobe and slippers and yell things at strangers." She tried to conceal a giggle behind one of her hands. "I shouldn't laugh," she said. "It's awful, isn't it?"

"Yeah." I leaned back, exhausted suddenly, and let my hands flop over the top of my head. "Let's talk about something else, okay? Anything else."

"Okay." Lucy sounded uncertain. "Like what?"

"I don't know. How's the Prom Bomb going?" Lucy had a list of potential dates she was going through, without any luck, to take her to the prom. So far, everyone she had asked had turned her down. Hence the name Prom Bomb.

"The same." She sighed. "I was going to ask Randy Duncan today after Mass, but considering the circumstances, I didn't think it would go over too well."

"Randy Duncan?" I stared up at the ceiling, trying to place him. "Doesn't he have that big birthmark over his eyebrow? And I'm pretty sure I've seen him picking his nose in class." He also had four cavities and a strange red orb in the back of his knee.

Lucy sighed again. "I'm sure he wouldn't do that at the prom."

"Lucy." I propped myself up on my elbows. "Come on. You can do better than that."

"How?" She looked dismal. "Do you know how many guys I've already asked?"

"Three?"

She raised an eyebrow.

"Four?"

"Six." She held up three fingers, flashing them twice. "I mean, I know I started at the top of the list. And okay, some of them already had girlfriends. But still, that's six rejections, Marin. Pretty soon I'll have to resort to sophomores and sneak one in. Or maybe I'll end up dragging you."

"Only when hell freezes over." I thought back to the lie I'd told her months ago about not wanting to go to the prom, that I hated dressing up even more than I hated to dance. Neither had been true. But there was no way I could go to prom. Maybe ever. The surge of shapes and colors all packed into such a small space, combined with a disco ball overhead spinning dime-sized fragments of light in every direction, would probably make me puke. "What's wrong with going with a sophomore, anyway?" I asked. "It's only a year age difference."

"Maybe physically," Lucy said. "Mentally, it's a whole different story."

I couldn't argue with her there. And I was starting to lose interest in the subject. I got up off the bed and walked around the room. I felt restless, irritated.

"You coming back to school tomorrow?" Lucy asked.

"No." I stopped in front of her dresser, gazed at a tiny statue of the Blessed Virgin on top. With her dark hair, long blue robes, and beautiful dark face, she looked like a wiser, older version of Lucy. "Nan thinks I should take a day or two off. You know, just to chill." I picked up the statue, held it out. "Are you guys Catholic?"

Lucy looked at me as if I were two years old. "Well, *yeah*. You're just figuring that out? I mean, we do go to a Catholic school."

"I'm not Catholic."

"You're not?"

I shook my head.

"Well, what are you?"

"I'm nothing."

She shrugged. "Okay. Well, I'm Catholic. Nice to meet you, Nothing."

I smiled, feeling foolish for having brought the topic up, especially since until this point, we had really never talked about anything more pressing than what movie we wanted to watch on TV or how hot Robert Plant was. I put the statue back on her dresser and turned around. "Well, I have to get home. I just wanted to let you know that I was going to be out of school for a few days. And that I really feel bad about freaking out on you like that in the nurse's office."

"You already apologized for that." Lucy stood up. "It's all good."

"I'll text you, okay?"

"All right." She looked down at the floor. The red glob in her mouth shimmered. "I was thinking about asking Randy tomorrow. I know he's kind of gross, but I asked around, and he's not going with anyone, so I figured what the heck. He'll probably laugh in my face, but I gotta try, you know?

I can't let the Prom Bomb down without a fight. What do you think?"

There was something so hopeful in Lucy's face that I couldn't bear to do or say anything to quash it. "Do it," I said.

"Yeah?" Lucy's face lit up. "For real?"

"Absolutely."

"Okay." She squeezed her hands together, rocked back a little on her toes. The yellow glob in her stomach swayed with her. "And, Marin? Be careful, okay?"

I looked at her sharply. "What do you mean?"

"Just"—Lucy shrugged—"I don't know. It was a lot today. Just be careful. Take care of yourself."

"I will." It was at times like this when I felt my own version of hopefulness. Maybe Lucy would turn out to be one of the good ones after all. Maybe she'd stick it out. Stick around. The feeling was like a porch light left on, a beacon in the dark. I didn't want it to go out.

"Night," Lucy said.

"Night, Luce," I said, just before closing the door. "See you soon."

Seven

I looked away from the Johnny Depp poster on my ceiling. My eyes were heavy, and my body was exhausted, but my brain was going at full throttle, still working over all the details of the evening. Dominic. The hospital. Cassie's black fingers, her eyes. The bird. Lucy. What if I'd told her? What if I'd just blurted it out right then, sitting on her bed, let her in on the crazy secret I walked around with every day? What would she say? What would she do? I reached up and rubbed my eyes again. The chances of getting any real sleep were looking slim to none.

A knock sounded on my door. "Come in," I said. It was Nan. I patted the side of my bed. "Here, sit."

Nan sat down a few inches away from me. The mattress sank beneath her weight, and the smell of lavender dish soap emanated from her hands. Her sleeves were still rolled up to the elbows from doing the dishes, and she had taken off her red kerchief. The blue beads in her hands rolled up and down in their never-ending trip along her knuckles, and the pink dot glowed inside her chest.

"How are you, angel?"

"I'm okay."

"It's late. I didn't hear you come in."

"Lucy and I got to talking. I guess I lost track of time." I wondered when or how I would get my bike back. If Dominic didn't return it within the next day or two, I'd have to ask him at school. Which was not something I wanted to do.

"You have a lot on your mind, Marin." It was a statement, not a question.

"Some."

"Do you want to talk about it?"

"Nothing to talk about, really."

Nan ran a finger over the space between her nose and upper lip. "How are your eyes?"

"The same."

"They don't hurt?"

"No."

"Anything blurry?"

"No, Nan." I glanced at the spot in her chest again and tilted my head to look at her. "How've you been feeling?"

She sighed, smiled. "Tired."

"Does anything hurt? I mean, like, besides your hands?"

"No." Nan looked perplexed. "Why, should it?"

I touched the front of her shirt with a fingertip. "You have a little pink dot," I said. "Right there."

"Here?" Nan touched her fingers in the same spot, dropping them again as I nodded. "My heart, eh?"

I nodded, watching her carefully. "Maybe you should get it checked out."

"I have a checkup coming just around the corner," she said, tweaking my nose. "Dr. Feinstein always checks my heart first."

She studied the pattern of my quilt for a moment, as if she might find what she wanted to say next somewhere in the stitching. "You know, I've been thinking about what Father William said when he stopped by earlier," she said. "About you seeing Cassie's epilepsy pain shape today? I don't know why, but it didn't occur to me that that might've happened. I'm sorry I didn't ask you about it."

I began to gnaw on the side of my thumb. "It's okay."

She hesitated. "And you . . . you're sure you didn't see anything, right?"

"Right. Everything happened so fast. It was hard to see anything, really."

My God. How many lies would I have to tell before this was all over?

Nan squinted, as if trying to reconcile my answer with what she knew, and then reached out and smoothed her hand along my forehead. "I know how difficult all this still is, angel, but it's such a blessing, what you have. Such a gift."

"Why do you always call it a blessing?" I turned over hard, something flaring inside. Nan's explanations always came back around to something religious, no matter what the situation. "It's not a blessing at all. It's horrible, walking around like this. I hate it. How could something that's so annoying, so"—I struggled for the right word—"*invasive*, be something that God gave me?"

Nan looked thoughtful. "God gives many people annoying things to bear. Look at me. I have arthritis. And a little bit of a mustache."

I smiled, but only a little.

"You know, some of the saints had visions . . . ," Nan began.

I rolled back over, disgusted. "I'm not a saint, Nan. And they're not *visions*." I sat up, clutching at my blankets. "The pain I see doesn't appear out of the woodwork or something. It's already there. In everyone. I see it all the time, every day. It's crazy."

"I can't even imagine." Her voice was a murmur. She rubbed my hand. "Oh, Marin. It's there for a reason. Maybe not one that you understand yet, but one that you will. Soon. I know it."

She sounded like Father William in his sermons, arguing that some things had no answers, that they were just for God to know. As if we were too stupid to be let in on the explanation, too dense to possibly understand how or why things happened the way they did. I dropped my eyes, defeated. It was too easy to pin something like this on God.

Too convenient. Plus, it didn't add up—especially for someone like me who didn't even believe in God anymore.

"Yeah." I was tired. I wanted her to go.

She stood up and gazed at me for a moment. She looked smaller somehow in the dimness of the room, as if the shadows behind her had shortened her physical size. The pink dot inside her chest gleamed a rich rose color. "You know, great things are expected of people who are given great gifts," she said, pressing the back of her hand against my cheek.

I closed my eyes. Another platitude that didn't add up. Another religious-tinted quote that was supposed to fix everything. Still, I let my hand linger on hers, and I watched the space where she had been for a long time after she left.

Once, when I was eight, Mom had drawn me into her lap, the sweet, clean scent of her hair swishing against the side of my face, and picked up an iris lying on the table.

"Look close," she whispered in my ear. Her breath was as soft as starlight, the flower inches between us. "Can you see the threes?" She touched each of the outer petals with the tip of her finger. "One, two, three."

I did the same, marveling at how velvety soft the flower was against my skin, how the color was the same saffron shade as the walls of my bedroom. "Ooh," I said. "Nice."

"And now look," my mother said, pointing once more. "Deeper, inside."

I leaned in closer, gasping with delight as I glimpsed the smaller trio of petals inside, and then, unbelievably, another set inside that. "Three threes!" I exclaimed, turning to look at her. "Like magic!"

"Like magic." My mother smiled, holding me close. "But better."

God, I missed her. My head hurt, thinking about it, a physical thing that throbbed inside my temple, and I winced under the beating pain of it. In the space above my curtain, I could make out a sky draped with stars and the edge of a swollen moon. Was she up there somewhere? Could she see me down here, flailing in her wake, struggling to put the pieces back together? Did she care? Had she ever cared?

I knew there were no answers to my questions and that there might not ever be. But I asked them anyway, a part of me demanding to know, deserving to know.

I closed my eyes finally and waited for sleep.

It was still dark when I woke up the next morning. I lay in bed, listening to Dad get ready for work. There was the telltale burbling of the coffeepot, followed by the pouring of Honey Nut Cheerios into a bowl, which he would eat standing up, the small of his back resting against the counter. There was the rush of water as he rinsed his dishes, the opening and shutting of the back door, and the crunch of his boots against the gravel as he made his way out to the truck. When I was little, I used to beg him to take me to work with him during the summer months, but he never did. He always said that a construction site wasn't a place for kids and that I needed to stay home with Mom. What he never understood was that I didn't want to stay home with Mom, especially when she started to get sad all the time and sit in her big bay window and stare out at the ocean. I just wanted to be with him.

I got up when I heard the roll of the car engine and stood in my window, watching his truck move down the road. I could see the back of his head inside the cab window. Tufts of hair stuck out beneath his baseball cap like sections of unmown grass. The red taillights got smaller and smaller until they were just two pinpoints in the distance. And then, nothing.

I lay back down and stared up at Johnny Depp. All right, so maybe I would just spend the day here like this, doing nothing, thinking nothing. Was it possible not to feel anything, either? Could I do that? Just for today? Above me, Johnny smiled, his smug, almost sardonic expression strung across his face like an uneven necklace.

I leapt up suddenly and tore the poster down. It came off in pieces, tearing at the bottom where it was still hinged with tape, and I swung furiously, yanking and shredding it to bits. Panting, I threw it in the trash, each piece crumpled into tight balls, and kicked the trash can over, just for good measure. Then I got back into bed and pulled the covers over my head.

I must have slept, because the sun was bright in my room when I heard Nan knocking.

"Marin?" She opened the door, knotting a clean kerchief around her neck. "Didn't you hear me calling you? There's someone here to see you."

"I don't want to talk to anyone."

"It's a *boy*." Her eyebrows were up high on her forehead. "I think he's from your school. He says his name is Dominic."

My heart rose and fell again. My stupid bike. The perfect excuse for him to come back over, just so he could find some reason to keep talking. Oh, he'd talk. Prod, was more like it. He'd find some way to get into it now as far as he could, probably. But why was I surprised? Had I really thought he wouldn't come back? There were too many unanswered questions. Too much at stake here. For both of us.

"Get up, angel!" Nan's voice drifted down the hall. "He didn't want to come inside, so don't make him wait out there on the porch all by his lonesome. It's bad manners."

I threw on some jeans and a white T-shirt, grabbed an old black cardigan and my blue scarf with the little bits of gold threaded throughout, and brushed my teeth. A few fingers through my hair, a settling of my sunglasses on my face, and I was set. I tested my breath, exhaling once into my cupped hands, and headed for the front door.

"Hey." He looked different. Cleaned up. Khaki pants, a white T-shirt, the same leather jacket. Brown shoes with leather laces instead of his running sneakers. His hair had been combed and was parted on one side. A map of lines spread itself across his forehead, and the blue disk inside his wrist quivered. "How are you?"

"I'm all right."

"I was a little worried." His eyes roved over me, as if looking for battle scars. "You know, watching you walk off like that. It was pretty dark."

"It was fine." I stared at his shoes—tan nubucks with scuffed toes. "I went to my friend Lucy's house."

"Oh. Well, good." He nodded, as if he understood. Which he didn't, not really. He turned, gesturing outside with his hand. "Do you think we could go for a walk?"

"Do you have my bike?" I asked instead of answering.

"I do!" He seemed startled. "Yeah, I do. It's still in the back of my Jeep. Come on. I'll get it for you."

I followed him out the door, inhaling the pine-salty scent of him, and leaned back inside again. "I'm going for a walk, Nan! I'll be back!"

"Take your time!" Her voice was a singsong.

I waited as Dominic lifted my bike out of the car. He set it down on the ground, moving the handlebars in my direction. "You obviously got home without this last night."

"I used my second speed." I wheeled the bike to the side of the porch and dropped the kickstand down. I could feel him smiling a little behind me.

"This way okay?" he asked, pointing to the dirt road.

"For what?"

"A walk." He pulled on one of his earlobes. "I asked you if we could go for a walk, remember?"

I inhaled and then let it out again, a balloon releasing air. "I really—"

"I promise I won't grab your arm," he said, cutting me off. "Or any other part of you." He bit his lip, realizing maybe how that sounded, and I forced myself not to smile. "We don't even have to talk about Cassie. We can just walk. And talk about whatever."

I looked at him suspiciously. He'd already returned my bike. And if he wasn't here to talk about his sister, then there was no reason for him to be here. Like, at all.

"Come *on*." He leaned toward the road, took a long step sideways. "It's just a walk, Marin. I'm not asking you to give blood or anything."

I fell into step beside him, keeping my gaze on the ground in front of me. Every few seconds, his hand would brush the side of mine, and he would apologize and then scoot over a little as if he had done something wrong. We were practically the same height; he had me only by an inch or so, and for a split second, I wondered what might happen if I turned my head and looked up a little, and he turned his head and looked down a little. The thought made me dizzy.

"You know, I've never really been out this way," Dominic said after another moment or two of silence. "It's sort of . . . off the beaten path a little."

I stared straight ahead, not sure what to say to such a thing. I guessed he was referring to the fields that stretched out on either side of us, or the road itself, which after another mile gave way to the scattered outskirts of town and eventually, downtown Fairfield with its multitude of stores and coffee shops. How had he known I lived here? I'd forgotten to ask him yesterday. Who gave him my address?

"I like it," he offered. "It's . . . quiet."

"Yeah," I said. "We like it too."

"You're not from around here, right? I mean originally?"

"No. We moved last year from Maine."

"Maine," he said, nodding. "I've never been that far north. I've heard it's nice. Lots of lobster, right?"

"Yep."

"You like it here?"

"It's all right."

He bit the inside of his cheek, scratched his forearm. The blue shape inside his wrist moved with him, a tiny spaceship getting ready for liftoff. "How about your parents? Do they like it here?"

"We live with my grandmother. She's been here all her life. My dad likes it, I think."

"What about your mom?"

"She's dead."

"Oh." He winced. "I'm sorry. I didn't know."

"It's fine."

Except that it wasn't fine. Aside from Lucy and a few of the wacky psychiatrists I'd been forced to talk to, I'd never told anyone here about Mom. It wasn't like I was in any kind of denial about her death or that I couldn't talk about it. I knew she was gone. And I knew she was never coming back. Still, saying the words out loud—*she's dead*—did something to me inside, shifting the pain to a place that hurt again. There was no telling what might happen or what I might say if he pressed the issue.

"How about siblings?" he asked. "You got any brothers or sisters?"

"No." I let the air stream out of my chest again. "Just me."

The sky was a pale blue, mottled with cottony clouds, and the tops of the trees swayed lightly under a breeze. A flock of geese trailed overhead for a few minutes, almost as if studying us from afar, and then, with a series of honks and shouts, moved on again. Maybe it was the sibling question, or maybe a part of me knew that he was restraining himself, forcing down the questions he really wanted to ask.

"How's Cassie doing?" I heard myself say.

He paused. "She's been better."

"Yeah."

"She's home." He looked at me, waiting for me to turn my head. "We brought her home this morning. She's on some medicine called Risperdal, and my mom and dad hired two nurses to stay with her around the clock."

"That's good."

"Marin." He glanced back at the house, as if he had needed to get a certain distance from it before he said what he really wanted to say. "I know I said we didn't have to talk about Cassie, but since you brought her up, I really need to tell you something."

My heart flip-flopped. "Okay."

"Last night, Cassie told my mother that when she saw you in the hospital, the pain in her head went away." He said the words in a rush, as if I might cut him off if he didn't get them out fast enough. "That might not mean a whole lot to you, but my sister has been in constant pain for almost six months now. *Six* months. She said it feels like someone is stabbing her with knives in the back of her skull and that it never lets up, not even when she goes to sleep. Can you imagine what that must be like?"

I raised my eyes the slightest bit until I could see just the edge of the silver zipper that lined his jacket.

"*I* can't imagine it," he went on, "and it's happening to my little sister less than ten feet away from me. Inside my house. At our school. Every single day. I don't know how she concentrates. I don't know how she's been doing anything. So do you know how big a deal it is, do you have any idea what it *means* that the pain went away—even just for a few minutes—when you came?"

"I'm glad she's feeling better," I said. "But I'm sure it doesn't have anything to do with me being there. She must've imagined it."

"She didn't *imagine* it." Dominic's voice was tight. "I'm telling you, she didn't. By the time I got back to the hospital, she was all tearful again, begging us to bring you back. But she wasn't crazed about it the way she had been. I don't know how to describe it. That weirdness in her eyes was gone, those constant jittery movements that she does with her hands and feet had stopped. We all noticed it. My mom, my dad, and me. It was like she had a little bit of hope inside again because you had come. And because the pain had left. Even just temporarily."

"Her pain didn't leave because of me," I said again. "I mean, I didn't *do* anything. Seriously. It must've just been a coincidence."

Dominic stopped walking and pulled something out of his pocket. My heart lurched at the sight of the dark green book in his hands, no larger than a deck of cards. The edges were embossed in a gold-tipped leaf pattern and an ornate drawing of a triangle inside a circle stared out from the front cover. A blue silk string dangled from the bottom, bookmarking a page. "What about this?" Dominic held the book out to me. "Is this a coincidence?"

I leaned back, as if he were holding a lit match under my chin. "What is it?"

"I don't know yet." Dominic made no move to pull the book back. "I found it in Cassie's room the other night. It's filled with all these weird words and writings and shit. I looked through it—there were a few things written in English, but I couldn't make anything else out." He moved the book another inch in my direction. "You don't know what it is?"

"How would I know what it is? I've never even seen it before."

"You're sure?"

"Positive." Lie number three, just in the past two minutes.

"Okay." He dropped his arm and then put the book back inside his pocket.

We walked on, the sun beating down relentlessly along the tops of our shoulders. The scarf around my neck felt too warm. I pulled it off and stuck it in my pocket. A ring of sweat dampened the neck of my T-shirt, and I rubbed my fingers under it. They were trembling.

"Here's the thing, Marin." Dominic's voice was low, ominous. "I don't think my sister has epilepsy."

"What do you mean? Your mother told us yesterday that the doctor said he was ninety-nine percent certain that was what she had."

"Marin." His eyes were steady, locked on mine.

"What?" My voice was rising and trembling at the same time. "I saw her have a seizure right in front of me. *You* saw it!"

"She did have a seizure. But I don't think it's because she has epilepsy."

"Oh, you're a doctor now? You know what's going on with her?"

"I don't know *what* the hell's going on with her. I just don't think it's epilepsy. All that shit she's been saying . . . the things she screamed out at Mass yesterday? The number she carved into her face? I mean, come on. Some people with epilepsy scream during seizures, but it's really rare. And they just . . . scream. You know, *aaaarrrgggghhh,* because their bodies are all out of whack. I looked it up on the Internet. I mean, I must've read fifty different sites, including the Mayo Clinic. People with epilepsy don't cut their faces up or yell stuff about Mass. About religion."

"So what are you saying?"

Dominic stopped walking. "I think something's been going on. Or something went on. Between the two of you. Maybe when you came to the house? Back in October?" He pulled the book out of his pocket again when I didn't answer and held it up. "Is this some kind of witchcraft manual or something? Did you guys get involved in some spirit thing that day she locked you in the closet?"

I could feel the blood draining from my face. "You can't be serious."

Dominic bit his lower lip, as if the movement might quell some of his frustration. He stared down at the book, thumbing slowly through the pages before closing it again. "For the last two days, my sister has been repeating your name over and over again. All she wants is to see you. And then you came and stood in the same room as her, and in less than ten minutes, she said the pain in her head left for a little while." His fingers closed around the book. "Why? Why you?"

"I have no idea."

"You're lying."

"Screw you." I whirled around, heading back the way we'd come.

He grabbed me by the wrist and I shook him off hard,

furious now. Leaning in as close as I dared, I stuck my finger inches from his face. "You *said* you wouldn't grab me, and you *said* we didn't have to talk about Cassie. Who's the liar now?" He didn't move, regarding me with wary eyes, and I moved forward another inch, my finger still under his nose. "I've been over to your house *once.* And if you remember, it was one time too many. You have the wrong person if you think Cassie's . . . condition . . . or whatever's wrong with her has anything to do with me. I barely even know her. And after what she did to me, I don't ever want to know her!" My voice rose to a shout, if only to force back the tears rising in my throat. "And the same thing goes for you! Now leave me alone! I mean it! Just leave me the hell alone!"

My flip-flops smacked against my heels as I continued walking back to my house. Or maybe it was the sound of my heart beating beneath my shirt. I was holding my breath for some reason, and the taste of vomit lingered in my throat.

"Marin!" Dominic called. "Come on, wait!"

But I didn't wait. I kept walking, staring straight ahead at the oak tree alongside the pond. Its enormous limbs jutted out from either side, the ends flush with wide leaves. From this distance, the top of it looked like hair. Green, leafy hair. A few hundred more yards, and I could turn into the driveway, walk up the steps, and shut the door.

He caught up to me and then surged ahead, turning around and jogging backward so that he could look at me as he talked. "Marin, please. I didn't mean to accuse you of anything. And I shouldn't have said you were lying. I'm sorry. Please. It's just . . . God, there's been so much going on. I'm just trying to put the pieces together. I gotta start somewhere." His knees were moving too high, and his elbows flapped up and down as he tried to maintain the awkward gait. "The only thing we have—*I* have—to go on right now is Cassie's connection to you. And maybe it's not even a connection. Maybe she just thinks it is. I'm just trying to get things to add up here, all right?"

I strode on ahead, pretending to ignore him. Behind my sunglasses, I could see the blue shape lodged in his wrist, like a piece of sea glass.

"Please," he persisted. "I didn't mean to jump all over you. You've got to believe me." He made a gesture over my shoulder, toward our previous destination. "Can we at least turn around and keep walking? And can you please stop walking so fast so I can stop running backward? I feel nauseous."

"Good," I said, but I didn't mean it.

"Good?" The side of his mouth lifted into a little grin. "You know what happens when people get nauseous while they're moving, don't you? This weird feeling starts in their belly, and then they—" He stopped, puffing his cheeks with air, pretending to gag. "That T-shirt you have on looks pretty clean. I'm sure you don't want to get anything on it." He heaved again, clapping a hand over his mouth.

"Bite me." I suppressed a smile and shoved past him.

"Marin, please." I could hear him stop and then a soft clapping sound as he lifted his arms and let them fall against the sides of his pants. "I've got nowhere else to turn. It's you or nothing."

I slowed at his words and then stopped altogether. *It's you or nothing.* Under any other circumstances, those four words would have meant something entirely different. But we weren't under any other circumstances. Still, I closed my eyes, let the weight of them drape over my shoulders.

"I don't have anything to tell you." My voice rang out over the dusty road. "I swear. I'm not involved in anything having to do with Cassie."

"Okay." Dominic trotted up next to me, took a deep breath. He sounded resigned, but I could hear a fragment of hope somewhere in there too. "So maybe I'm jumping to conclusions here. Or maybe it's just something you and Cassie have to work out."

"There's nothing Cassie and I have to *work out.*" I turned around, heading back down the road again toward town. My voice was fierce. "I don't even *talk* to your sister. I haven't said a word to her in over six months, and that's not going to change any time soon."

"Okay. Then just tell me this." He raised both his arms and draped them over the top of his head, surrender-style. "What really happened the day I found you in that closet?"

I bit down hard on my lip, stared out at the traffic up ahead as it rushed by, the spin of metal, the blur of color. It was here. The moment I'd been waiting for, without realizing it, since the day it had happened.

And yet.

"Nothing." It came out in a whisper.

He nodded, as if he'd been expecting me to say such a thing. "You know, I've been thinking a lot lately, trying to remember back to that day, and I realized that it was right around the time when my sister started acting really strange. I mean, even stranger than bringing someone home and locking her inside a closet. You might not believe this, Marin, but that's not who my sister is. She's never done anything like that before."

"Well, there's a first time for everything."

"True." Dominic raised an eyebrow. "Very true. But right after that was when her behavior started to get really weird. She wasn't sleeping, for one. She'd get up late at night and wander around the house for hours, like she was looking for something. And then just a few weeks ago I found her in the kitchen when I came down for a drink of water. She was opening and closing the cupboard drawers, rummaging through things, and then moving on to something else. When she saw me, she got this strange expression on her face, like she didn't know who I was. When I asked her what was wrong, she just blinked, like she hadn't heard me. And then when I went over to her and asked her again, she hissed at me. *Hissed!* Like a cat." Dominic made the noise between his teeth—*sssssst.* "I leaned back a little, you know, because it kind of freaked me out, and she laughed. And, Marin, I'm telling you, it wasn't her laugh. I don't know how to explain it, but it was this completely foreign sound, this deep, weird noise, like someone else's voice had gotten stuck inside her throat. It was all of three seconds, but it was the freakiest thing I ever heard."

"What'd you do?"

"There was nothing I *could* do." Dominic shrugged. "She just turned around and walked back out of the room. Went inside her bedroom and shut the door, like nothing had ever happened. The next morning, she was up and dressed, ready to go to school." He rolled his bottom lip over his teeth. "I just . . . God, I have so many things running through my mind that I don't know what to think. I just want to figure out how to help her."

We were on the sidewalk now, on the corner of Market and Main Streets, a bus stop looming ahead of us like a wide plastic cave. The bench inside it was empty. I headed toward it and sat down, glancing at the scrawl of graffiti marring the smooth surface: *Jesus loves you. Go fuck yourself. Brian-n-Lacey Forever!* The juxtaposition of the phrases was so stark that looking at them, I didn't know whether to laugh or cry. How was it that love continued to exist alongside such ugliness? Or did it?

Dominic followed, settling himself in the space next to me. "Can you please just tell me what happened in the closet that day, Marin?"

"I don't know!" I burst out. "I don't know *what* happened that day! I swear to God I don't! It wasn't my fault!"

"I'm not saying anything's your fault," Dominic said. "I'm not blaming you for anything. I just want you to tell me what happened."

"Why?" My voice was ragged, the sound coming out of my throat like something torn. "Why do I have to keep being involved?"

"Because you already are. You were there." Dominic touched my arm. "Don't you understand, Marin? You're the only one who knows what really happened. Which means that you're the one who holds the key to fixing it."

"*I* can't fix it!" I shook my head. "I can't do anything! I didn't even want to be there! She forced me to go inside that closet!"

"I know." He winced, remembering. "But, Marin, listen to me. There's got to be some kind of connection between whatever happened that day and what's happening now." He reached over and took my hand, sliding it inside his. "Think about it. All of this can't be a coincidence. I know it's not."

I wasn't sure if I heard anything else after he took my hand in his. It was such a natural move, completely devoid of self-consciousness, as if he'd done it a million times. Which of course, he probably had, with other girls. His fingers looked too big to be wrapped around mine, the nails short and neatly clipped alongside my stubby, gnawed ones. But they felt just right there, too, as if they belonged somehow. The blue disk inside his wrist seemed to fade a little as I regarded it from this angle, and I fought the urge to reach out with my free hand and run my fingertips over the top of it.

"Marin."

Oh my God. What was I thinking, getting all worked up about him taking my hand? He wasn't interested in me. Not that way. He was here for a singular objective only, one that involved me finding the "key" to unlocking the crazy box his sister had gotten herself into. I glanced away from his pleading eyes and stared instead at the cracks in the sidewalk beneath us. A weed sprouted up between the cement, green and flourishing despite its tiny prison. I crushed it under the sole of my shoe.

"Can you please—"

"Why can't you just leave me alone?" I pulled my hand away from his and turned on him. "Seriously! I mean, first it's your sister, and now you!"

He didn't answer right away, looking stunned by my outburst. Then: "I just want you to be straight with me. Tell me what really happened that day at my house." His eyes looked like pieces of glass in the sunlight. "I'm on your side here, remember?"

My side? Since when had things been divided into camps? And who was in the opposite one?

I closed my eyes, trying to steady myself.

I had to start telling the truth about something.

To someone.

Even if it was him.

And even if it meant I might lose everything because of it.

Eight

Cassie had been riffling through a rack of clothing inside her closet that day when she paused and threw a dress on the bed. "How about that one?" Her tone was careless, bored even. "I never wear it anymore. Actually, I don't even think I wore it at all. It's a four. You wear a four, don't you?"

I nodded, gazing at the dress, which was floor length, with a bias cut and deep neckline. Molded cups had been sewn inside the navy blue material to accentuate the bust, and tiny rhinestones glittered around the waist.

"You like it?" she asked over her shoulder.

"It's beautiful." I fingered the silky material, letting it slip through my fingers like oil. The rhinestones looked like little balled-up pieces of tinsel. I'd had lots of dresses before, but none like this. This was like something a woman would wear at a movie premiere. On Johnny Depp's arm. It had to be exorbitantly expensive. "What about the other girls, though?" I asked. "Maybe we should wait till they get here and have a chance to look at everything too."

"Oh, Dawn and Krista?" Cassie threw another dress on the bed. It was short, crimson colored, with thick straps that crisscrossed in the back. "Didn't I tell you? They both texted me on the way home. They forgot they had tutoring after school. They can't come."

"Oh." I stood there awkwardly, the hem of the dress still in my hands. That hadn't been the deal. Cassie had said there would be four of us coming to her house after school. "Well, are you sure you don't want this one anymore?"

"Totally." Cassie walked over and sat down on her bed. She reached for one of the black and white throw pillows arranged like dominoes across a matching comforter and hugged it to her chest. "My mother went out and bought it for me last year after my shrink told her that he thought I had dyslexia."

"Dyslexia?"

"Yeah, you know. When you see some words backward instead of forward? Apparently I've had a mild case of it since before I even started to read, but my parents never noticed." She rolled her eyes. "Anyway, I don't see words backward exactly. Some of them just look jumbled up a little. Like someone went"—she made a scrubbing motion with one hand—"like that to them. Switched 'em all up." She shrugged. "That's why I'm in Mrs. Randol's class every morning now with all the rest of the retards. Actually, it's not too bad. More a pain in the ass than anything." She studied me, waiting for my reaction, but I said nothing. "Go ahead! If that one fits, I have another one just like it you can have. Let's see what it looks like. Try it on!"

I hesitated. "Right here?"

"Well, yeah." Cassie shrugged. "It's just us. You're not *embarrassed* or anything, are you?"

I looked away. Embarrassed or not, there was no way I was going to take my clothes off in front of this girl; aside from the sudden revelation about her dyslexia, I still only knew her for all of ten minutes. Plus, it was weird. I never undressed in front of anyone. Ever. "Can I just use your bathroom?" I asked.

Cassie opened her mouth as if she were about to object, and then closed it again. "All right," she said. "Whatever. Just don't touch anything."

The bathroom, which was directly off the bedroom, was bigger than Nan's kitchen. I steadied myself against the marble sink as I slipped off my shoes and wriggled out of my jeans. The mirror above the sink was as big as my bureau back home; bordered with white lightbulbs the size of tomatoes, it looked like something out of a movie star's dressing room. The faucet was gold, the sink molded like a shell. I had just taken off my T-shirt when another door, on the opposite side of the bathroom, opened a crack.

I gasped, clutching my T-shirt against the front of my

chest, but Cassie stepped inside and pressed a finger to her lips. "I'm . . . I'm not done yet," I stammered.

"That's all right." She looked me over, taking in the worn bra Nan had gotten me at JCPenney last summer, and then hitched herself up along the surface of the sink. "I just need to ask you something."

An uneasiness settled over my shoulders, and I shivered, as if a cold wind had blown into the room. I understood then that the invitation to come to Cassie Jackson's house had been a ruse, that the absent girls were in fact no accident. I was here for another reason entirely. The knowledge descended so quickly, like a plastic bag snatched over my face, that I had no time to react. No time to breathe.

Cassie swung her legs a little, holding on to the edges of the countertop with both hands. "Your mother committed suicide, didn't she?"

The question was so shocking, and I was so unprepared for it, that I staggered backward. *"What?"*

"I don't mean to be rude. It was just something I heard from someone at school, and I want to know if it's true."

"That's none of your business." The words came out of my throat painfully, shards of glass being dragged against the skin. I was aware of my nakedness again, of standing there dressed only in my underwear, and it made me furious. I clutched at my shirt, moved quickly to retrieve my jeans.

Cassie sighed and hopped off the sink. "Oh, just *tell* me,

all right? I told you about my dyslexia. Besides, it's important that I know."

"You're sick." I grabbed my sneakers, stuck my free hand inside them. "You know that? You're seriously—"

She was on me before I could finish, pushing me by the shoulders into the flat of the door and then holding me there. I staggered backward under the movement, dropping my clothes, freezing as Cassie's hand closed around my throat. Her face was inches from mine, a thick strand of blond hair caught between her lips like the tail of a mouse. She grabbed at my jaw with her other hand and held it tight between her fingers. "Is. It. *True?*"

For a terrible moment, I held the girl's gaze. Her eyes were like nothing I had ever seen before, hard and clouded, like brown and blue marbles. Her fingers tightened around my jaw, squeezing the soft skin along the inside of my teeth. *"Yes."* I ejected the word forcibly, hatefully.

Something eased in Cassie's face. She released her fingers, dropping her hand inch by inch, and studied me. "Good," she said. "Then we can begin."

"Your mom killed herself?" Dominic's voice sounded hollow, as if something inside had emptied itself. We were sitting in his Jeep, parked fifty feet or so past the farmhouse, the only private place either of us had been able to come up with to talk. Twice, Nan had pushed back the curtains to peek at us and then disappeared behind them again.

Dominic's hands were clasped between his knees, and his eyes roved over the side of my face.

I stared straight ahead, hoping he didn't notice the quivering in my chin, and nodded once.

"Shit." He turned his head again. "That must've been awful, Marin. I'm so sorry."

I blinked, remembering the countless times the words *I'm sorry* had been thrown my way afterward, and the countless times I'd wanted to pick them up and throw them right back in the giver's face. It had felt like such a trite, easy thing to say, just a small conglomeration of words that let people off the hook and meant nothing to me. Now, I realized, maybe some of them hadn't known what else to say and this was what had come out. Maybe it was all they had.

"My grandmother did the same thing," Dominic said. "Just a few years ago. Cassie took it really hard, probably worse than any of us. They were tight, the two of them. Like, ridiculously tight. Especially since our parents were always gone. Gram used to have Cassie over to her place all the time and took her on trips. She was always helping her with her reading, too, trying to get Cassie more into books and stuff." He looked at me. "I probably would have gotten some kind of complex about how close they were if I hadn't been so into sports."

"Was she sick before she died?" I asked, remembering what Lucy had said. "Your grandmother?"

Dominic nodded, tapping the side of his head. "She was

always a little off, but she kind of lost it toward the end. Like, she started wandering through town, yelling random stuff at people. She had to be put in a hospital. On lock-down." His face hardened. "That was where she did it."

"I'm sorry too."

"Thanks." Dominic was still staring out the window. "Anyway, I interrupted you. You were right at the part where Cassie was freaking out on you in the bathroom." He shook his head. "Go on. I mean, if you don't mind."

Now it was my turn to stare out the window.

Bring myself back to that place.

Again.

"Begin what?" I asked, watching Cassie with wary eyes.

"I have a secret." Cassie brought a finger to her lips. "Shhhh . . . Come with me."

"I'm not going anywhere with you." I started to put my jeans on, but Cassie reached out and grabbed me around the wrist. Her grip was like a dead bolt; her fingertips turned white.

"It won't take long," she said. "I promise." I winced as her thumb ring dug into my skin. What could she possibly want from me? I twisted my arm, trying to wrench myself from her grasp. But it was no use; Cassie began to drag me toward a closet on the other side of the room.

"Let me *go*!" I yelled. "What are you doing? Are you crazy? Just let me go!" I could see her jaw clench as she dragged me inside, her arm muscles flexed tight as cords. She began to feel around the floor molding with one hand, still holding me firmly with the other. I leaned back with my whole weight, trying to throw her off balance, anything to loosen the suffocating grip, to break free and run. "Cassie, if you don't let go of me, I'll scream," I said. "I swear to God, I'll scream so loud that—"

She cut me off, yanking my arm so hard that I fell to my knees next to her. Her mouth was twisted into an ugly snarl as she leaned in close, but I could see the slightest glimmer of hesitation in her eyes, a break in the clouds. "Don't scream," she said. Her voice was hoarse, a tight whisper. "No one's going to hurt you. Nothing bad is going to happen. I just need you to do something with me. Something that no one else can do with me except you."

I stared into her face, a picture of rage, perspiration, and anxiety, and tried to steady my breathing. "What is it?" I asked.

"You'll see." She refastened her grip around my wrist. It was so tight that I winced.

"You're hurting me," I pleaded. "You're breaking my wrist."

She ignored me, pushing the hems of hanging clothes aside and feeling along the baseboards. Suddenly, she stopped, her fingers settling on a small, indented button.

* * *

"Wait." Dominic interrupted me again. "*What* little button?"

I shook my head. "The one in her closet. In the wall. Behind her clothes. You know, on the left-hand side. There was a button or something that she pushed, and part of the wall opened."

"Part of the wall *opened*?" He looked dazed. "Are you sure?"

"What do you mean, am I sure?" My annoyance flared. "Do you seriously think I would make something like that up? Right now?"

"No, no." He held up his hand, warding off a rabid animal. "But I . . . I just don't know what you're talking about. A button? *In* the wall? Can you show me? I mean, if we went back to my house? Could you show it to me?"

"What?"

"If we go back. Right now. To my house. If I take you up to Cassie's room and we go in that closet, will you show me that button?"

"*You* find it," I retorted. "I'm telling you, it's there. You don't need me to point it out to you."

"Marin. It's a walk-in closet. I don't know if you remember, but it's filled to the brim with shoes and clothes. I mean, I wouldn't be able to find my way around that thing with a magnifying glass. Please."

I glanced out the window. The front curtains stayed shut. "I don't know. I mean . . . what about Cassie? Didn't you say she was home now?"

Dominic shook his head. "Yeah, but she's not in her

room. We had to take her upstairs. To the third floor. She's in a room with no windows."

I reached up, pressing three fingers against my forehead. My skin was damp despite the coolness in the air, and my fingers felt cold. "Okay," I heard myself say. "I'll show you where the button is. But that's it. After that, I really have to go."

"That's all I need." Dominic stuck his key into the ignition.

"I have to tell my grandmother I'm leaving."

"Oh." He looked startled. "Yeah, right. Of course. Sorry. I'll wait."

I could feel his eyes on me as I raced across the yard and opened the front door.

"Nan?" I stuck my head inside.

"Yes, angel! In the kitchen."

I didn't move. It was harder to lie when I had to look at her. "I'm going into town for a little bit. I won't be long."

"Be back for dinner, all right?"

"No problem!"

"Have fun!" Again, a singsong.

If she only knew.

"Shit," Dominic said when I got back inside. "That was fast."

I fastened my seat belt, moved an empty Pepsi bottle to one side of the floor with the toe of my shoe. "You say *shit* a lot, you know that?"

"Yeah, I know." He backed up the car, resting a hand on

the side of my seat as he looked out the rear window. His fingers were inches from my face, and the dull blue shape in his wrist was still, almost as if it was resting. "It's a bad habit, I guess. I don't even think about it. I'll try not to say it anymore. I mean, around you."

"I didn't say it bothered me." I looked out the window, flushed by his offer. We drove in silence for a few minutes, the possibility of what was to come pressing down on us like a wall of mud. I was off and running, I realized, back on this road again despite all my efforts to stay off it. There were no directions this time either, no signs or maps to tell me if I was going the wrong way.

I was just as lost as I'd been the first time. Maybe even more so. The only difference was that now I had someone with me. Someone who could help the situation. Or make it worse.

Only time would tell.

Nine

If I had felt out of place walking into the Jackson house all those months ago as Cassie's guest, walking in now for the second time felt borderline surreal. I had to force myself not to stop and stare at everything, astonished all over again by the obviousness of the Jacksons' wealth. The inside of the house still looked like a museum, complete with black and white marble floors, corridor-like hallways, and an enormous chandelier that hung inside the front foyer like a glass jellyfish. A gold mirror edged with delicately hammered leaves hung at one end of the main hallway, and large oil prints depicting various ponds and trees decorated the walls.

The only normal-looking object in the house was the large, sepia-toned family portrait that hung just inside the front door. Mr. and Mrs. Jackson were standing on a white beach behind a very young Dominic and Cassie, a cloudless sky above. I paused again, just as I had that first day, marveling at how happy they all looked with their arms around one another, hair tousled and windblown, tanned faces filled with contentment. Beneath the photograph, etched into a tiny gold plaque, was the word *FAMILY.*

"That was almost ten years ago," Dominic said, slowing behind me. "One of the last family vacations we ever took together."

"In ten years?" I stepped away from it, embarrassed, and ran my hands along my arms.

"*They* go," he said, indicating his parents with a thrust of his chin. "But we don't. At least not anymore." He shrugged. "Whatever. Come on."

The situation regarding Cassie and Dominic's parents sounded more muddled than ever. What kind of parents went on vacation without their kids? And where were they now, considering their only daughter was so obviously ill?

"Where *are* your parents?" I blurted out.

"They're at work."

"At work?" I tried not to sound aghast. *"Today?"*

"Well, my dad is. He's the head of a major corporation based out of L.A., which means he more or less lives at the office here or the one in California, no matter what's going on. My mom was here all morning. But now I think she's at her shrink's office. She'll be back later." He sounded defensive. "They don't leave Cassie alone or anything. The nurses are with her."

"Okay." I followed him up the wide marble steps, forcing myself not to steady my hands against the glossy serpentine railing that ran down the length of it. I didn't want to touch anything else in this house again if I could help it.

"All right," Dominic whispered, stepping into Cassie's bedroom. "Here we are. It might look a little different. They're redoing a lot of it. She wrecked most of the big stuff during some of her fits."

My stomach turned as I looked around. Most of the furniture was gone; only the periwinkle carpet bore the faded outline of where Cassie's four-poster bed used to be. The walls had been stripped bare; there were no more posters of David Beckham or Justin Timberlake. Still, I would have recognized this room anywhere. Maybe even blindfolded. The smell of Cassie—a blend of sunscreen and ruthlessness—was everywhere, hanging like an invisible presence in the air.

Dominic opened the door to the closet, but only a little, as if something might jump out. "You okay?" he asked. "Can you do this?"

I'd had bad dreams for weeks afterward, ones in which I would find myself naked and chained in a basement, the floor around me wet and moldy. Once at dinner, when Dad had said something about a walk-in closet in the home he had just built, I'd burst into tears. Later, I heard Nan tell him not to worry, that I was going through puberty, which made girls cry about everything.

They had no idea. No one did.

"Marin?"

"Yes." The answer surprised me, coming out of my mouth louder than I thought it would. "Yes, I can do this. Go ahead."

He swung the door open wide. I looked in. All of Cassie's clothes were still in there, rows of sheer blouses and denim skirts, silk dresses and skinny pants. The wall of boxed and loose shoes was still beneath them, each pair packed neatly next to the other and arranged by color. Even the shelf of stuffed animals hadn't moved; there was the black and white panda with the pink paws crammed into one corner, and the white and purple polka-dotted giraffe, both of which I'd glimpsed when Cassie had first pushed me inside.

"Okay." Dominic pointed to the wall on the left, where Cassie's skirts were hanging. "This side?"

I nodded. "I think so."

"Do you think you could show me?"

I moved forward quickly, shoving hangers and tops to the side, until the pale wall behind it appeared. Nothing. I squatted down, moving more clothes, staring at more wall. Still nothing. A vague panic began to rise inside my chest, a trapped bird fluttering. He was going to think I lied about this too. That I was a first-class freak who—

"There!" Dominic said. "Right there! I saw something!" He pushed his way around me, crouching down on his hands and knees, and pointed to a spot on the baseboard along the wall. I followed his finger until I could see it too: a small sunken circle, barely visible, embedded in the woodwork.

"It could be," I whispered. "Push it. See what happens."

Dominic put his finger on the circle. For a split second he looked at me, and when he did, I thought, *Yes, we are on the same team.*

He pressed down.

Cassie and I watched as a panel in the wall slid open. It moved heavily, as if being pushed by invisible hands, and then disappeared into a space inside the opposite wall. At the sight of it, Cassie's whole face relaxed, like she had just been injected with some kind of drug. She yanked me to my feet and forced me inside. "Come on."

I gazed around the tiny space. It was less than a third of the size of Cassie's regular closet, with a low, dropped ceiling and an unfinished hardwood floor. The faint smell of wax and spices hung in the air. Red drapes had been pinned up against the walls—maybe there was a window behind one of them, I thought, something I could throw myself out of—and the absence of light cast a sickly pallor against Cassie's face as she closed the door behind her. "Go over there and sit down," she demanded, pointing to a space on the floor. "Don't worry, I'll be right across from you."

A lock sounded, clicking into place behind me as I shuffled across the small space, and I whipped around, gasping. "Go on," Cassie ordered. There was no key in her hand, nothing that gave any indication as to how the door had just locked, but I was sure I had heard it. I sat, clutching at myself, still trying in vain to hide my exposed body. Was this some kind of sick joke? What was she going to do? Torture me? Keep me prisoner?

"What is this place?" I whispered. "What are you—"

"Marin, relax, okay? I already told you, no one's going to hurt you." Cassie walked over to a table pushed against the far wall. It was covered with a heavy red cloth, etched in a black and gold scroll pattern. Two white candles, the edges thick with dried mounds of wax, flanked either side. I wasn't sure if I was even breathing anymore as Cassie pulled a lighter out of her pocket and lit the candles. First the right one. Then the left. The flames cast an eerie glow throughout the room, throwing wide, flickering shadows against the red walls. She picked something off the top of the table and came back over to where I was sitting.

"Okay, now," Cassie said. "We're just going to play a little game, all right?" I stared at the little green book in her hand. On the front cover was a picture of a triangle inside a circle, the edges tipped in gold. She held it up, as if reading my mind. "All the rules are in this book."

"What kind of game?" I could feel the muscles in my neck spasming beneath my skin.

"You'll see. It's gonna be amazing." She put the book down, smoothing a page with the side of her hand, and arranged the blue silk bookmarker along the crease. "First you have to take my hands."

I did as I was told, biting my lips to stop them from trembling. Cassie's hands were damp with perspiration. They felt like paws around mine, her fingernails like talons.

"I know you're scared." Cassie sounded almost sympathetic. "But you really don't have to be." Her face softened. "You're gonna be so happy when you see what happens. You'll be so surprised."

"At what?" I tried not to cry.

"Trust me." Her eyes got wide. "You'll see."

"I don't want to see." My voice was pathetic, a whimper, but I couldn't help it. "I really just want to go. I don't know why you need me to—"

"Marin." Cassie leaned forward, her face straining with earnestness, her hairline damp with sweat. "Listen to me, okay? There's no one else. Don't you understand? You're the only one."

"The only one what?"

"Who can complete the ritual with me."

"Ritual?" The word filled my head like blood pooling. "What ritual?"

"The conjuring ritual." Cassie squeezed my hands, as if to reaffirm the benign nature of the experiment, and scanned the inside of the book again.

"Conjuring?" My voice was a whisper. I couldn't remember exactly where or when I'd heard such a word before, but I seemed to recall that it had something to do with evoking spirits. Calling on the dead. "Oh my God, Cassie, please. I don't want—"

"Shhh . . ." She repositioned my hands inside hers, gripping them with a little more pressure this time, as if I might try to make a run for it. "Okay, now that we're holding hands, I have to read." She looked up at me, her eyes wide with excitement. "Ready?"

I stared at her, blinking back tears.

"Holy shit," Dominic breathed as the wall slid aside. His eyes swept the inside of the room as he entered, ducking his head so that it wouldn't knock against the ceiling. "Holy *shit*. I can't believe this. This is where she brought you?"

I nodded.

"This is unreal. I mean, what *is* this place?"

I said nothing. The truth—the honest to God truth—was simple. I still didn't know. My primary thought, racing over and over again throughout my head after Cassie pushed me inside the closet, was only how I could get back out. As quickly as possible. Afterward, when it was all over, I hadn't let myself think about it. At least not in detail. I'd shoved it to the back of my head, tied it up in a neat package marked "Fine," just like I'd told Nan and Dad that night at dinner. And then I'd tried to forget about it.

"How'd she get this in here?" Dominic sounded dumbstruck as he pointed to the table with the gold and red cloth covering. His fingers moved over the cloth absently, as if trying to place it. "And these candles . . ." His voice drifted off as he picked one up, studying the heavy glass holder up close. "These look like the crystal candlestick holders my grandmother used to keep in her china cabinet." He turned it upside down and then set it back on the tabletop. "Oh my God," he said. "This must've been my grandmother's room."

"Your grandmother's?"

"This is her house. *Was* her house, before she died and left it to us. She must've . . ." He did not finish the thought. His eyes took on a vacant look, as if trying to recall something from long ago. "There were rumors once, when I was a little boy, about my grandmother being a medium—"

"A medium?" I interrupted. "Like someone who calls on spirits?"

"Yeah." Dominic looked at me. "That was the rumor, but we never took it seriously. I already told you she was a little weird. Kinda off. Like, she was always wearing big rings and crystal necklaces. It was easy to pin stuff on her, you know? I even asked my dad about it once, and he said it was bullshit, that people were always spreading lies about his mother because they were jealous of her money." He paused, examining the bottom of the candlestick holder again, and then nodded as if finding another piece of proof. "And because every so often, she acted a little strange. But this . . . the tablecloth, the drapes, the candles, this is all her stuff. This must've been her little room . . . where she . . ." He bit his lower lip, letting the thought trail off. "No wonder Cassie insisted on getting her old bedroom when we moved in. She must've already known about the closet and the secret room. All of this." He raised his eyes until they were level with mine. "Which means that even after my grandmother died, Cassie must've kept on doing the same things in here."

"Evocatio Spiritualis de Endor . . ." The strange words came out of Cassie's mouth awkwardly, as if she had tried to say them before and failed then too. But what language were they? And what did they mean?

"Endor! Endor!" Cassie uttered the word with reverence, almost as if she was pleading with someone. *"Pareo pactum quod servo mihi!"* She tripped over another word, and then two more of them, pausing to recollect herself and say it again. *"Recolligo, phasmatis flamma!"*

She repeated the odd phrases two more times, still with difficulty. After the third time, she tilted her head back, exhaled, and closed her eyes. *"Fiat, fiat, fiat. Amen."*

I wondered if I was in a dream, one of those sickeningly real ones where even the smell of things felt tangible. Any minute now I would wake up, stare up at Johnny Depp, feel the softness of my quilt beneath my arms, wait for the day to begin.

Cassie's hands were still clutching mine, the perspiration even more slick against her palms. With less than six inches between us, I could smell her breath, a mixture of strawberry gum and cigarettes that mingled with the burning scent of the candles still flickering across the room. I felt faint, as if I might pass out, and I fought against it. Cassie's eyes were still closed. Should I lunge now, start swinging until I tasted blood, heard the breaking of a bone? Inside my shoes, my toes curled; the cords in the back of my neck tightened.

Cassie opened her eyes. She got to her feet and walked over to the little table, where she retrieved the two candles. I made a quick, sudden movement, as if to run, and then eased back down again as Cassie glanced at me over her shoulder. "Don't try anything, Marin." She sounded more annoyed this time than angry. "You don't want to make us both regret something we don't have to." I swallowed hard, watching as she moved toward me again. The faint, rubbery scent of burning wax drifted across the room as she held out one of the candles. I took it, wondering what might happen if I lunged forward and shoved it down her shirt.

"All right." Her voice was low and tremulous as she sat back down and closed her eyes. The flames flickered across her hard features, softening them around the edges, and for a split second she looked like just a regular girl. "Now we wait."

"Go back a minute," Dominic said, digging inside his pocket for the little green book. "To the very beginning of the ritual, when Cassie grabbed your hands. What was the word she used? What kind of ritual did she say it was?"

"Conjuring," I said. "She said it was a conjuring ritual. Like she was trying to conjure someone up, I guess. To talk to them. I don't know."

Dominic thumbed through the pages, stopping at one of them. His lips moved, forming words without sound, and his face turned pale. He turned the book around so I could see the heading, and I leaned in to read it:

CONJOINING SPIRIT RITUAL.

"Conjoining?" I repeated.

He nodded. "There is no conjuring ritual in this book. Only conjoining."

I shook my head. "I don't get it."

"Cassie read it wrong. She must've thought it said *conjuring,* which means to summon, right? To call on someone? Conjoining is a whole other word."

"That means to bring together," I finished. "To make as one."

Now we wait? My blood ran cold at Cassie's words. Wait for what? I sidled a glance to the right of me and then to the left, hoping Cassie didn't notice. Was something going to come rushing out from behind another panel? Some wild animal or . . . Panic filled my chest, and I held my breath, trying to suppress it. Okay. All right. What had she said this was? A game, right? It was just a game. Nothing was going to *happen*. Nothing *could* happen. We were just two teenage girls from Connecticut in the good old United States of America, sitting in a closet. Yes, one of us had muttered some strange words in an attempt to lead some kind of "ritual," and sure there were candles burning on an altar across the room, but nothing was actually going to come of anything. We weren't witches, for God's sake. This wasn't Salem.

I could do this. I could "wait" with Cassie until nothing happened and we had no choice but to leave. She would be disappointed no doubt, and maybe even take her frustration out on me, but I could bear anything now as long as it meant we were getting out of this room. I crossed my legs and leaned back against the red drapes, trying to steady my breathing. My heart knocked against my rib cage like something trying to get out, and my bladder was uncomfortably full. In our hands, the candles flickered to and fro, the flames dancing like pale scarves in the darkness. I closed my eyes and then opened them again as something shifted behind them.

Cassie's eyes were still closed, but the flame on her candle had extinguished itself. My eyes widened as I stared at the trail of smoke drifting toward the ceiling. The room smelled like something burning; the air was thick with heat. Had she just blown her candle out while my eyes were shut? Was she trying to scare me even more? Maybe it was the lack of oxygen in the room, the absence of fresh air. I sat frozen, the only light in the room now coming from my candle, which swayed back and forth, delicate as seaweed. A small egg-shaped shadow loomed on the floor, growing wider at the bottom and then narrowing again. My flame flickered. Once. Twice. Three times it sputtered, as if trying to make up its mind, and then it, too, went out.

The room plunged into darkness, a horrible blackness that settled over the top of my bare arms like a skin, smothering the front of my face. I heard a noise, a dull thumping sound as if something had hit the wall or the floor, but I couldn't see Cassie at all; the blackness had swallowed her up. I reached out with two hands, moving them throughout the inky space, until my fingers bumped into the side of Cassie's leg.

"Cassie?" I whispered, still feeling around with my hands.

She was on her back, flat on the floor, but she didn't move. In fact, I couldn't even be sure she was breathing.

A faint clicking noise sounded in the corner. I paused, my trembling fingers hovering midair, and listened. A strange heaviness seemed to descend over the top of me, as if the space around me had just been filled with a dense air. We weren't alone anymore. Someone—or something—else had entered the room. A movement, light as a breeze, brushed against my shoulder, and I whirled, staring into darkness. The faintest sound of breathing drifted out from a corner on the other side of the room, and the unmistakable knowledge that I was being gazed upon settled like a stone inside my chest.

I began to scream, groping around the room like an animal and flailing my arms and legs. I tripped over Cassie, who gasped once, as if she had been holding her breath, and then began to pant, her breath coming in short, shallow bursts. I screamed again, pulling at her T-shirt, shrieking her name. "Cassie, get up! Get up!" She lay inert, oblivious to my prodding, and jerked her head to the right. If not for the sudden movement and the panting noises coming out of her mouth, I might have thought she was dead. Maybe she was dying. Maybe something really had happened, and she was breathing her last breaths.

My scalp prickled as the faint sound of fingernails—or were they claws?—emerged from the opposite corner. I screamed again and clutched at Cassie's shirt. "Get up, Cassie! Please! Wake up! Get us out of here!" I yanked again at her shirt, pulling so hard this time that it ripped. Still she lay motionless. The scraping noise sounded again, closer this time, and I scrabbled in the opposite direction, my survival instinct going into overdrive. Staying as close to the drapes as possible, I crab-walked on my hands and legs, feeling around with my fingers along the baseboards. There had to be a way out from the inside; Cassie had to have done something to close the door behind her. A lock, another button, maybe even a lever. I just had to keep moving until I found it.

My fingers raced along the dry wood, feeling, searching, pleading, until they came into contact with something smooth and silky. I lurched backward, bumping into the back of the table, hitting my head on a corner. The soft material brushed against my face; it was only the tablecloth, nothing else. Furious, I pushed the table over, wincing at the deafening crash it made against the floor, and resumed my search for the wall button. My eyes were shut tight, and my body, electric with fear and adrenaline, moved of its own accord. The air was dense; beads of sweat dropped like tears from the edge of my face. A hoarse panting sounded behind me, and I could not be sure if it was coming from Cassie or something else. Just when I thought I might collapse, my fingers came across a small indented circle, and as I pressed it, the wall slid back open. I stared in amazement as the bright lighting from Cassie's closet illuminated the small space, and then I rushed from the room.

But my excitement was short-lived. Cassie had locked the outer door as well, dead-bolting it shut, imprisoning me twice. I gasped and pulled at the handle, but it was no use. I whirled around, scanning the floor for a key, but the floor was bare. Standing up on tiptoe, I felt around the edges of the door, my fingers clamoring desperately for something, anything that might let me out. But there was nothing. For another twenty minutes, I pounded and screamed, pausing only to snatch one of Cassie's sweaters to cover myself with and to glance over my shoulder in case Cassie or whatever had made the scraping noise had followed me. I even hurled myself against the door in the desperate hope that it might give, but nothing worked. It would be another thirty minutes before Dominic heard my cries and came into Cassie's room.

I fell out all at once as he swung open the door, knocking

him down against the floor. "Let me out!" I screamed. "Let me go!"

"Whoa, whoa, whoa! What's going on?" He scrambled back up again, his face a map of bewilderment.

I slammed the closet door shut and sank to the floor against it, sobs racking my body as the realization that I was safe—at least for now—settled over me.

"Hey." Dominic's voice was soft. He reached out with one hand. "What's going on in here? What happened?"

I stopped crying and struggled to my feet. This was no time to start a conversation or answer any questions. I just wanted to get out of there. I had to leave. Now. Darting past him, I flew into the bathroom, searching for my clothes.

"Hey!" He paused at the bathroom door, one hand pressed against the frame. "What's your name? Are you here with my sister? With Cassie? Where is she?"

"I'm right here."

I screamed as her voice drifted out behind us, nearly falling over as I whirled around.

"Cassie?" Dominic stared at his sister.

Except for a few pieces of her hair being mussed and loose along the right-hand side of her face, her appearance was just as it had been before: calm, poised, unconcerned, all at the same time. Her eyes had a glossy quality to them, as if she'd just been sunbathing out by the pool, and except for the bottom of her T-shirt, which now hung ripped and untucked outside of her jeans, there was no sign of disarray, no indication that anything at all had happened.

"What the hell is going on?" Dominic demanded. "What happened?"

Cassie smiled, the edges of her mouth curling into a faint sneer. "Nothing happened," she said. "We were just playing a game." She paused, her eyes shifting from her brother's face to mine. "Weren't we, Marin?"

Ten

"'To conjoin with the dead,'" Dominic read aloud from the little green book, "'you must have a red room devoid of all light, two burning candles, and . . .'" He paused and then sat down, his legs giving way beneath him like pencils snapping.

"And what?" I asked.

"'Two people whose loved one has died by their own hand.'" He looked up at me, pain swimming behind his eyes.

Don't you understand, Marin? There's no one else. You're the only one who can do this with me. The realization hit me all at once, a fist between the eyes. "*That's* why she picked me," I whispered. "She needed another person who had survived someone's suicide." It was so awful that I wanted to cry; so horrifying that I wanted to scream. "How'd she even know?" I said instead. "I mean, how'd she find out about my mother?"

"You know how it is in school." Dominic was making an effort to talk. "Some people make it a point to find out everything they possibly can about someone new. Someone different." He shrugged, a mixture of embarrassment and distress crossing his face. "Cassie must've asked around about you, found out somehow."

"I just . . ." I sank down against the wall directly across from him, holding my head in my hands. "I just can't believe it."

Dominic was quiet.

"That's so sick." I lifted my head, stared at the front of his knees. "It's demented." I bit my lip, lifted my eyes to meet his. "I know she's your sister and everything, but that is just freaking crazy. I mean, who *does* that to someone?"

"I know." Dominic winced, as if the admission hurt him physically. "You're right. It is sick. But that's what I think Cassie is right now. Sick."

"You can say that again."

"Marin, you don't have to believe me when I say this, but this isn't really who Cassie is. I'm telling you, she's a good person. She didn't used to be like this. Something happened to her. . . ."

"Yeah, *something* happened to her," I blurted out. "She turned into a psychotic bitch." I leaned down and fiddled with my shoelace. He couldn't possibly blame me for being so pissed off. Still, I was talking about his sister here, his only sibling, someone he still had a connection with, still loved. I hoped he didn't freak out on me.

"Because of all this shit she's gotten involved in," Dominic pleaded. "And yeah, it's her fault she got involved in the first place, but it's only because she misses Gram so much. She hasn't been able to move on since Gram died, and with my mom and dad gone all the time, and with me doing all my sports, she probably feels like she has no one. She's desperate, you know? She's lonely, Marin, and she's just been trying to make that loneliness go away."

"Lonely?" I almost spat the word back out at him. "Are you kidding me? She's the most popular girl at St. Anselm's! She must have two hundred friends, Dominic. Give me a break."

"You want to know how popular Cassie is at St. Anselm's?" Dominic asked, hooking a thumb into his belt loop. "She pays people to be friends with her."

I squinted over at him and raised an eyebrow.

"Ask around. Ask anyone. Cassie'll give you whatever you want, buy you anything you need, as long as you say you're her friend. You know Rachel Vernits with the red hair? Olivia Randall, who's captain of the cheerleading team?"

I nodded slowly as he reminded me of the other two popularity queens: tall, lithe girls with big boobs, impeccable hair, beautiful teeth. They barely glanced at me in the cafeteria and rarely, if ever, deigned to move out of the way when we crossed paths in the hallway. Cassie was always planted in the middle of them.

"Cassie bought Rachel a membership to our country club last year. Olivia smokes Pall Malls. She had Cassie promise that she would buy her cigarettes for a whole year if she wanted to be part of their group."

"What?" I was aghast. "Why would she do something like that? Cassie can be friends with whoever she wants."

"No, she can't," Dominic said. "Cassie puts on a good show, but underneath, she's just a scared little kid."

"Scared?" I repeated. "Of what?"

"She was always shy," Dominic said. "But when she was younger, she was so nervous about school and not being able to read well that she started stuttering. Then she got so embarrassed about her stutter that she barely said a word at all. It got a little better in middle school, until she got placed in some of the special classes for her dyslexia and her friends started dropping her like a hot potato." He shrugged. "Maybe she thinks it's a guarantee of some kind, paying these girls. Maybe that way they won't dump her like the other ones did."

I felt a wave of pity for Cassie, followed immediately by a flood of aggravation. I didn't want to feel sorry for this girl. Not even a little bit. So she'd had a stutter once. And maybe she still struggled with dyslexia. Neither of them were the end of the world. She didn't have *cancer,* for crying out loud. Or one leg. She wasn't fat or ugly, and she hadn't been disfigured by some terrible accident. And even if she had, none of those things gave her the right to mess with people's lives the way she'd messed with mine. End of story.

"She's lonely, Marin. That's all it is." Dominic's voice sounded far away. "That might not be something you can understand, but when I think about the lengths she's gone to just to be in touch again with someone who loved her . . ." He swallowed a sound coming out of his mouth and shook his head, forcing it back down.

I opened my mouth to say something when a scream sounded above us. There was a crash, followed by the sound of something breaking. Another scream, higher than the first, echoed through a hallway, and we could hear feet running.

Dominic's face seemed to drain of blood. "That's Cassie. And the only one up there right now is Miss Peale, the day nurse. We have to help."

I pulled my hand out of his and held back. "I can't. I don't want to go up there."

"Marin." Dominic braced himself. "Please. I know it's not fair that you're involved in all of this, but I can't change that now. I need you." He paused, breathing hard. "She needs you. She'll feel better when she sees you're here. Remember? And then she'll calm down again. Just like last time."

A door slammed. Another scream.

I resisted, a sob clutching at the back of my throat. *I don't want to see it again. I don't want to see any of it.* But Dominic's face was so wrought with terror, the pleading in his eyes as real as anything I'd ever seen before; I couldn't bring myself to turn away. I was still part of this, however unwillingly. There was no point in denying it anymore, no use in running.

"Don't you leave me," I ordered.

He held out his hand, and I took it. Side by side, we raced up another flight of stairs and then stopped, trying to survey the situation.

The third floor looked nothing like the first two. The floors were bare, and the smooth hardwood matched the timber beams that arched across the ceiling like the skeleton of a ship. A narrow corridor of doors, combined with the absence of windows, gave it an almost monastery-like appearance, and in direct contrast to the noises we had just heard, it was eerily quiet.

"Miss Peale?" Dominic said in a low voice. "Are you there?"

A whimper emerged from inside one of the rooms, and we took a step toward it. "Miss Peale?" he said again. "Do you have Cassie with you?"

Silence.

I stayed inches behind him as he moved toward the door, holding on to one of the belt loops on the back of his pants. My whole body was hot, as if it might explode, and the top of my scalp prickled. Dominic reached out and gripped the door's black iron handle. "Miss Peale?" He pushed open the door.

It was hard to take everything in all at once, but my eyes

fell first on the nurse, a short, chubby woman, who was standing in the corner next to Cassie's bed. At the sight of us, she flattened her hands out in front of her, as if to say, "Not yet." Dressed in pale blue scrubs with a mass of black hair pulled back in a ponytail, she had two orange globs beneath her shirt, one loose and watery-looking, lodged inside her breastbone, the other small and tight as an acorn inside her armpit. Next to her on the floor, a lamp lay on its side, the shade dented and torn. Remnants of the smashed lightbulb littered the space next to it like tiny teeth.

"What happened?" Dominic asked. "Where's Cassie?"

The nurse brought a finger to her lips and pointed to a spot directly behind us. Slowly, Dominic and I turned around.

Cassie was stooped over in the opposite corner, bent in half at the waist, clutching her right side with her free hand. Her clothes appeared clean enough—blue athletic shorts, a white T-shirt, soft socks—but her hair, which hung on either side of her face, looked as if it hadn't been washed in weeks. Both arms were swathed in cocoons of white gauze, some of them still dotted with bright red spots of blood. Beneath them, I could make out tiny shapes in all different colors, miniature specks, darting one way and then another, from where she had cut herself again. Her breath went in and out of her mouth in shallow, ragged spurts, and her eyes were riveted to the floor.

"Cassie?" For the first time, Dominic sounded frightened. "Cassie, are you all right?"

A low growl drifted out from beneath her hair.

"Don't startle her." Miss Peale's voice was very soft. "She's just settled down again, I think. I'm going to give her a shot in a few seconds."

"What happened?" He did not take his eyes off his sister.

"She just bolted," Miss Peale whispered. "One minute she was sleeping, and then she sat up and started screaming. She tipped over the lamp when she jumped out of bed, and I think that really spooked her. She took off down the hall after that."

A snarl came out from the corner, the sound a dog might make before it lunges at someone's throat.

Dominic turned, gripping my hand. "Go to her?" he mouthed. "Let her know you're here."

I stared at him, unable to answer.

"Just let her see you," he whispered. "Let her look at your face." He squeezed my hand. "I'll go with you."

"What are you doing?" the nurse said sharply. "You need to leave her alone now. She's very skittish after these episodes. I have to—"

"I know," Dominic said. "Please. Just give me a minute."

Miss Peale did not reply.

I forced one foot to move. Then the other. Cassie's hands had moved up toward her face; she was twisting small pieces of her hair, wrapping them around her fingers. Suddenly, she dropped to the floor in a heap. I stopped, frightened. She stayed there for a moment, her face buried between her arms. The grunting noises began again, slowly at first and then gathering speed, a wolf panting. Inside her arms, the red shapes danced and throbbed, but there was no sign of the blackness in her head.

Not yet.

Not yet.

"Cassie?" The name coming out of my throat was barely audible, but the growling ceased, as if someone had pulled a switch in Cassie's back. I took another step, watching as she lifted her head. "Cassie, it's me. It's Marin."

Her face appeared like a mirage behind her hair and she gazed at me for a moment, transfixed. Under the bandage on her left cheek, I could make out the large carving wound again; it looked like a piece of raw meat, the edges clotted with dried blood and tissue. I opened my mouth, my lips forming a word, but nothing came out.

"Talk to her." Dominic's voice sounded tremulous in my ear. His fingers squeezed mine. "Say her name again."

"Cassie, it's Marin." I tried to steady my voice. "I'm here again, like you asked. Do you remember?"

Without warning, the girl's blue eyes rolled up inside her head. For a split second, her pupils vanished, a cloudy whiteness filling the void. Her eyelashes fluttered, tiny wings desperate to take flight, and then they rolled back down again, settling on me with an eerie deliberation. My blood seemed to freeze as I tried to understand what I was seeing. These were not Cassie's eyes looking out at me any longer. These eyes were reptilian, glossy and hooded, the pupils dark and cylindrical instead of round.

I took a step back, whimpering, pulling on Dominic's hand.

"No, it's okay." Dominic was holding my hand so hard it hurt. "Just say her name one more time, Marin. Maybe it'll help."

I shook my head, pushing at him now, trying to twist my hand out of his grip. "No, I can't. Please! Let me go!"

A terrible giggling drifted out from the corner, a throaty cackle that got louder, filling the air in the room with dread. The hairs on my neck stood up, and I could hear the sharp intake of Dominic's gasp.

"That's the laugh," he whispered. "That's the one I heard that night. In the kitchen."

"We have to get her back in bed." Miss Peale strode across the room, sounding both irritated and frightened. "Right now."

Dominic dropped my hand as Miss Peale reached for his sister. He followed her lead, grabbing Cassie's feet as she took the girl's arms. The strange laughter dissolved into shrieks as they carried her across the room, Cassie's body writhing and twisting under their hold. She arched her back and threw back her head, shoving her legs in and out like pistons, struggling to break loose. The awkward movements caused Dominic to drop her feet, and he moved in quickly, desperately, to grab them again. Somehow, the two of them got her back into bed, pinning her down against the mattress and then holding her with their arms.

"Keep her down on your side!" Miss Peale barked. "I've gotta tie her arm down over here."

It was hard to know if Cassie heard she was going to be tied down or if she had run out of energy and decided to relinquish the fight. But she suddenly stilled, a decision so immediate and unexpected that everyone, including Miss Peale, took a step back. Cassie lay there for a moment on the mattress, limp and unmoving. The restraint closest to Dominic still hung down on the side of the bed, forgotten.

"Cassie?" Miss Peale said her name as the girl sat up in the bed. She looked disoriented, confused. "Cassie, honey, what is it?" If she heard the nurse's question, Cassie gave no indication of it. She began to breathe hard again, her nostrils flaring, as if something was building itself up inside. A murky gray thread appeared behind her eyes, snaking between the spaces inside her skull. I watched as it morphed into a rich blackness, the thickest, deepest absence of light I had ever seen, ten times blacker than her fingertips had been the night before, one hundred times deeper than what I had seen in the hospital. It filled every crevice inside her brain, swallowing the tiniest of cells, obliterating them one by one from sight. It was so deep that it was not even a color. Or a shape.

It was more of a thing, a presence.

"What's going on?" Miss Peale's voice was sharp again. "What's that on her neck?"

The right side of Cassie's neck had begun to swell, as if being pushed at with a fist from the inside. Slowly, a section of skin morphed into a small, round shape. Inch by inch, it grew, expanding to the size of a golf ball, and then a peach, before it seemed to stop, hovering just a few inches below her jawbone. The skin around it was as taut as a drum, the edges ringed with red. Cassie reached toward us with her one free arm, the fingers on her hands twisting like claws. She opened her mouth wide, as if she might scream, and then closed it again without a sound.

"What's happening?" Dominic shouted. "Is she choking?"

"I'm getting the Risperdal." Miss Peale raced over to the dresser on the other side of the room and grabbed a syringe. She watched Cassie with one eye as she held up the needle, flicking at the bottom half with a shaking fingernail.

The other side of Cassie's neck began to twitch and then swell. "Mariiiiiinn . . . ," she whispered. Her voice sounded far away, as if trapped inside a box. "Mariiiiiinn . . ."

Miss Peale lunged at the girl, grabbing her wrist and plunging the needle deep into the muscle of her upper arm. Cassie did not turn her head, did not even blink.

"Mariiiiinn . . ." Her voice was a wheeze, the last fragment of air being pushed from her lungs.

"Oh my God." Dominic's voice was louder. "She can't breathe! Help her, Marin. Please!"

I took a step forward, an inch closer, my eyes still on Cassie's neck, which was distorted now beyond description, but she recoiled at the movement as if I had touched her with an electrical current. The sinewy blackness seemed to be bleeding now, oozing its way behind the features of her face, swallowing the insides of her throat. It dipped lower, spreading like a wave into the tops of her shoulders, her lungs, her heart.

"Cassie?" My lips shook.

She gazed at me for half a second with her terrible eyes and then lifted her hand to point at me. "You can do nothing to me," she said. The faraway whisper in her voice was gone, replaced now with a new, gravelly voice that sounded warped, as if she was speaking in slow motion. "Nothing!"

I felt faint, listening to the sound coming out of Cassie's mouth, my fear a tangible thing now holding me by both shoulders. And yet just like in the hospital, I could not stop staring, could not tear my eyes away from the horrific image. My eyes did not blink. They could not. Riveted, I remained where I was, locked in a nightmare of unbearable proportions.

Cassie continued to stare at me, the blackness inside of her seething. Her eyes darted first to the right and then to the left. All at once, she dropped her head and clutched one side of it with her free hand. She rocked back and forth in the bed, pulling at her hair, and then stopped. Without lifting her head, she pointed at me again and began to scream. "Why do you keep looking at me? Stop it! You'll kill me! You'll *kill* me!"

I staggered backward, gasping for breath, the fear like

a claw making its way up the back of my throat, siphoning off breath. What was happening now? Nothing made sense anymore. Hadn't Dominic said that she *wanted* to see me, that she derived some kind of comfort from my presence in the room? I wasn't helping at all. In fact, it looked like I was only making things worse.

Cassie flung herself against the bed; sprawled out on her back, her arms and legs beginning to flail like pieces of a broken windmill. Miss Peale was on top of her again, her mouth pinched in a tight line, struggling to tie her down. Cassie screamed and cursed. "Get out! Stop looking at me! Get out of here before you kill me!"

I moved back. Way, way back, past Miss Peale and Cassie and Dominic, into the corner, where I slumped down, pressing myself into the tiny space. If I could have, I would have merged somehow through the wall. Anything to get out of here. Anything to forget the ghastly scene unfolding before my eyes.

"Get out!" she continued to scream, although there was a desperation to it now, a begging tone that had not been there before. "Please," she moaned. "Please just leave me alone."

It took a full five minutes for Cassie to settle down again. Even after the screaming stopped, her fingers and legs continued to twitch, as if ridding themselves of the last of her energy until she was still again, a tangle of limp limbs beneath Miss Peale. Like a tide ebbing, the blackness left her body, a swirl of movement down a drain. Her panting slowed, and after another few seconds, her eyes refocused, the pupils shrinking back to their normal size.

"Is she . . . ?" Dominic started.

"Give me a minute." Miss Peale's voice was tight. "Let her relax all the way. I don't know if she'll start up again."

The room was silent for several moments, the only sound the deep intakes of Miss Peale's and Cassie's breathing.

"All right," Miss Peale said. She cradled Cassie like a baby in both arms, repositioning her against the pillows. "I think this one's over."

Dominic ran to her. "Cassie," he said.

With great effort, Cassie lifted her head off the pillow and looked around the room, her head hanging low against her chest. Her eyes drifted, unfocused, as if she were drunk, pausing only when she caught sight of me, still hovering in the corner.

For a full minute, she stared at me without saying anything. Even from across the room, I could see the normal blue of her eyes again, and then a blur as they filled with tears.

"Marin," Cassie whispered. It was her regular voice, verging on the edge of a sob. "Oh God, Marin, you're here."

Eleven

Cassie wept with abandon, her face a picture of anguish. She tried to stretch an arm toward me, but the restraints made it impossible for her to move it more than a few inches. "Marin," she whimpered. "Please, come here. Help me."

But I didn't move. What in God's name had just happened? Were my eyes, my ears, all of my senses deceiving me? I searched Cassie's face, straining to see something—anything at all—still lurking there inside her head, but there was nothing. Was the blackness really gone? Was whatever had just happened really over?

The veins along the outside of Cassie's neck tightened as she tried to lift her head some more, but there was no sign of the softball-sized shapes that had been there, no trace of any distortion at all along the smooth slope of skin.

"Please," she whispered, still stretching her fingers in my direction. "Marin."

Was it really safe? Cassie looked like a baby, a toddler who had been punished and was pleading for forgiveness. But was it just a trick? Another ruse to get me closer so that she could hiss at me again, spit curses in my direction?

"It's okay now, Marin." Dominic was beckoning me forward with his hand. "She can't move out of the restraints, and the Risperdal is starting to work. She's calm. It's all right."

I got up, moving toward her on wooden legs, and then stopped a foot away from the bed. Cassie's face, splattered with drops of saliva, was still pink from exertion. The figure eight on her cheek looked darker, as if the scabs had loosened and bled during her outburst, and the white bandages around her arms were unraveling.

I stretched out my hand until it came into contact with Cassie's, but it was not until my fingers closed around the other girl's that she began to cry. Her body heaved up and down as she wept, taking in air, breathing in oxygen. "Marin, don't leave me. Please, don't leave me."

I struggled to wrap my head around everything that had just happened. First of all, what was the blackness I kept seeing inside Cassie? And secondly, where had it gone? Was it just hibernating again, the way it obviously had since I'd seen her in the hospital, waiting to emerge when it needed to? What made it come out? And then withdraw again?

"Cassie." I pulled back a little and lowered my hand. "Is that really you?"

"It's me." Cassie's voice was a whisper, but it broke on the word *me*. "Oh, Marin, please don't leave. When you're here, I can't feel it anymore. It's gone. She's gone." She was breathing hard again, but her eyes were still the same clear blue, the voice definitively hers. The muscles inside her face relaxed as her sobbing slowed. She smelled like sweat and body odor, and despite my terror, I reached out and touched her hair.

"Who is 'she'?" I asked, just as I had in the hospital. "Who are you talking about, Cassie?"

"I don't know." The girl was starting to panic again. "But when I see you, she leaves. The pain leaves." She talked quickly, as if running out of time. "You're the only one who can take it away. Don't go." She clutched at my arm. "Please don't go. Don't leave me alone with her again. Please."

She had to be wrong. Nothing I had just done—or didn't do—could have had any effect on such a situation. The fact that I had been here was just a coincidence. A fluke. None of it had anything to do with me. "I won't leave," I whispered, sitting down on the bed next to her. "I'll stay."

Cassie's head lolled to one side at my words. Her whole body trembled, and her breath emerged in raspy gasps. She shuddered once, something catching and then releasing deep inside her throat. For a full five minutes, she remained like that, silent, pressed up against me. Maybe the Risperdal was working after all. Or maybe she was just exhausted from the events that had just transpired. Whatever it was, it did not take long before I recognized the sound of deep, measured breathing. I looked over at Miss Peale, who nodded. "She's asleep," she mouthed.

I got up as slowly as I dared, extricating Cassie's hold on me with gentle hands, and lay her back down on the pillow. The skin on her face was a milky white, as if she had just come in from the cold, and her mouth was parted, the lips loose and slack. Ragged strands of her hair hung down against her chest, and the terrible carving on her cheek flickered beneath the bandage. I felt a tugging inside, a pain that made my eyes fill with tears, which made no sense at all after everything this girl had put me through, but there it was.

"Come on," Dominic whispered. "Let's let her sleep now."

He pushed through the door first and then stood there for a moment, his back to me, and lowered his head. For a full moment, his shoulders rose and fell as he pressed his thumb and forefinger along the inner corners of his eyes, and I wanted to go to him, I did, but then I remembered how I hadn't wanted anyone around me after Mom died, not even the people I loved the most. Their presence hurt physically, as if the part of her she had taken away from me was still with them. I couldn't bear it.

He turned back around after another moment, wiping his face with the back of his wrist. Without moving, he met my eyes. Held them for a moment. "Sorry," he said.

"Please don't say that. There's nothing to be sorry for."

He nodded. "You okay?"

"I think so."

"Did you see those . . . ?" He winced, bringing his fingers to his neck.

I nodded.

"What *were* they?"

"I don't know. But they went away after she calmed down."

He nodded again, his eyes sweeping the rug beneath his feet. "And that laugh . . ." He looked up. "You heard it, right?"

"Yeah."

"I *told* you. That's what I heard that night. In the kitchen. The same exact thing." He tilted his head to one side. "It's not just me, is it? I mean, I wasn't imagining it. That wasn't her voice, was it?"

"It didn't sound like her."

He ran a hand through his hair and rolled his shoulders back as if shaking off some last vestige of fear. "Well, at least she'll sleep now. She'll be out for a while too. That stuff they give her could flatten a horse."

"Good."

He hesitated as I looked at my watch. "You need to go, probably."

"Yeah."

"I'll take you home."

But I lingered as he moved past me, something still tugging inside.

"Marin?" He turned around.

"What do you think it is?" I didn't want to know, and yet a part of me already did. Still, I needed to hear someone else say it. I needed to hear him say it.

Dominic pushed his hands inside his pockets. He took a deep breath and then let it out, a loud whooshing sound. "I think when she said those weird words in the closet that day, when she was holding your hand and trying to get our grandmother to talk to her . . ." He paused, wincing. "I think it worked. I mean, I think my grandmother's spirit came into that room. And then it must've moved into her." He lifted his head. He looked drained, as though he hadn't slept in days; the hollows beneath his eyes were shrouded with faint circles. "You heard her just now, right? When she was describing it. She used the word *she*. It can't be anything else. That's gotta be what happened."

"You . . . I mean, you really think it's your grandmother's spirit in there . . . ?" I could barely bring myself to finish the sentence. "I mean, in *her*?"

"Yeah." Dominic's face was anguished. "I do. And we've got to find a way to get it back out because for some reason, it's torturing my sister. Maybe it's upset at being trapped inside Cassie's body. Maybe it doesn't know how to get back out. I don't know." He ran his hands through his hair. "Oh my God, I don't know how any of this shit works."

I could hear the tremor in his voice, a shaking that I knew my own voice would assume if I said anything else, and so I took his hand instead, holding it between both of mine. The gesture was as natural as his had been, maybe even more so, and I cupped his big fingers inside my palm and pressed them against mine.

"I'm scared," I whispered.

"I know." Dominic made no movement to adjust his hand, except to squeeze mine more tightly. "So am I."

Twelve

We went out to a sun porch on the side of the house, an enormous room with a white floor and three ceiling fans spinning overhead, so we could sit and talk. I followed Dominic's lead, collapsing next to him on a white wicker couch with lemon-colored cushions. Palm plants rose up from stone pots in each corner, and crisp eyelet curtains hung over the windows. The air smelled like oranges and fabric softener, and I wished that I could lay my head down and go to sleep. I wondered if I would ever be able to fall asleep again after everything I'd just seen. Would Cassie?

"Maybe there's an undoing ritual in the book." Dominic was riffling through the pages of the little green book. "You know, that'll tell us how to get the spirit out."

"What do you mean, *us*?" I already missed the feel of his hand in mine. And right now, I wanted it more than ever, if only to help ease my own fear, which was starting to encompass a lot more than just the facts of Cassie's situation. Things were happening too fast, charging ahead at full speed before we had a chance to come to any real conclusions about anything. What if we were wrong, and it didn't involve Cassie's grandmother at all? What if it was some kind of evil demon or crazed spirit? Then what? "Dominic. There's nothing *we* can do about this. We have to get a—"

"Wait, look!" His eyebrows shot up as he pointed to a page. Across the top of it, the heading read EXORCISM OF CONJOINED SPIRITS. He slapped the back of his hand against the book. "I *knew* it! We can undo the conjoining ritual with this. We can totally help her!"

"An exorcism?" I repeated. "You're not serious."

"It's right here." He pointed to the page again. "Look, it's right here."

"You're out of your mind." I made a point not to look at the book. "Have you ever seen *The Exorcist*? Do you know what happens during those things?"

"That's just a movie, Marin." Dominic was studying the page, his eyebrows furrowed into a knot. "You know, like *The Exorcism of Emily Rose* and *The Haunting* and all those other ones. They amp up all the special effects to make more money. None of that shit really happens."

"Oh yeah? You know that for sure?"

"Marin." Dominic looked up from the page. "This is real life, okay? Just listen for a minute."

I swallowed hard, a slow dread already beginning to

move through my veins. "Dominic, I really don't think that—"

"It doesn't say anything here about the red room or candles or anything." He began to read aloud, his excitement mounting: " 'Before a conjoined exorcism can begin, the afflicted person must be lying supine on the floor.' " He looked at me. "Supine?"

"I think that means flat on her back. But, Dominic, I don't—"

" 'After the afflicted has been settled comfortably,' " he pressed on, " 'he or she must be in the presence of a single being that possesses a buried heart' "—his forehead wrinkled and his voice slowed—" 'and a hidden trinity. BE FOREWARNED! This ritual cannot be completed without specific said objects, and should not even be attempted unless both are present.' " He looked up at me. "What the hell is 'a buried heart' and 'a hidden trinity'?"

"No idea." I paused, and then unable to help myself: "They're not talking about a real heart, are they? Like in a dead person?"

"I don't know." Dominic's eyes were as wide as nickels. "What do you think?"

"It doesn't matter what I think." I shook my head. "But getting a real heart is totally impossible, unless you're some kind of crazy person who goes and digs up corpses. And the hidden trinity must be some kind of code that, like, only your grandmother understood. Neither of those things makes any sense."

"I agree." He reached up to pull on his earlobe. "Help me figure it out. Just keep talking."

"I don't want to keep talking." I got up and paced the length of the room. Sunlight filtered through the big windows, illuminating a pocket of dust motes; they hung suspended in the air like tiny stars and then vanished again. "The only reason I'm even here is because I wanted to find out more about what happened that day in the room behind the closet."

"All right." He interlaced his fingers and locked them behind his head. "Fine. Then I'll just talk to myself."

I gazed out at the beautiful scenery through the glass pane: a white, kidney-shaped pool surrounded by deck chairs and tables looked out over a sweeping vista of manicured lawns and cypress trees. A man in jeans and a red baseball cap was riding a mower over the grass, and farther out beyond the pool, another man was washing a black car in the driveway of a four-car garage.

"A buried heart," Dominic murmured behind me. "Buried as in what? Literally buried? Like in a graveyard, maybe? Or maybe it's just underneath something. Closed off, in some way. Shit, I don't know. How about just a heart? Heart as in . . ." He exhaled again, a loud, painful sound. "As in love? As in . . . what?"

He'd said his father was in the local office today, that he lived more or less in the tall building downtown. So who was the guy on the lawnmower? And who was the man washing one of their four cars? Did they have a staff?

People who just took care of the grounds? I'd never known anyone like that.

"Maybe it doesn't have to be a real heart," Dominic continued. "Maybe it can be fake or plastic. You know, like something the Tin Man gets. In *The Wizard of* Oz. A symbol, you know?"

"The Tin Man gets a plastic heart with a stopwatch on it," I said without turning around. The man on the lawnmower was creating wide, even swaths in the grass, neat as a ruler. "I doubt that's what the people who wrote that book had in mind for an exorcism ritual."

"Yeah." He cleared his throat. "I just . . . I mean, I can't imagine my grandmother ever doing anything with a real heart. She used to freak out if she saw a *worm* on the sidewalk. Besides, the only thing I ever heard about her was that she was just a medium. She wasn't into black magic or anything. As far as I know, she didn't go around visiting graveyards or sacrificing dead animals for exorcisms."

"Maybe she never did a conjoining exorcism," I said. "And no offense, but I think there's a lot about your grandmother that you probably never knew."

He didn't respond, and I squeezed my eyes shut behind my glasses, wishing for the second time today that I could take my words and put them back in my mouth. I waited, biting my lip. The lawnmower guy had started back down the slope again. Tiny bits of grass spit out from one side, and I could see a series of dark blue ovals under his right arm.

"You're right," Dominic said. "She might've been

someone else entirely when she went into that closet and did her witchcraft. Probably someone I wouldn't even recognize." He sighed. "All right, what about a hidden trinity? Do you think that could be as literal a thing as the heart?"

I turned around, crossing my arms over my chest. I'd talk him through this last part and then I was done. I wanted to go home. Besides, it was getting late. "The only time I've ever heard anything about a trinity was in church."

"Right. God the Father, God the Son, and God the Holy Spirit."

I raised my eyebrows. "Are you Catholic?"

"Marin," he said, smiling a little. "We both go to a Catholic school."

I rolled my eyes. He sounded like Lucy. "I'm pretty sure there's lots of students at St. Anselm's who aren't Catholic."

"Yes, we're Catholic," Dominic said. "We used to belong to St. Ignatius's, but we haven't been in a long time. My dad knows the priest there. Father William?"

I nodded. "He's friends with my grandmother."

"Do you think the trinity means something inside a church?"

"Maybe. Except that it says it has to be hidden."

"Well, the only Holy Trinity I've heard of isn't exactly visible. But it's not exactly possible to get, either."

I thought for a moment. "The word *trinity* actually means anything with three parts, right?"

"Yeah, I guess."

"Well, then, maybe it can be anything. You know, like

a branch with three leaves on it. Or a set of something, like three pictures or three cups." I shrugged, getting frustrated. "Except that they all have to be hidden. So I don't know."

"No, no, I think you're right about the first part, though." Dominic wagged his finger in my direction. "I think that's the way we've gotta be thinking. Now we just have to find a set of three things that's hidden."

"You mean *you* just have to find a set of three things that's hidden."

"Yeah." He leaned back into the couch again. "Shit. This is going to be a lot more complicated than I thought."

"And you might not get it," I added. "Or you might get the wrong things and make something even worse happen."

"We'll get it," Dominic said, and then caught himself. "*I'll* get it." He paused, watching me. "I have to. This is my only chance, Marin."

"It's *not* your only chance." I moved away from the window and took a step toward him. "If you really think there's a spirit inside your sister, Dominic, you should go tell someone—"

"Who?" Dominic's eyebrows narrowed as he cut me off. "Who am I going to tell? My parents? They don't know jack-shit about my sister and me, okay? As far as they're concerned, Cassie and I are two of the most perfect children on the planet. If I went and told them that I think my grandmother's spirit is living inside her, they'd laugh in my face."

"Then tell them about what happened in that room! Tell them what she did! What happened that day!"

"You're not listening to me." Dominic clenched his jaw. "They won't hear me, Marin. They don't ever hear me, because they're not here."

"They're here now," I protested.

"Just to get Cassie settled." His voice fell, and he wrinkled his nose, as if trying to hold back tears. "My mom told me this morning. Now that they've gotten a diagnosis and everything's set with the nurses and the medication, they're going back. To Florida."

I staggered backward, aghast. Who *were* these people? And how could they treat their own children like strangers? *Worse* than strangers.

"I probably should tell someone." Dominic's voice was conciliatory. "And I will. But I've got to try this first. I have to. And then if it doesn't work, I'll tell whoever we need to tell about everything that happened. I swear."

I stared at the floor, running a fingertip over the curve of one eyebrow. An already insane situation had somehow just leapfrogged into complete madness. Dominic Jackson was going to perform a conjoining exorcism on his sister in the hopes of extricating their dead grandmother's spirit from her body. It sounded so ridiculous that I might have laughed if my heart wasn't lodged in my throat.

Dominic leaned forward, trying to catch my eye. "I know you think I'm crazy, but there's a really good chance that it'll work. The ritual that Cassie did worked, right?

Why wouldn't it work for me?" His face twisted in desperation. "If I can just figure out what a buried heart and a hidden trinity are and then find some way to get them, I can save her without anyone ever being the wiser."

"I don't think *you're* crazy," I said. "I just think your idea is."

"What idea?" We both turned as Mrs. Jackson appeared in the doorway. She was as beautifully dressed as she had been yesterday, this time in a silk dress that wrapped around at the waist and cobalt blue heels with gold trim. The yellow ball in the center of her chest looked slimy, as if it had been coated in fungus. It swayed like Jell-O as she moved, and she had too much makeup under her eyes, which gave her a strange, alien-like appearance. I felt a surge of hate as I looked at her. She was an awful, selfish person.

"Oh, hey, Mom." Dominic shoved the little book inside his back pants pocket. "Marin and I were just talking."

Mrs. Jackson's eyes swept up and down the length of me. Her red lips pursed. "Oh, hello, Marin." She looked reproachfully back at Dominic. "What are you two doing here? You didn't go up to see Cassie, did you? I don't want her getting all—"

"No, Mom, she was just helping me with some of Cassie's school stuff." Dominic glanced in my direction, shooting me a "just go with this, okay?" kind of look, and then refocused on his mother. "You know, filling me in on the stuff she's been missing. It's no big deal. Don't get excited. She was just going home anyway."

Home. The word had never sounded so good.

"Yeah, I have to go," I said. "I'm actually kind of late." I took a step out of the sunroom, avoiding Mrs. Jackson's stare.

"Right behind you," Dominic said.

I waited until he brought the Jeep to a halt at the first stop sign inside the development. Then I turned in my seat, shifting my knee up, a fence between us. "I know you're hoping I'll change my mind about all this, but I won't. If you're that set on doing it, you're gonna have to do it by yourself. I'm sorry, but the first time was too much. I just can't go there again."

"I know." A muscle pulsed in his cheek. "It's okay."

I lowered my leg. I'd expected a fight. An argument, at least.

He pushed down on the gas, navigating the car onto Reynolds Avenue. Between us, his track-and-field medal swung behind the mirror; sunlight glinted off the edge, splashing pale, watery shadows across the upholstery. I picked at the trim along the edge of my seat, trying to ignore the vague disappointment curling up in my chest. How could I be disappointed? I didn't want to do this. Not even a little bit.

"What's the real deal with your parents?" I asked, switching subjects. "You know, with them not being around and thinking you guys are perfect?"

His hands tensed on the wheel, and for a moment, I wished I hadn't asked. But then he rocked his head from side to side as if warming up for a fight and took a deep breath. "I probably made it sound like they're terrible people, but they're not. They're just really into their own lives." He shrugged. "They're used to doing their own thing, living life on their own terms. They were raised the same way. Their parents were always jetting to one place or another, so I guess that's all they know." He bit the inside of his cheek as he made a right on Main Street. "As far as thinking that we're perfect, they just sort of follow our progress through the nannies' reports, which are usually glowing." He lifted one eyebrow, allowing a tiny grin to slip onto his lips. "The not-so-glowing ones usually don't get sent. Which means that my parents are pretty much in the dark when it comes to any of the bad stuff that happens. Unless it's an emergency or something, like with Cassie the other day."

I stayed quiet, listening. For as absent as Mom had been, sleeping through her days, sometimes for weeks at a time, she had always been there for me. Or at least she'd tried to be. I'd gone into her bedroom once or twice during those times and sat next to her on the bed, holding her hand, asking her how her day went, and she had made the effort to sit up both times and talk. The conversation had been stilted and I'd gotten the feeling that part of her, maybe even most of her, wasn't hearing the things I'd said, but still. She'd sat up. She'd tried. From what Dominic was telling me now, Mr. and Mrs. Jackson didn't even try.

"They do love us." He glanced in my direction, checking to see if I believed him. "I mean, there's nothing they haven't given us. Ever."

"Except their time."

He squinted, as if the light behind the windshield had gotten too bright. "Right. Except their time." He snorted, and the movement seemed to drop something he'd been holding in, crack some part of the façade. "Sometimes I think they see us more as pets than kids. You know, just something to have because everyone else has one. We add a little bit more to the status report in their social world."

"Doesn't that bother you?"

"It used to a lot more when I was younger." He shrugged. "Not so much now that we're older. You can get used to anything, right?"

"Depends on what anything is." I paused. "Do you really think they'd laugh at you if you told them you thought Cassie had somehow summoned your grandmother's spirit? I mean, that's serious stuff, Dominic."

"I know. But even if they didn't laugh, it would take a lot to convince them. In their world, the doctor's word is golden—nothing else matters. As far as they're concerned they've already been given a diagnosis and medication to treat it. Throw in the twenty-four-hour nurses, pay the bill, and the case is closed." There was a bitterness to his voice that hadn't been there before, and I wondered if he ever had moments where he missed his mother the way I still missed mine. Even if she wasn't there for him. Even if deep down, he wondered if she loved him at all.

"Sometimes I think the worst thing about parents is that they forget they were kids once," I said. "And that they used to feel things too. Just like we do."

"Yeah." Dominic turned his head, startled for a moment, and then looked back out at the road. "Yeah, I think you're right."

We'd reached the dirt road by then and drove in silence down the length of it. My legs felt rubbery for some reason, as though I'd just gotten off my bike after riding thirty miles uphill, and my hands were cold. It had been a long time since I'd had such an intense conversation with someone, and while parts of it had been uncomfortable, I wished other parts of it would never end.

"Well, here we are." He pulled the Jeep into my driveway and leaned his head against the seat. He looked drained, as if he had just run a race, which he sort of had. It had been a long day. For both of us. He let his head loll to one side until he was looking at me. "You're a really incredible girl, you know that?"

I dropped my head, traced an imaginary line on the fabric of my jeans.

"Hey." He reached out and rested a hand on top of my wrist. "I mean it."

I looked down at his fingers, at the blue sphere inside his wrist. It would take less than a second for me to bend down and put my lips over it, let them linger there for a moment until he could feel how much I felt for him. I slid my hand on top of his instead, felt my fingers close around his. He leaned closer, brushing my unkempt bangs along the top of my forehead. "It'd be nice to look into your eyes one of these days," he said. "Instead of always looking at my reflection in your sunglasses."

I dropped my head and pushed them farther up along the bridge of my nose. "I have to wear them," I lied.

"Why?"

"I have bad eyes."

"Oh." He studied me, perhaps deliberating whether to probe any further.

"I really have to go." I wasn't going to give him the chance. Not now. Not ever. I pulled my hand out of his. "Thanks for the ride."

"Any time." He looked disappointed as I slid out of the car. My hand was on the door when he said, "Marin?"

"Yeah?"

He hesitated, as if wanting to say something else, and then pulled on his earlobe. "Thanks. For today. For everything."

"You're welcome." I shut the door and headed inside, standing just behind the curtain in the front window so I could see the back of his head as he drove down the long road and then out of sight once more.

Thirteen

Nan was slumped in her big easy chair when I came into the living room, fanning herself with one of her kerchiefs. Her white hair lay in limp curls along the tops of her ears, and her cheeks were pink. It was all I could do not to run to her, to throw myself into her lap, spill out the whole story. "Nan?" I said instead.

She dropped the kerchief and opened her eyes, a smile flitting across her broad features. "Hi, angel. How are you?"

"I'm okay." I went over to her, slid down in the space next to the chair. The blue beads along her knuckles were very bright, and the rosy egg just below her shoulder had grown at least another inch. I squeezed her arm and left my hand there. "You feeling okay? You look tired. What were you doing?"

"Oh, I had a heck of a day." She resumed fanning herself.

Her skin was paler than usual and she had an uneasy look on her face, as if she had eaten something that hadn't agreed with her. "I went out to the greenhouse and swept the floor and rearranged all the pots, and then I weeded the vegetable garden and planted another row of carrots, and then I came in here meaning to lie down, but I caught sight of an enormous cobweb in the corner of the dining room ceiling and the next thing you know, I had the entire house dusted."

"Nan." I leaned over, resting my chin on her arm. "That's too much for anyone. Why don't you go upstairs and lie down for a while? I can make dinner."

"No, no, angel. I've been sitting here for the past twenty minutes or so. I'm good and rested again." She reached over and ran her hand through my hair. "I don't like getting older, Marin. My energy just gets zapped. It stinks."

I grinned, even as something pulled at me, deep inside. "Just the way it goes, I guess."

"You got that right." She moved the kerchief back and forth in front of her face. "So how was your date?"

"Nan!" I pulled back as if she had tossed a bug at me. "It wasn't a *date*!"

"Boy, girl, car, lunch. Hours and hours and hours away from the house." She raised her eyebrows. "Sure looked like a date to me."

"Well, it wasn't."

"He's someone from school?"

"Uh-huh."

"Dominic? Was that his name?"

"Uh-huh."

"Wonderful name. You know, Saint Dominic had a phenomenal life. He was a—"

"He's not a saint, Nan," I cut her off. "He's just a boy."

I could feel her eyes on me for a moment, and then she reached out and tucked a piece of hair behind my ears. "Well, all right, then, Smarty-Pants, if it wasn't a date, what was it?"

I hesitated. There was no way I could get into anything that even resembled the truth. And maybe a partial lie didn't really count. At the very least it wasn't as bad as a full-blown one. "It wasn't anything," I said. "He's actually Cassie's older brother."

The kerchief halted. "Cassie *Jackson*?"

"Yeah."

"Marin, I really don't think—"

"He just wanted me to give him the rundown on her classes. You know, because we're in the same grade. She's going to be missing a lot of school because of being sick and he's helping her out so she doesn't fall behind." I shrugged. "That's it. No big deal."

"Oh." Nan eased back into the chair again. "Well, all right, then."

God, I hated lying to her more than anyone else. She deserved better from me. *I* deserved better from me. "Is Dad home?"

"Not yet." She hauled herself partway out of the chair and I stood, extending my arm so she could pull herself all the way up. "You want to help me with dinner?"

"Sure." I waited for her to link her arm inside mine. She leaned her whole weight against me as we moved toward the kitchen, her feet shuffling a bit as she walked. "I'm starving. What're we having?"

"What'd we have last night?" she asked.

"Um . . . pork chops."

"We had leftovers, didn't we?"

"Nan. We always have leftovers."

"Good." She nodded once. "Then that's what we're having tonight."

Sleep was impossible. I tossed and turned in bed, kicking the covers off at one point and balling my pillows up under my head to adjust my position. Nothing worked. Every time I closed my eyes, all I could see was the scene in Cassie's room—the weird shape her eyes had taken, the blackness in her skull, the disgusting growths on her neck. There was the horrible giggling and then the words she'd said in that odd, distorted voice: *You can't do anything to me. Nothing.* If it was her grandmother's spirit in there talking, where had such a comment come from? And what did it mean?

Deep down, I knew that Dominic's crazy theory was probably right, that it was some sort of spirit inside Cassie. I couldn't deny the fact that I had heard and felt something that day in the locked room. It had been an otherworldly *thing,* seeping into the room like a fog and then breathing and scratching the walls. Whether it was their grandmother's soul from the dead or a life force all its own, I would probably never know. And maybe it didn't matter. But it was time to admit that whatever it was, it had knocked Cassie flat on her back. And then invaded her being. Now it seemed as though it were eating her alive, from the inside out. And there was nothing anyone could do about it, unless someone summoned a priest or Dominic's insane exorcism worked.

I got out of bed and headed for the kitchen, but the dusky glow coming from the TV in the living room made me change course. Nan always stayed up late watching *I Love Lucy* reruns, or David Letterman, and sometimes I fell asleep on the couch next to her. I stopped, though, when I saw Dad in the easy chair, watching a war story on the History Channel, and tiptoed backward, trying to escape without being seen.

"Hey," he said, turning to look at me. "I thought I heard something." He patted the wide arm of his chair. "Come sit."

Damn it. I bypassed his chair and sat down on the couch instead, leaning over my knees so I could study my bare toes.

He ignored the rebuff, watching me with steady eyes. "How was your day?"

"It was okay."

"Mine was, too, thanks for asking." He kicked up the foot portion of the chair and leaned back. "Although it was a digging day."

Digging meant foundation work, which was Dad's least favorite part of his job. It was interminable labor, he always said, and boring to boot. His favorite part was when the skeleton of the house was finally up and he could sit on the thick beams and hammer ten thousand nails into the wood. Dad had always been good with a hammer and nails, but these days, he took a sincere pleasure in hitting things over and over again.

"'Bout midmorning, Dave and I found these crazy fossil-like things on one side of the foundation that had the whole crew excited," he said. "It was kind of fascinating."

"Cool." I fiddled with my big toenail, which needed to be clipped. "What kind of fossils?"

"They were embedded in these real thin pieces of rock. They looked like bird skeletons. Or maybe bats. I don't know. But they were perfectly preserved. I mean, you could see the tips of their feathers. Right there in the rock."

"You bring one home?"

He looked startled, as if he hadn't thought of such a thing. "There were only three," he said. "Dave took them to show a scientist guy he knows over at the college. He thinks they might actually be worth something."

"Nice." I stood up and glanced in his direction. The yellow globs along the bridge of his nose were so small they looked like sequins. "Well, night."

"Nan says you were hanging out with the Jackson boy today." Dad looked at the TV as he spoke.

My heart lurched. "Yeah, just to go over homework stuff. For his sister."

"I don't want you to see him again." He flicked his eyes away from the screen and fastened them on me. "Understood?"

"Why?" A rush of anger washed through me. "I didn't do anything wrong."

"I'm not saying you did. I just don't want you to see him again. Cassie's parents can worry about her homework. It's not your place."

"I *know* it's not my place. I was just trying to help."

His eyes narrowed and then eased again, as if considering this. "Help someone else," he said, looking at the TV again. "Okay?"

I strode from the room without answering and slammed the door to my room before flopping onto my bed. If I could stand one more day with him in this house, it would be a miracle. He was such a rigid *jerk,* throwing his authority around like I was a piece of property, as if he *owned* me. The ironic thing was that he probably thought he'd just gone and gotten all personal with me because of the stupid conversation about bird fossils. Which was a joke. He never came right out and asked me anything of any real significance when it came to my life. God forbid we had a conversation about anything important. Anything that *mattered.*

Right after we moved to Connecticut, Nan had asked Dad and me to accompany her to a therapist she talked to every so often, just to "get things out in the open, to make sure we were all on the same page." The therapist had been a nice-enough lady, with short blond hair, a long green dress that showed a little bit of cleavage, and brown sandals. But the thing I remembered about her the most was the enormous piece of amber hanging from a silver chain around her neck. It had a bug inside it, a mosquito maybe, or some kind of beetle, and it was perfectly preserved, its papery wings and minuscule legs suspended there inside a honey womb. She'd watched Dad and me as Nan recited the whole story of Mom's death, and how Dad and I had just moved down here from Maine, and how we were all going to live together now even though we'd never done such a thing before. She'd leaned forward when Nan finished, resting her elbows on her knees, and waited until Dad and I looked up at her.

"Don't be afraid to tell each other when it hurts," she said. "That's all you have to do. You can whisper it or shout it. Just let each other know when it hurts."

It had sounded like okay advice, except that I knew neither of us would ever do such a thing. We weren't built that way, hadn't ever come right out and said words like that before, even when things hadn't hurt. Dad had nodded and grunted, but I studied the small insect nestled inside the chunk of amber around her neck and wondered what it would feel like to be smothered in warm sap, to be buried alive in something sticky and suffocating like that. Or maybe I already knew. Maybe this was how it felt.

I sat up in bed all at once, yanked from my thoughts.

A buried heart.

Why hadn't I thought of it before?

I knew exactly what a buried heart was.

Better yet, I knew just where to find one.

Fourteen

I held my breath as I pulled on my jeans and a clean T-shirt; there was no telling what might happen if Dad heard me and came snooping around my room, checking to see if I was asleep yet. Nan was dead to the world; I could hear her snoring through the walls, but it would take Dad a little longer to lose consciousness. No matter. It was better to be safe than sorry. I glanced at the clock—12:42 a.m. Eighteen more minutes until his History Channel show ended, which meant that he'd probably either doze off in the chair or head back into his bedroom. I waited, my fingers gripping the windowsill, as the numbers on the clock ticked by. 12:58. My whole body was tensed; a pocket of sweat pooled inside my bra. 12:59. The sound of sweeping music drifted down the hallway, which meant the credits were rolling, and I winced, holding my breath again as Dad's footsteps made their way past my door and into his room. But it was not until I heard the click of his ceiling fan—something he switched on every night to help his allergies—that I opened the window and slipped out.

I'd taken lots of bike rides at dusk and a handful or two at night. But I'd never ridden this late, and never with such a mission in mind. I would have felt gleeful if the situation had been in any way positive, thrilled if the hour had been anything other than one in the morning. Now I realized that I was dumbfounded, startled, and terrified all at the same time. How had I thought of the buried heart so suddenly? And what made me lunge to go get it myself instead of calling Dominic and telling him about it? Was I making a mistake? Did it matter?

I pedaled harder, as if to overtake the darkness, and sped toward town.

Even at this hour, Elmer Sudds was still open; I pedaled toward the yellow light spilling out from under the front door like a punctured egg yolk, and then moved past it, my shoulders hunched up around my ears. It sounded like a circus inside: blaring music, people laughing in high-pitched screams, the scrape of heavy furniture against the wooden floor. Too much going on in there, I noted, for anyone to notice me out here. I maneuvered my bike down the alley behind the bar and skidded to a halt as a figure stepped out of the shadows.

"What the . . . ?" Someone jumped back, startled.

"Dominic?"

"Marin?" His face relaxed, his fists unclenching. "Jesus, I thought you were some drunk coming back here to take a leak." He paused, squinting at me under the dim streetlight overhead. "Wow, I didn't even recognize you at first without your glasses."

I brought my fingers to my face, felt my neck flush hot. "Yeah. I don't have to wear them at night."

He nodded. Took a step toward me.

"What are you doing out here?" Even I could hear the accusation in my voice.

He stopped walking. "You won't believe it."

"What? The buried heart?"

He clapped his hands together once, as if catching a fly. "You thought of it too? That . . . that's why you're here?"

I swung my leg off the bike, dropped the kickstand. "Yeah. It just came to me. Like, totally out of the blue."

"Me too!" He sounded excited, motioning me forward with his hand. "I was just starting to dig when you got here."

I followed him over to the space by the fence, kneeling down next to the little mound of dirt. The smell of garbage and stale beer lingered in the air, and for a moment I wished we'd thought of a better place to bury the little bird, that we hadn't stuck him in an abandoned lot behind some cheap bar. Especially now. I brushed my fingers over the top of the pile. Dominic hadn't gotten very far; there were only a few indications of the dirt being poked at. I wondered if he was feeling as hesitant about the whole thing as I was. "You think it's still here?" I asked.

"None of the dirt had been touched," he said, sinking next to me. "And the little rock I put on top of it was still there. It's gotta be here."

I watched him dig, undoing the very work he had completed just twenty-four hours ago, until he stopped, breathing hard, and sat back on his heels. "There," he said.

I leaned in to inspect the tiny animal. Except for a layer of dirt, which coated its body and wings like a filthy blanket, it looked just as I remembered. The tiny beak parted ever so slightly. Eyes shut tight, the thin lid like a transparent shade, frond-feet curled up beneath it. Asleep, not dead.

Dominic squeezed my shoulder. "You want to take it out?"

I lifted the bird from the hole and held it in my hand. "Dominic," I said. "You're not gonna . . ." I glanced down at it, feeling an infinite tenderness toward the tiny animal, an unexplainable protectiveness.

"What?"

I shook my head, erasing the mental picture from my head.

"What, Marin?"

"Cut it," I said, wincing. "You're not going to cut it open, are you?"

"God, no." Dominic reared back, as if smelling something rancid. He reached up and pulled on his earlobe. "I don't think I'm even capable of doing something like that. I fainted in Mr. Kosloski's science class last year when we had to do the frog lab."

"You did?"

He nodded and made a face like he was gagging. "Keeled right over as soon as they opened them up. Hit my head on the edge of the lab table and had to get six stitches."

Without thinking, I leaned in close, my eyes running over the width of his forehead. Sure enough, I could see a faint ridge just above his eyebrow, the scarred skin thick and pink. "It's not so bad."

"No?" His voice was faint.

I didn't move. "No."

He reached up and ran the tip of his index finger down the side of my face. My whole body trembled. "Has anyone ever told you how beautiful you are?" he whispered.

I pulled back and stared down at the dead bird. "You probably ask all the girls that."

The expression on his face was comparable to having been struck. "Seriously? Is that what you think?"

"Well." I shrugged, embarrassed. "I know you've had a lot of girlfriends."

"Oh yeah?" He chewed the inside of his cheek. "What else do you know?"

"Nothing. That's just what I heard."

"From who?"

"My friend Lucy."

"Lucy?" His forehead crinkled into little lines. "Lucy who?"

"Cooper. In my grade. You know, the really tiny one? With the beautiful face?"

He crossed his arms over his chest. "All right, why is it okay for you to say someone's beautiful, but not for me?"

"Because I'm telling the truth."

The same look as before filled his eyes. "You think I'm lying?"

"I don't know." I struggled to my feet. "Who cares? Come on. It's like three in the morning. I have to get home before my dad gets up for work. He'll kill me if he knows I snuck out of the house."

He didn't move, just stayed there on the ground, looking up at me. If I'd been brave enough, I would have leaned down right then and there and kissed him on the lips. Anything to erase the stunned look on his face, the sting in his eyes. "Did you bring something?" I asked instead. "You know, for the bird? A box or a bag to put it in?"

He blinked and then dropped his head, as if realizing the moment was over. "Yeah." His voice drifted out under him. "In the car."

We walked in silence toward his Jeep, the chirp of crickets the only sound in the air. A million different apologies ran through my head: *I'm sorry. I didn't really mean it. Sometimes things come out before I have a chance to think how they might sound. I'm not good at this. I want you to like me. I want you to love me. I don't want you to like me. I don't want you to love me because that means I will have to love you back, and loving someone is too hard. It hurts too much.*

He opened the back door to the car and reached inside, pulling out an empty iPod box, white with a fitted lid.

"That's perfect." My voice was just above a whisper.

He opened the box, holding it in both hands as I deposited the bird inside. I watched as he closed the lid carefully, taking pains not to bump any part of the animal. "You know, Marin—" he started, but the buzz of my cell phone cut him off.

I froze as my phone buzzed again. There was only one person in the world who would be calling me at this hour of the night. I pulled my phone out of my pocket. Dad. "Shit," I said. "It's my father."

"Don't answer it," Dominic said.

"I have to." I was already flipping the top up. "It'll be worse if I don't." I pressed the phone to my ear. "Dad, listen. I know you're mad, but I'm on my way home."

"Marin." His voice was choking. "Where are you?"

"Downtown. But I told you, I'm on my way—"

"Turn around," Dad said. "Meet me at the hospital. Nan fell in the bathroom about a half hour ago. They think she had a heart attack. The doctors aren't sure if she'll make it through the night."

Fifteen

"You have to go faster." I was up against the dashboard of Dominic's Jeep, pressed so far into the front of it that I could have merged with the windshield. "Seriously, just go around that guy. There's no one in front of him."

"Marin, I'm going as fast as I can. I don't want to get either of us killed, all right?" Dominic glanced in his rear-view mirror and then stepped down hard on the gas, swinging the Jeep around the car in front. He clenched his jaw and sped faster down the highway. "Three more minutes and we'll be there. Just let me know if you see a cop."

I didn't answer. I couldn't be sure if I had heard him or if the words Dad had just told me—that Nan would be undergoing emergency surgery in less than twenty minutes—were real. I had the sensation of floating as he'd talked on the phone, as if some part of me had drifted away, and I could not, or would not, listen anymore. Maybe I was shutting down. Maybe everything had finally started to take its toll, just like it had with Cassie, and I was cracking up. For real.

Dominic swung the car in front of the hospital, braking so hard that I bumped my head against the windshield. "Shit." He touched my sleeve. "I'm sorry. Are you all right?"

"I'm okay." I opened the door and got out. "Thanks for bringing me."

"You're welcome." The door was almost closed when I heard him say my name.

"I'll be thinking of you." Dominic was leaning over the seat, toward me. "Let me know how everything goes, okay?"

I nodded and slammed the door.

Dad was talking to a doctor dressed in blue scrubs when I raced down the hall, but he stepped away when he caught sight of me and caught me at the shoulders with both arms.

"Can I see her?" I gasped. "Please. Just let me see her."

"Not yet." Dad's eyes were bloodshot, his hair mussed. "She's being prepped for surgery right now. Dr. Andrews here was just going over everything with me." He dropped his arms, pulling me to one side by the wrist. "Doctor, this is my daughter, Marin. Marin, Dr. Andrews is going to operate on Nan."

"Is she going to die?" I demanded.

Dr. Andrews, who was a good head taller than Dad and had cropped gray hair, seemed unfazed by the question.

"She's an older woman," he said. "And the blow was a big one. Honestly, it's going to be touch and go for a few hours after the surgery, which will probably take most of the night. But we'll take very good care of her. If she makes it through tonight, I think she'll be over the worst of it."

His head was covered with a blue cap that creased sharply in the middle, and a gold chain peeked out from beneath his scrub top. I could make out a purple, kidney-shaped blob resting behind his right ear, as well as a smaller yellow one inside his mouth. *"If?"* I repeated.

The doctor nodded. "The first twenty-four hours after heart surgery are the most crucial. We'll know where things stand afterward." He nodded at Dad and stuck out his hand. "I really have to go. They're waiting."

I watched him leave, glancing at the blue paper covers over the tops of his shoes. They looked ridiculous, like clown feet. Nan's doctor had clown feet. What if he wasn't good enough at what he did? What if his hands shook or something slipped?

I felt Dad's hand on my shoulder, and for a moment, I wanted nothing more than to turn and sink against him, to let him take everything the way he once did, a long time ago. Except that I couldn't. We weren't the kind of people who did that sort of thing. We might never be that kind of people.

"Where were you?" The tightness in his voice was unbearable.

Nothing I said now, short of going to see a dying friend,

would justify my absence from the house at this hour. There was no point in lying. "I had to go downtown."

"At two-thirty in the morning?"

"I know it looks bad, but if you—"

"It doesn't *look* anything, Marin. It *is* bad."

I stared at the lines along the linoleum floor, the squares within the squares, the sea of tiny speckles that you wouldn't even know were there unless you concentrated really hard. It was coming. Again. A wave out at sea, gathering strength as it rolled into shore. Pretty soon it would be another tidal wave. A tsunami, crushing everything in its wake. I could feel it.

"If you think finding my mother bleeding from the head and clutching her chest in the middle of the night isn't terrible enough, try calling your teenage daughter for help only to realize"—he stopped and glared at me to emphasize his point—"that she's *nowhere* in the house."

"Bleeding from the head?" I repeated. "Why was her head bleeding?"

"Because she cracked it on the sink when she fell down." A pain shot through my chest, and I closed my eyes against it. Dad's eyes narrowed into little slits. "Tell me, Marin, what was so interesting downtown that you felt you had to sneak out of the house without telling anyone?"

What was I going to say? That I'd thought of something Dominic Jackson could use to help get some kind of spirit out of his sister? That I'd ridden my bike downtown and dug up a dead bird in the back parking lot of a bar? Seriously?

"Nothing." I stuck my foot out, toeing the tip of my shoe along the floor. "I just . . . we were talking. Just hanging out."

"Who's we?"

"Me and Lucy."

"You and Lucy." He cocked his head. "All of a sudden, the two of you have a burning urge to see one another. And talk. At two-thirty in the morning." He inhaled once through his nose, and I could feel the wave rising up inside him. Any moment now, it would come flooding out, maybe drowning both of us this time. Well, I wouldn't let it. I wouldn't.

"I made a mistake, Dad," I said. "So don't, okay? Just *don't.*"

He let me go, watched wordlessly as I walked down the narrow perimeter of hall, the soles of my red Keds making light peeling sounds against the floor. I stepped through the yawning doors that led outside and glanced around. The narrow ribbon of road in front of me was marked "EMERGENCY ONLY," but it was cluttered with cars. A green Honda. A red SUV. Two silver Mercedes, their windows tinted as black as coal. Small bushes had been arranged on either side of the door, and a welcome mat in front spelled out the words FAIRFIELD GENERAL.

God, I was at another hospital.

The image of Nan falling, of cracking her head on the corner of that awful bathroom sink filled my head, and my legs gave way beneath me, buckling with such force that I almost fell over. Stumbling, I reached out at the last moment and caught myself on the edge of a bench. I sat down, willing the heaviness inside my head to lift.

Nan.

Oh, Nan.

She'd been so tired this afternoon, so drained. I should have known, the way she'd been sagging there in the chair, waving at her damp skin with a kerchief. I should have *known*. How long had she been lying there in the bathroom bleeding, gasping for breath? Had she called for me? *Marin! Marin, my angel, come help me!* Why hadn't I stayed in the house, instead of heading out to try to impress some stupid boy? I would have been with her, could have reached her before it even happened, kept her head in my lap as I called the ambulance on my cell phone.

I brought my knees up to my chest, resting my forehead against them. The knocking inside my head felt like feet banging against the floor. Were things really supposed to be this hard? And if they were, could I get through it?

My cell phone went off. A text from Lucy. *Hey stranger! Where r u? Call me!* I stared at the words for a moment, watching as they bled and swam together in a swirl of black. It was after three in the morning. What was she doing up? There was no way I could call her right now; I wouldn't know where to begin, wouldn't know how to stop. Still, I pulled the phone closer, began stabbing at it with my two thumbs. *Can't talk now, but need u to cover 4 me if my dad calls. More later.* I clicked my phone shut and put it back in my pocket. She'd do it. I knew she would.

"Marin?" I startled as I heard my name and then stood up as Father William hobbled toward me. "Am I interrupting?" He hesitated. "I don't want to intrude."

"No, it's okay." I frowned. "Did my dad call you?"

"He did indeed. May I?" I nodded as the priest indicated the seat next to me. He sat down with a sigh, the red spheres in his spine pulsing under his movements, and removed his hat. "I just talked to him inside," he said, inching the brim between his fingers. "He told me she's been taken into surgery."

"Yeah." It hurt to talk. Especially about this. I looked at the green Honda parked across the street instead. The back windshield had one of those glow-in-the-dark stick-family stickers on it, complete with a mother, a father, three kids, two dogs, and a fish. The fish was last in line, jumping out of a little fishbowl, flanked by fat droplets of water. It was hard to imagine what kind of a stick-family bumper sticker Dad might put on the back of his truck. I doubted one that represented us accurately even existed.

"She'll be okay." Father William rested both of his hands atop his cane, which he held between his splayed knees. He did not look at me. "She will. I know it."

"Uh-huh." The annoyance in my voice was obvious. Adults loved to say stuff like this in these kinds of situations, as if they knew something us teenagers did not. But I was starting to get the feeling that they didn't know either. They just hoped like we did and pretended they knew about everything else.

"She will." The priest took a handkerchief out of his back pocket and blotted his eyes. "She's a trouper, that girl. Stronger than I'll ever be. That's for sure."

I watched him out of the corner of my eye and then looked down at my hands. Maybe he was afraid too. It was possible that he loved Nan in a way that I had no idea about, or maybe ever would. They'd been friends for over fifty years; he'd presided at her wedding, had baptized Dad, and had buried her husband, all before I was even born. Maybe the thought of losing Nan felt insurmountable, like it did for me. Maybe he needed to throw that pretend knowledge out there, say it aloud, just so someone could hear it.

"I think she has a pretty good doctor," I heard myself say. "He seemed okay to me, anyway. Aside from the clown shoes."

Father William laughed, a short, barking sound, and stuffed the handkerchief back in his pocket. We watched a few cars drift by, looking for parking, and move on again. A couple walked down the sidewalk, their arms around one another, heads touching. The woman cried softly while the man looked straight ahead, his face stoic and impassive. Next to me, Father William shifted. Out of the corner of my eye, I could make out the red spheres; they shimmered around the edges, as if lit from within.

"Can I ask you something?" I said.

"Of course."

"How did you hurt your back?"

"Oh, it was a long time ago. When I was a child, actually. My little brother fell into our pool, and I dove in to get him." He sighed, a weighted sound I could not place. "It was too shallow. I broke my neck, severed three of the disks in my spine. I was in the hospital for six months. I wasn't supposed to walk again. Ever."

"But you did."

"Yes, I got better." He shrugged. "Stronger. I tackled my rehabilitation program like nothing I'd ever done before. Total commitment." He smiled. "Being sentenced to a wheelchair for the rest of my life didn't sit well with me. I had things to do. Places to see."

"Wow." I was impressed. "It still hurts, though, sometimes?"

"Most of the time." He turned to look at me. "Speaking of which, have you heard anything more about the epileptic girl? From your school?"

I had to tell him. Someone else had to know in case Dominic's crazy idea didn't work, in case he got himself into even deeper trouble than he was already in. And a Catholic priest, who as far as I knew was the only person supposed to be *doing* any kind of ritual in the first place, was the ideal person to tell. "Not too much," I started, then paused. "Father, can I ask you something else?"

"Sure."

"Have you ever helped someone who had a spirit inside them?"

He looked at me, a curious expression crossing his face. "You mean have I ever performed an exorcism?"

"Yes."

"No. No, never. Only a very few priests are selected as exorcists in the Catholic Church. They're sent to Rome to study the practice. Some of them are there for years. Exorcist priests are a rarity, even in this country. I don't think we have more than nine of them living in the United States."

"But you're a priest," I said. "Couldn't you do one if you had to? I mean, if it was an emergency or something?"

He shook his head, rubbing one of his white eyebrows with the side of a finger. "I really don't have any idea about that kind of thing, Marin. Like I said, you need special training. It's a very, very delicate process. Not to mention dangerous." He shifted in his seat, realigned his cane between his feet. "May I ask why you're asking?"

I held my breath for a moment, and then let it out. "I saw one," I said.

"You saw one what?"

"A . . . a spirit, or something. I saw it. Inside Cassie, the girl they're saying has epilepsy."

Father William's face contorted, as if he had just tasted

something rotten. "You saw a spirit?" he repeated. "Inside her?"

I nodded.

He opened his mouth and then shut it. "That's impossible," he said. "And I mean that with all due respect. But that's completely impossible. You must have imagined what you saw. Or maybe you saw something else. Some other part . . . of . . . of her illness. Her mental state. I'm sure things look completely bizarre right now, in the condition she's in."

"I didn't imagine it. I know what I saw."

"And what"—he paused—"what did you see?"

"I saw blackness."

"Ah." Father William nodded, as if playing along. "Blackness."

"I've been seeing pain in people's bodies for almost a year now," I said. "Shapes and colors of all different kinds, all different shades. And in all that time, I've never seen a black one. Ever. It's so black that it's almost impossible to describe. And it moves, Father. It moves around inside her head, down into her chest."

The priest's face blanched. He stared at the sidewalk for a moment and then ran a hand over his eyes. "It must have been the epilepsy," he said finally. "Have you ever had the chance to look at someone with epilepsy?"

"Maybe." I shrugged. "Half the time, I don't know what kind of pain I'm seeing in people. I've seen a lot of different things."

"I'm sure that's what it was, then." The look on his face

had become patronizing again. Maybe even with a bit of condescension mixed in.

"I don't think so," I said. "This is different. I'm telling you, it *moved*. Nothing I've ever seen inside a person has ever moved like that. It's like . . . like this black ribbon that slides in and around her cells. . . ." I shook my head. "It's crazy."

"I'm sure it's the epilepsy." Father William drew his fingers around his mouth.

I was starting to get angry. "You'd believe me if you could see it," I burst out. "It would scare the shit out of you." I winced as the expletive came out of my mouth and hung my head. "I'm sorry. I didn't mean to swear."

"That's all right." He patted my back. "I understand how upsetting all of this has been for you. Really, I do. And now with Nan. It's a lot. Things are going at full tilt here."

"But there's other things," I said. "Today, when I saw her, she talked in a weird voice that wasn't hers. And her fingertips turned black. And then her eyes changed."

"Changed how?"

"The pupils turned sideways, like a lizard's eyes or something. And then these horrible things started growing out of her neck!" I squeezed my eyes at the memory, clapped my hands over my ears.

"Marin." Father William's hand on my shoulder made me jump. "You've got to calm down, dear. There are things that can happen to a human body during seizures that are very difficult to explain, let alone witness." His hand moved in circles between my shoulder blades; it felt irritating and comforting at the same time. "You've been through so much this past year. It's starting to have an effect on you."

"No!" I squeezed my eyes even tighter. "That's not it!"

"Listen to me. I know you think you understand what's happening to this girl, but let me tell you something. Spiritual possession is incredibly rare. From the little I know about it, less than one percent of all cases turn out to be real situations in which a spirit has actually entered the body. Less than *one* percent! Plus, it takes *years* to diagnose. There are all sorts of experts who have to come in and examine the person and eliminate every other medical and mental possibility."

I opened my eyes, staring out at the sea of cars again. Maybe Dominic's parents weren't the only people who wouldn't listen to us. Who wouldn't hear. "You don't believe me," I said. "You just think I'm some dumb kid, getting hysterical."

"I don't think you're a dumb kid at all." He was somber. "I really don't. You're actually one of the most interesting people I've ever met. And I mean that."

"Why? Because I can see pain?"

"Well, yes, partly because of that. But also because you're intelligent. And sensitive. The way you've dealt with your particular affliction has been—"

"Affliction?" I interrupted.

He paused, staring down at his hands. "I'm sorry. What do you call it?"

"I don't call it anything." I waited. "Nan calls it a blessing."

He smiled, looking out over the parking lot again. "Yes," he said. "Of course she would. That's exactly what it is. A blessing."

I stayed quiet after that. Now that Nan had been brought up again, I didn't feel like arguing anymore.

Father William apparently felt the same way. Clutching his cane, he pulled himself to his feet. I stared at the knees of his black pants as he donned his hat and straightened his sweater. "Marin, look at me." His voice was gentle, soft. I raised my eyes. "You must be very careful about dabbling into anything having to do with spiritual realms. That's not something to fool around with. In any kind of way. If it turns out this girl is indeed possessed by some kind of spirit or, God forbid, a demon, she'll have to be cared for by professionals. A real exorcist will have to be brought in, someone who will invoke the name of God through a series of specific prayers and rituals. That's the only way a spirit can be cast out. It can take weeks. Sometimes even months. And even then sometimes, it doesn't work."

My blood ran cold at his words. But I didn't answer.

"Marin," he said again, "promise me you won't get involved."

"I'm already involved."

"Then promise me you'll un-involve yourself." His eyes were grave. "I mean it. Promise me."

"Only if you'll help." My knees were shaking.

"I am not an exorcist. And even if that's what that girl needs, I can't just go out and get one. The bishop has to be alerted first and then he assigns one."

"Then alert the bishop." I bit my lip. "You can do that, can't you?"

"Cassie would have to be examined first. By a priest who has experience with these kinds of situations. Then he would make a request to the bishop."

"Do you know of any special priests who could do that? Who could come examine her?"

Father William rested a hand on my shoulder. "I'll look into it," he said. "But, please, dear, in the meantime, promise me you'll stay out of it. It's much, much more complicated than you could ever imagine. Please walk away and don't look back. For your own sake. And for Nan's."

He left me with that, shuffling down the sidewalk without saying goodbye. I sat there for a long time after, still a little stunned that I had told him anything at all. But there was no one else. Literally. And I was scared. For Dominic. And for Cassie too. Had I just created a whole new set of problems by telling Father William? Or would the people who needed to be involved, the ones who should have been involved from the very beginning, finally be brought in?

The moon overhead was as full as a coin. Gauzy clouds

moved swiftly behind it, and a constellation of stars seemed to have been flung against the dark sky by an invisible hand. For a brief moment, it seemed that everything was looking down at me, gazing from a great distance, an entire world I did not know about and would not ever comprehend in this lifetime.

I got up finally and went back inside to find Dad.

Together, we would continue to wait.

Sixteen

It was 4:37 a.m. when Dr. Andrews came back into the waiting room, cap in hand. I was stretched out on a brown vinyl couch watching a steak knife infomercial while trying to keep my eyes open. Dad was sprawled on the smaller sofa across the room, one leg slung over the arm of it. His eyes were wide open. Neither of us had said another word to each other. However, at the sight of Dr. Andrews, we both sprang to our feet. Without his blue cap, I could make out a bald spot on top. The purple orb behind his ear had diminished somewhat, although the yellow one in his mouth looked bigger.

"How is she?" Dad asked.

"It went as well as it possibly could have," the doctor said. "But five out of the six arteries were blocked, which, combined with the heart attack, has left her heart severely damaged." He swept his eyes over me. "Now we wait. As I said before, the next twenty-four hours are critical."

"Thank you." Dad stuck his hand out. "For all you've done." His lower lip trembled as they shook. I might have thanked him, too, if I had not caught sight of the blood all over his ridiculous paper shoe coverings, drops and spatters adorning the blue paper like some kind of bizarre painting. Nan's blood. The sight of it left me mute.

A few minutes later, a nurse led us into the ICU, where Nan lay on a vast stretcher, her body covered with tubes and wires and blankets. For a split second, I thought we were too late, that Nan had breathed her last while we had been out in the waiting room, talking to Dr. Andrews. Her skin was the color of an eggshell, the edges of her lips dry and cracked. Thin tubes snaked out of her nose, and another one ran down the length of her arms. A white bandage had been taped to one side of her head; a dull bruise bloomed on her cheek. Still, nothing prepared me for what I saw beneath her hospital gown, inside her chest cavity. Even ten feet away, the shape of her pain was staggeringly large, the size of an orange, mealy and fibrous-looking, as if the muscle had been dragged against a cheese grater. I pressed my hand against my mouth so that I would not scream.

"Come on," Dad said in a tight voice. "It's okay."

I made my way to the bed, following Dad, holding my breath. The only sound in the room was the steady, faint beeping of a machine hooked to one of Nan's fingers. On a screen in front, a red digital heart blinked on and off—once, twice, three times—in sync with the beep. There was a pause. Then once, twice, three times again. Dad stared at it for a minute, as if it might start talking to him. Then he put his hands on the bed railing and looked down at his mother. His face was gray, and the backs of his arms trembled.

I stayed to the left of him, motionless except for my fingers, which fluttered at the tips. The blue beads inside Nan's hands, still running the length of her knuckles, skittered abruptly, as if caught, and then resumed again. Still! Despite everything else! I let out a sob then and ran to her, sinking down against the other side of the bed. I clutched at her hand, pressing my face against it. "Oh, Nan, I'm sorry! I'm so sorry!"

I wept for a long, long time, until I could not cry anymore, until I was dizzy from it. My eyes and nose were swollen; the inside of my head felt as though it had been packed with cotton. I lifted my head, swaying a little under the bright lights. Dad was gone. I stared at the place he had been—just inches away, across the bed—as if he might rematerialize if I looked hard enough. But he had left.

I lurched as a low moan, barely audible, drifted up from the bed. "Nan," I whispered. Her eyes were still closed, but another groan came out of her mouth. "I'm here, Nan. I'm right here." I smoothed her white hair back from her face. It was matted on top, as if someone had put honey in it, and damp around the edges. "It's okay," I whispered. "I know you'll get better. I know it. I'm here, Nan. I'm right here."

I stayed there for the rest of the night, sitting in a chair pulled close to the bed, resting my head on the only available inch of mattress space, Nan's soft hand in mine. Dad came back after a while, settling into the soft blue chair in the corner, but I did not lift my head, did not acknowledge him. I dozed off and on, waking when another one of Nan's unconscious moans sounded, a gasp here, a low, wet rumble there. Then I would stare at the purple wound of her heart, my eyes boring into the ripped mass under the bandage, unable to look away. I fastened my gaze on it in a way I never had before, in a way I knew I might not ever do again, all the while holding her hand, pressing my lips, the side of my cheek against it. There was no reason for someone like Nan, who had done nothing but good things all her life, to have to bear this kind of pain. Life was hugely, breathtakingly unfair. And the worst part was that there was nothing I, or anyone else for that matter, could do about it.

We would just have to wait.

Again.

I squinted as a shaft of light gazed in from between the hospital curtains and then opened my eyes all the way. Morning.

Morning!

I sat up and looked at Nan. Her eyes were still closed,

but a little bit of pink was back in her face, as if someone had pinched her cheeks, and her breathing didn't seem quite as shallow. The machine behind her bed was still beeping, but faster now and without any hesitations. Most shocking of all was the shape inside her chest cavity; it was half the size of the one that had been there last night, the once-tattered material now a smooth, slick band of muscle.

I stared at it for a moment, as if I might be imagining things, but no. It was better. I could see it. It was *better.* I rubbed my eyes and got up out of my chair. My back was stiff, and my neck hurt. I could hear water running in the bathroom. "Dad?" I whispered.

He opened the door, wiping his hands on a piece of paper towel. His eyes were bright, but the circles underneath said otherwise. "She made it. She made it through the worst part, Marin." His voice shook. "She's gonna be all right."

I nodded, willing it to be true. "Are you sure?"

"I'm sure." He threw the wad of paper into a wastebasket. "The woman's an ox. Always has been. I wouldn't be surprised if she sits up in the next ten minutes and asks for breakfast."

"No bacon and eggs for a while!" A nurse with curly red hair appeared in the doorway. A tiny blue disk wedged itself along her thumb where the cuticle was bleeding. "I'm Sharon," she said, shaking Dad's hand. "The day nurse. I'll be taking care of things in here today."

I tried to keep quiet as the nurse examined Nan's tubes,

pressing a button on the heart monitor, inserting a thermometer into one of Nan's ears. Then: "She's doing okay, right?" I couldn't help myself, still didn't trust what I saw beneath her hospital gown. "Even though she's not awake yet? She's still doing all right?"

"She's doing very well." Sharon smiled and folded back the edge of Nan's blanket. "Much better than expected, actually. She's a fighter, this one."

"When do you think she'll wake up?"

"It's hard to say." Sharon took a chart off the wall behind Nan's bed and opened it. "It's different for everyone. Sometimes the older folks need a little extra time to come out of it." She wrote something inside the chart and then closed it again. This time, she looked at Dad. "You know, the night shift told me you've been here all night. Why don't you two go home and shower? Try to get a few hours sleep, if you can. We can call you when she wakes up."

Dad hesitated.

But my reaction was immediate. "No," I said. "I want to be here when she opens her eyes. I want to be right here."

"Okay." Sharon's tunic was dotted with a horde of multicolored balloons, each one dangling a string. Clown shoes. Balloon shirts. This place was a circus. "Your decision, of course. But it might be a while."

"Come on, Marin." Dad moved his head, gesturing toward the door. "She's right. At the very least we can get cleaned up, have something to eat. Then we'll come right back."

"I'm not hungry. And I don't care about being clean right now."

"Marin." He looked defeated, exhausted. Was it because he'd barely slept? Because he'd waited up all night, waiting for his mother to live or die? Or was it from this constant back-and-forth between us? I felt drained, too, just thinking about it.

"All right," I said. "But not too long."

"An hour," Dad said. "I promise. Tops."

Seventeen

Neither of us spoke on the ride home, the momentary exhilaration replaced by the usual awkwardness. Some things never changed. I sat close to my door inside Dad's truck, as if I might disappear through the other side, and watched the inside of town as we passed through it. People rushed here and there, their faces pinched with anxiety and distraction, different colored orbs glowing out from under their skin. I looked at them carefully, trying to gauge whether their pain looked unusual, but nothing stood out. Nothing seemed different than what I saw on any other day.

I leaned my head back against the seat and closed my eyes. Had Nan's heart really looked different just now? Or was I imagining things? There was no way I could bring it up to Dad; my uncertainty was bound to upset him even further—especially if I was wrong. And what if I was wrong? What if I just wanted to be right so badly that I was overlooking all the other stuff that said I was wrong? I wondered if the sudden urge to laugh was the result of exhaustion, or if the absurdness of the situation had started to get the best of me after all.

I took a long, hot shower at home and tilted my face up against the stream of water, letting it run down my face, my chest, all the way down to my toes. God, it felt good. On days like this, water could feel like a salve, or a cocoon, enveloping all the aches and bruises, holding them tight inside the warmth. I wondered when Cassie had last showered; was such a routine thing even possible for her now? And what about food? When had she eaten last? Could she even swallow anymore?

The kitchen was full of morning light. It settled over everything like an invisible film, illuminating the copper teakettle, brightening the handles on the cupboards. Dad was at the stove, cracking eggs into a frying pan. His hair was wet, and he had changed into jeans and a white collared shirt. On the counter, the coffeepot gurgled.

I opened one of the cupboards, took out a mug.

"You want some eggs?" Dad asked, not turning around.

"No, thanks." I filled the mug almost to the brim, added a splash of cream, three sugars. "I'm not hungry."

"You should eat something." He lifted the pan and slid the eggs onto a blue plate. "Even if it's just a piece of toast."

I leaned against the counter, sipping my coffee as Dad

sat down at the table and began to eat. He stabbed one of the soft yolks with the corner of his toast, and I stared at the yellow blood as it began to spread against the plate, ooze along the edges. I looked away. "You think she's awake yet?"

Dad withdrew his phone from his front shirt pocket and checked the screen. "No one's called."

I nodded, picking at the chipped rim of my mug. "Where'd you go last night for so long? I mean, when you left Nan's room?"

He didn't answer right away, chewing with a new ferocity, the muscles in his neck straining. "I could ask you the same thing," he said.

"I just went outside. Sat on a bench for a while. Got some air."

He nodded. "Me too."

Something rose inside at his words. Maybe we were not so different after all, not so far apart. I sat down, arranging my hands over the top of the mug. "You see the moon?" I asked. "It was full."

He glanced up, exhaustion etched on his face. "I don't remember."

I looked down again.

"I was kind of in a daze, I guess," he said. "I'm pretty sure people were walking in and out; cars were pulling up and driving away." He shook his head. "But I can't remember what any of them looked like. It was like I was in a tunnel or something. I don't even know how long I was out there."

Eleven months and twenty-six days, I thought to myself. *Since the day Mom jumped. That's how long you've been out there.*

He got up to refill his coffee cup. When had his jeans started hanging around his waist? And why hadn't I noticed? "Dad."

"Hmmm?" The sound of liquid pouring sounded in his mug. He set the coffeepot back.

"It hurts."

His eyes creased. "What hurts?"

I stared into my cup, blinked back tears. *Just say it. Out loud. Just let each other know when it hurts.* I'd just done that. So why did I have to explain it? Didn't he know that it hurt even more when I had to go into details, that it felt like something was ripping inside when I had to say the words? Out loud? "My head." I rubbed my temples. "I'm just tired, I guess."

"Well, that's what happens when you stay up all night running around town."

"Yeah." I got up from my chair and walked across the kitchen, then stood for a moment against the counter. Dad's dirty frying pan was sitting in the sink next to me, the edges already crusty with dried egg. I put my coffee cup down and curled my fingers around the plastic handle of the pan. For a moment I just left it there, feeling the blood course through my arm and under the thin skin of my wrist, down into each of my fingers until they tightened their hold and squeezed, and then I lifted the pan and hurled it with all my might across the kitchen. It bounced off the wall, leaving a wide, scalloped dent, and then slid across the floor, scuttling like a large insect before coming to rest again under the table.

"Jesus *Christ*!" For a split second, Dad ducked, and then he jumped out of his seat, his eyes large as quarters. "What the hell is *wrong* with you?"

"I hate you!" I screamed.

"What are you talking about, you hate me? What did I do?"

"Nothing!" I shrieked. "That's the problem! You never do anything!"

"About *what*?"

"About Mom! About us! About anything!" I could feel the rage in me ebbing as I spoke, as if making room for the grief, and it came all at once, a hurricane of trembling and tears. I hung on to the counter so I wouldn't fall over.

"What do you mean, about Mom? You want to talk about Mom right now, Marin? Is that it?"

Oh my God. I hated him so much. Why couldn't he just take me into his lap and hold me and tell me that he knew what I was feeling, that things would take a while but that they would get better? They would, they would, they would. I stared at him, willing him to see what I needed, daring him to give it to me. But he only shook his head at my silence, then leaned down and picked up the frying pan. "Do you know what could have happened if this thing had *hit* me?"

"I wasn't aiming for your head."

"Oh." He nodded, sputtering. "Well, I guess that makes it okay, then."

"Do you want to know the only person I hate right now more than you?"

He shrugged, placing the frying pan back in the sink. "Sure. Why not?"

"God."

I could tell by the look in his eyes that my answer was unexpected. Maybe he thought I would say no one. Or Cassie. Or even Sister Paulina. He walked back over to the table and pulled out a chair. Sat down. He set his elbows on the table and linked his fingers together. Then he looked up at me. "It's not God's fault that Mom did what she did."

No. It was mine.

"I didn't say it was God's fault." The words felt like marbles in my throat. "I just said I hated Him."

"Because of Mom."

"*Yes,* because of Mom, okay? What kind of God lets someone suffer like that and not do anything to help them? Nan's always saying that God can do anything, that He even knows what we're thinking. So what am I supposed to think of someone who lets a person kill herself?"

He sat back in his chair, regarding me for a moment.

"You don't know, do you?" I pushed myself away from the counter, crossing my arms over my chest. "You don't have an answer."

"People have choices, Marin. They make up their own minds."

"He could have changed hers!"

"How? How could God have changed Mom's mind?"

"*I* don't know! He's supposed to be able to do anything, isn't He? She was one single person in the whole world! It wouldn't have taken Him more than three seconds to help her start thinking differently. Why couldn't He do that? Why couldn't He do that one single thing for her?"

"I don't . . ." He stopped, bringing his hands to his forehead. His fingers clutched at the hair on top, rooting for something, and then released it again. "Jesus, Marin."

"Yeah, Jesus." I kicked a cupboard door. Behind it, a pot rattled. "That's always what people say when they don't have anything else to say. You just don't have an answer." I walked out of the room. "No one does."

I could feel his eyes on me as I pushed through the back door, could feel the weight of them along the length of my shoulders as I ducked my head and started walking. It was still cool enough to make me shiver, and my wet hair didn't help matters. I wrapped my arms around myself, moving in an unknown direction, and then stopped when I reached the garden, regarding the edge I had kicked to pieces just two days before. What a mess. All of it. Such a frigging, goddamned mess. And yet, I didn't want to go, didn't want to turn my back on it just yet.

I walked to the middle of the plot instead and lay down. Above me, the sky was a robin's egg blue, the smooth curve of it dropping off in the horizon. I could smell the loamy scent of dirt as it pushed into my hair, could feel the coldness of it as it pressed against my back. *She was just one person, one single person. He could have helped her. It wouldn't have killed Him to help her.* But that's what we all were, weren't we? Just one single person. Why was one of us more important than the other? Who was to say that Mom's needs were any more pressing than someone else's?

I stretched out my arms, grabbing handfuls of the moist earth, and squeezed it hard inside my fingers. What did any of it matter, really, if we all ended up back here, buried in the ground, disintegrating into nothing? What was the purpose of any of it if that was what we had to look forward to? Where was the hope, if such a thing even existed? Where was hope when Mom had needed it? When I did?

I paused as my fingers came into contact with something hard. I picked at it distractedly, unearthing a rock, I guessed, or a root. It came out all at once, with a faint ripping sensation, and I brought it into my line of vision. It was dry and bumpy, like a tiny potato. I sat up. It was the rhizome root I had pushed down into the dirt a few days ago, the rotted one, covered with fungus. And yet unbelievably, little white roots, delicate as tendrils, had begun to sprout

out of the bottom, where they had anchored themselves deep into the earth, ready to grow again.

I positioned myself on my hands and knees, pushing the rhizome back into the soil, tamping it down with my fingers. It would take another year probably, maybe even two, but I would have bet anything at that point that it would push its way back out of the earth again. Maybe even bloom.

I sat back on my heels, watching an ant as it raced along a mound of dirt. It had something in its mouth, a seed maybe, or even an egg, and it barely hesitated as it made its way to a tiny hole off to one side and then disappeared down into it.

There was a whole world under there. An entire living world that breathed and grew and then died again. . . .

I stood up so fast that something in my knee cracked.

An invisible trinity.

Why had I made it so complicated?

It was so simple.

And it had been right under my nose the whole time.

Eighteen

The call came ten minutes later. Nan was stirring; she would probably wake soon. I got back in the car with Dad and stared out the window as he drove to the hospital. It would have been nice to tell him about the rhizome, nicer still if we'd been able to have a conversation about it. But it wouldn't happen. Aside from throwing a frying pan across the room, there were too many other things hanging in the air, too much hurt. And so neither of us said anything.

At first glance, it seemed that nothing had changed. Nan was still flat on her back, the same tubes in her nose, her mouth agape. The wound inside her chest was pulsing a faint purple color, but it looked stronger, too, maybe even stronger than before. Sharon was standing next to her bed, folding a blanket. She smiled as we came in. "She must have heard you come in the building," she said. "She just this moment opened her eyes."

I flew to the bedside. Nan's eyes were open, but barely, small slits from which tiny slivers of blue looked out. "Oh, Nan," I whispered, taking her hand. "Nanny, I'm here."

Dad moved in next to me, gripping the side rails with both hands.

Nan did not move her head, but her hand closed around mine. It was as weak as a child's, no strength at all. A noise came out of her mouth, something between a cough and a gasp. Dad spun around, looking for the nurse. "Is she okay? I don't know if she's choking."

Sharon moved to the other side of the bed and leaned in. The blue shape in her thumb pulsed. "No, no, she's okay," she said. "Her throat is just very dry. And she won't be able to move her head for a little while, since everything is so sore. But you can feed her ice chips if you want." She handed me a cup filled with shaved ice. A tiny spoon jutted out from the side, like a shovel buried in snow. "Just little amounts. You can slide it right down her throat. Good, good, that's it. Perfect." Nan made another grunting sound, and Sharon nodded, smiling. "See? She wants more. Go ahead, you can give her a little more. Uh, uh, uh! Just a little! That's it. Just a few at a time."

I fought back tears as Nan's lips closed around the spoon and then lingered, looking for more; she was desperate for water, dying of thirst. The color was still in her cheeks, but I had never seen her so helpless. So feeble.

"Dr. Andrews ran a few tests while you were gone," Sharon said, busying herself with an untouched food tray. "I think he might have some good news for you."

"Like what?" My head whipped around. "What did he say?"

"Don't worry; he'll tell you." She headed for the door. "He should be here any—oops!" Sharon sidestepped Dr. Andrews by inches, laughing. "Almost got you on that one, Doctor!"

He laughed, too, showing a mouthful of crooked teeth. For a moment, I wasn't sure it was the same person I had seen last night. This guy was dressed in a blue suit, complete with a jacket, shiny brown shoes, and a tie. A gold tiepin accentuated the middle of the silk fabric, and his hair, or what was left of it, had been slicked back neatly. Even the purple orb behind his ear looked smaller, as if it had rested too.

"Good morning!" he said.

"Doctor." Dad extended his hand. "How is she?"

"She's doing unbelievably well." Dr. Andrews took a stethoscope out from his jacket pocket and inserted it in his ears. Pressing it against Nan's chest, he listened for a moment. Beneath her hospital robe, I could see the purple shape vibrating, keeping perfect time with her heart. Dr. Andrews stood back up and shook his head.

I felt something clutch inside. "What? What is it?"

"It's borderline surreal, is what it is." He folded his stethoscope and reached for the chart on the wall behind Nan's bed.

"Surreal?" Dad repeated. "Why? What do you mean?"

We waited as he scribbled something in the chart. The yellow orb simmered in his mouth. Snapping the file shut, he looked first at me and then at Dad. "What's happened here is impossible." He shook his head again. "Almost to the point of ridiculousness. I've never seen anything like it in my life. Certainly never during my time in the medical profession."

"Like *what*?" Dad pressed. "What is it?"

"I don't mean to frighten you, but this woman should have died last night." He held up his hands, as if surrendering, and then dropped them. "For all intents and purposes, she was more than halfway there. Between her age, the condition her arteries were in, and the attack she suffered as a result, her heart had almost completely stopped. I did everything I could last night in surgery, but there's only so much we can do. I was almost certain that when I came in this morning, I was going to be signing a death certificate. Her heart was hanging on by a thread. A thread that I've seen hundreds of times over in surgery patients who end up dying the next day." He took a breath. "I know it's hard to hear, but there's no medical reason why your mother is still alive, Mr. Winters. Or at least none that I know of."

"Then maybe we should find someone who does." It came out before I could stop it. But why was he being so negative? Why was he being such a jerk about it?

"Marin." Dad's voice was sharp.

Dr. Andrews smiled. "Maybe you should. And please be sure to bring that person here when you do. Because whoever can explain to me how your grandmother's heart was able to withstand not only the stress of a quadruple bypass operation on an already massively weakened organ, but also somehow repair itself by almost forty percent overnight is definitely someone I want to meet. Someone a lot of people in the medical community would like to meet."

I glowered at him, not sure if he was mocking me.

"I've been a heart specialist for over twenty years. I know how hearts work, what can be done to fix them, and when their limits have been met. I have never, in all my years practicing medicine, seen a case like this. On a scale of one to ten, her heart went from zero to six for no reason whatsoever. Right now, it's beating with the strength and intensity of a forty-five-year-old runner. That thread it was hanging from? As strong as a rope." He shrugged. "It's impossible, but there it is."

"So now what?" Dad asked. "Can we take her home? Can she—"

"Oh no, she'll have to stay here for a few more days, at least." Dr. Andrews smiled. "Her heart may be in decent shape, but the rest of her will have to catch up."

"Okay." Dad nodded. "I just . . . I don't know how to thank you. Again."

"Don't thank me," Dr. Andrews said. "I didn't do much. Like I said, whatever reversed that chain of events was . . . I just don't know. Maybe we'll never know." He looked up as a figure appeared in the doorway. "Looks like you have a visitor. I'll check back later."

Father William hobbled into the room, his face drawn and worried. I moved toward him, straining over his shoulder to see if Dr. Andrews was still in sight. "Come in," I said, pressing the priest's hand. "I'll be right back."

I strode down the hall, gnawing at the edge of my thumb. Dr. Andrews was at the nurses' station a few yards away, writing inside another chart. "Doctor?"

He glanced at me and then went back to his scribbling. "What can I do for you?"

Behind the counter, two nurses looked over, waiting to hear what I would say. "Can I talk to you real quick?" I gestured toward the opposite wall with my head. "Over there?"

"Sure." He followed me over to the wall, leaned against it with one hand. A perspiration stain, wide as a fried egg, spread out beneath his arm, and a heavy silver watch slid down his wrist.

I looked down at my shoes, fumbling with my hands.

"I know you want answers about your grandmother," Dr. Andrews said. "But I don't have any to give you. Believe me, I wish I did."

"I know. But do you think . . ." I hesitated, hoping I didn't sound crazy. "I mean, do you think something outside of medicine did this?"

His eyes creased, as if I had blurred in his line of vision. He pushed himself off the wall, crossing his arms over his chest. "Are you asking me if I think God did this?"

"Sort of." I nodded, unable to look at him. "Something like that."

"Anything's possible," he said. "But as a rule, medicine steers clear of using God as an answer for anything, even if we can't explain it." He grinned. "We're a proud group. It goes against the cold hard facts, I guess. But I'd be a fool to tell you that the possibility doesn't cross my mind from time to time. Especially in situations like this."

"Really?"

"Really." He paused, smiling again. "Have you ever heard of Albert Einstein?"

"Yeah, sure."

"One of the most brilliant scientific minds ever, right? Found the answer to just about every problem he was ever faced with. I have a quote of his in my office, something that my wife gave me when I first started here at the hospital. Do you want to know what it says?"

I nodded.

"It says, 'Mysteriousness is the true source of all art and all science. He who can no longer pause to wonder and stand rapt in awe, is as good as dead; his eyes are closed.'" He paused. "I don't know if God healed your grandmother last night. We'll never know, I guess. But I like to hold on to the idea of the mysterious, the way Einstein did. I'm going to stand rapt in awe at this one. I'm okay with that."

I ducked my head. "Thanks," I said softly.

He put a hand on my shoulder, the chunky silver watch glimmering. A heavy, spicy scent emanated from his wrist.

"You take care of yourself. Get some rest. You're going to need it, keeping up with that grandmother of yours. I have a feeling when she's up and around again, she's going to give all of you a run for your money."

I watched him walk away and disappear inside an elevator. A few feet away, the nurses bustled behind the counter and a phone rang.

His eyes are closed. His eyes are closed.

Maybe I was right.

Maybe it did come down to seeing, after all.

Inside my pocket, my phone buzzed. I unlocked the screen.

It was Dominic. *How r things with yr Gram?*

She's stable, I texted back. *Doing okay.*

So glad. I'm right outside. Can you talk?

Right outside? What was he doing right outside?

Give me a minute.

I ambled into Nan's room, sidling next to the bed. She was asleep again, her mouth parted, breathing in and out. Dried saliva lay in white patches at the corners of her lips, and her tongue looked swollen. Still, she looked like a different person than last night. Alive. Dad and Father William were speaking softly in the corner.

"I'm going to get a snack." I spoke to Dad in a low voice, not wanting to disturb Nan, not wanting her to hear me lie for the millionth time. "And then check out the gift shop. Is that okay?"

"Yeah, good." Dad didn't take his eyes off Father William.

Dominic was outside the emergency room, leaning against the door of his Jeep. His damp hair indicated that he had showered and he had on a clean change of clothes, but the shadows under his eyes were darker, as if they had deepened over the past twelve hours. Could I tell him what I was thinking? Did I dare? What if I was wrong?

"Hey," he said, pushing himself off the car as I emerged from the electric doors. "How are you?"

"I'm okay. Relieved, mostly." I fought the urge to fall against him, to let him wrap his arms around me and press me against his chest. "Last night they were saying she wasn't even going to make it."

"Wow." He shook his head. "You must've had a hell of a night. I can't even imagine."

"She's up there, sleeping like a baby now. The doctor says she can go home in a few days." I paused. "How's Cassie?"

"She's worse." He looked down at his shoes. "Like five hundred times worse. Last night was a nightmare."

"What happened?"

"She just went berserk. Put both hands through a bathroom window, cut her arms and face. They had to bring a doctor over so she could get stitched up." I winced behind my sunglasses. "She's still on the third floor. My dad . . . had to tie her up with rope because she kept ripping herself out of the restraints." He coughed once behind his hands and then pressed his fist against his lips. "I don't think it's my grandmother's spirit in there."

"What do you mean?"

"It can't be. It's . . . whatever it is . . . is trying to kill her. Literally. It's got to be some kind of demon inside her, Marin. Some kind of evil. My grandmother would never do these things to her—dead or alive. And look." He shoved a hand inside his pocket and withdrew a slip of paper. The number eight was drawn on the front in black marker. "You know the carving on Cassie's face? The number eight? I looked it up. Eight is the symbol of infinity, eternity." He turned the paper to the right so that the number was on its side. "But when it's on its side, like this, exactly the way Cassie has it, it turns into a symbol of evil."

"Evil?" My chest tightened.

"Yes." Dominic shoved the paper back inside his pocket again. "Any form of purity that's corrupted or turned on its side like that becomes a symbol of darkness. Like the upside-down cross. Or the Star of David with the circle around it." He shook his head. "It can't be a coincidence. It just can't. There's too many things that are all adding up now. It's got to be a demon doing all this shit to her. It's got to be."

My skin prickled at his words and my mouth felt cold. "If you really think that, then you should tell your parents. Or a priest. Listen, Dominic, I talked to Father William last night. At the hospital. He came to see Nan. He told me that he would look into finding a real exorcism priest to come examine Cassie."

His eyes lit up. "He did? When?"

My heart sank. "I don't know when, exactly. He just said he'd look into it. Apparently, these kinds of priests are hard to get ahold of."

But Dominic was already shaking his head. "We don't have time. I have to try the conjoining exorcism as soon as possible. Like in the next day or two. Once I get everything together, it'll work. I know it will."

"Listen to me!" I protested. "Father William said we shouldn't be messing around with this stuff! I'm serious. You don't have any kind of experience with this, okay? Please don't stand there and tell me that you're really going to do some kind of ritual on a demon!"

"The ritual Cassie did brought it into that room." His voice was determined, unswayed. "Which means that the one I do can take it out again." His eyes were pleading. "I've got to at least try. You don't realize what bad shape she's in, Marin. No one does but us."

Did I dare? Even though the stakes had just been raised, the bar of fear inalterably heightened? I chewed on the inside of my cheek until I tasted blood, studying the tips of my shoelaces.

"Marin?"

I lifted my head, aligned my gaze with his. "I think I know where to get an invisible trinity."

His face blanched, but his eyes lit up. "What?"

"I think I know where to get an invisible trinity," I repeated. "We'll have to go downtown, but I'm pretty sure I'm right."

"What is it?"

I winced, not willing to divulge my secret just yet. Without tangible proof, he might laugh. Scoff, even. "Get in the car. I'll show you."

Nineteen

Dominic darted toward his side of the car so fast that I almost flinched. I got in on the passenger side, fastening my seat belt, hoping beyond hope that what I was about to show him would suffice, that at the very least, he wouldn't dismiss it outright. And yet, I didn't want it to work, either. Leading him down this road, plying him with false hope, wasn't only dangerous, it was also stupid.

"Oh my God, Marin, I can't believe you're actually telling me this." He spoke with a new energy; a light had come back behind his eyes, and his shoulders had righted themselves again. "Just this morning, I was lying in bed thinking that we were going to lose her. And then you tell me you've found an invisible trinity. We'll have both things now! The buried heart and the invisible trinity! We can do it!"

I nodded, wishing he would stop using the word *we*.

"You're not going to lose her," I said as he braked at a red light.

He looked over at me again, the lines in his face softening. "No?"

"No." I dropped my eyes, pretending to study the back of a Smartfood Popcorn bag.

"God, I hope you're right."

I took a deep breath. It was time. It was. I could feel it. "Listen. I have to tell you something else."

"Okay."

My heart thudded in my chest; a roaring sound filled my ears. "I can . . . see things."

"What do you mean? What things?"

"Pain. I can see people's pain." I held my breath.

"Pain?" Dominic's head flicked back and forth between watching the road and looking at me. "Like, you can tell when someone's hurting inside?"

"No, I can *see* it." I scanned the front of Dominic's blue T-shirt, his arms, legs, and pointed to the spot on his wrist with two fingers. "Like right there. There's a bright blue blob there, right inside your wrist."

Dominic looked down and ran his fingers over the spot I had indicated. "That's where I sprained my wrist. Just this year, during preseason javelin tryouts. It's actually been feeling a lot better lately." A curious expression came over his face. "But you already knew that, right? Someone told you?"

"No." I shrugged, pushing my glasses up along my nose. "Who would've told me?"

He stared at me for a moment and then looked back down at his arm. "And *what's* there? What can you see?"

"It's just a blue shape." I looked at it again, more intently this time. "About the size of an egg. It's a little bit darker on the right, and the left side is flatter than the right. Blue usually means some kind of joint or muscle injury or—"

"Wait, *usually means*?" He sat up straighter. "As in you've seen this kind of thing before?"

"Well, yeah. You think you're the only person out there who's injured something? I'm not one hundred percent sure that all the blue shapes I see are joint injuries, but . . ." I stopped, letting my head fall back against the seat rest, realizing how ridiculous everything sounded. "I'm pretty sure they are."

"So you see other ones?"

"Hundreds. All the time."

"Shit, Marin." He ran a hand through his hair. "Have you always had this?"

This. As if it were a disease of some kind, a cancer. "No, it just started last year. Right after my mother died."

"After your mother died?" His eyes were still round with disbelief. "Do you think the two are connected?"

"You mean do I think my dead mother, who didn't even leave me a note saying goodbye before she stepped off a cliff, gifted me with the paranormal ability to see pain?"

He didn't answer.

"I'm sorry." I ran my thumb over the window lock. "I didn't mean for that to come out that way."

"It's okay. I shouldn't have pushed." He paused, maybe considering his next question a little more carefully. "Did you get it checked out by doctors?"

"Four different ones. Three shrinks too."

"And none of them could give you an answer?"

"About twenty different tests came back negative. The shrinks were even worse. One of them asked me what kind of *scents* accompanied my visions. Another guy said I was just trying to get attention from my dad."

"That sounds like something a shrink would say." He sat forward on the seat, his eyebrows knitting into a thick line. "Is *that* why you wear those glasses all the time?" Things were falling into place for him; he was starting to connect the dots.

"Yeah. I'm sorry I gave you the bad eyes explanation. That's what we've told everyone else. I mean, everyone who needs to know, like Father Nickolas and Sister Paulina. No one knows the real reason."

"What is the real reason?"

I shrugged. "It's just too hard being there all day at school, staring at everyone's pain. Everyone has something inside them. Well, almost everyone. And every time I walk down the hall or go into a classroom, it's like being bombarded with hundreds of different colored stars or something. I wouldn't be able to concentrate at all if I didn't have my glasses."

"They help?" He leaned over a little, as if trying to detect if I were actually human. "Like they make things less bright?"

"Yeah. Pretty much." I looked out of the corner of my eye. He was glancing between me and the road, trying to keep the wheel steady.

"Wow." He blinked a few times, his lashes so long that they looked like tiny feathers. "Holy *shit.*"

The sensation of having just peeled back an entire layer of skin came over me then. Once again, I was standing in front of a boy who had flung open the door and stared, trying to comprehend what he was seeing. But, I also realized slowly, he believed me. Given time, of course, the realization might also lead him to conclude that I was just plain weird. A freak, even. But right now, he believed me. I was sure of it.

"Does this . . ." He yanked on an earlobe. "Does this mean you've seen what's inside my sister?" His voice was soft, as if he was afraid of my answer.

I hesitated. Admitting what I saw inside Cassie would make it that much harder to keep trying to weasel out of everything. I could *see* the damn thing. Any medical doctor or exorcist priest who examined Cassie would probably want me there next to him, just to tell him what was happening, where in her body it was moving next. And as much as it frightened me, was it fair that I kept relinquishing that right? Did I have a kind of responsibility in a way to be there? It wasn't Cassie's fault that something so insidious had slipped inside her. Yes, she'd been terrible to me, and yes, she'd performed the ritual, but she hadn't wanted *this* to happen. She was a victim of her recklessness just as much as I was. Maybe even more so.

"I see blackness," I said. "Around her eyes, and then inside her head, behind her eyes. It isn't like anything I've ever seen before. It's bigger than pain. Deeper."

He had stopped breathing and was squeezing the steering wheel so tightly that the knuckles under his skin turned white. "And then what?"

"What do you mean, and then what?"

"What happens to it?"

"I don't know. It just slips away again."

"It slips away?" Dominic stepped on the gas. "Why? Because you're looking at it?"

"No." I bit my lip, staring back down at my jeans. "I don't know. I mean, it never even occurred to me that it might . . . you know, go into hiding again or whatever it does because I look at it. But honestly, I don't know anymore."

Or did I? Was it really possible that the amount of time I had spent staring at Nan's heart last night had something to do with how much better it had gotten? Were the two things connected, even remotely? Even as I watched Dominic plowing through traffic, I could feel something clicking into place. I didn't doubt anymore that I could see pain inside people's bodies. So why wasn't it possible that when I looked at that pain directly, it somehow lessened or that area of the body restored itself? Yes, it sounded ridiculous. Yes, it sounded impossible. But somehow, in some inexplicable way, it had also worked. Hadn't it?

"There's so much about it that I still don't understand," I went on. "I don't even know where it came from. It's just so confusing. I want to do the right thing, but I don't even know what it is I'm doing."

"Maybe you don't have to know." Dominic put a hand on my shoulder, left it there. "Maybe you just have to go with it. Try to trust it and see what happens."

"Maybe." I stared out the window again, watching as two little kids chased after one another in their front yard. They were so little, so carefree, shrieking with joy, their hair blowing back in the wind, that I felt envious of them.

Try to trust it. See what happens.

It sounded so easy.

And yet I already knew it would be the single hardest thing I would ever do in my life.

Twenty

Randy's Floral was located across the street from Elmer Sudds, a small, pristine shop that smelled of rosewater and mint leaves. It was dark inside, as if someone had drawn the shades, and large white buckets of flowers littered the floor. A large bookcase lined the length of one wall, each shelf decorated with various pots of greenery. I walked past the begonias and sunflowers, the big heads bowing beneath the weight of their thick stems, and moved through an aisle thick with potted pansies, tulips, and Gerbera daisies. Tiny white lights strung in and around the pots gave the impression that they were floating in midair, and every few feet or so, a garden gnome peeked out from behind one of the leaves.

"Flowers?" Dominic asked for the third time. "For the trinity?"

I ignored him, moving toward the back of the store where most florists kept their coolers.

"May I help you?" A small man appeared from behind a wall. Dressed in jeans, a white button-down, and cowboy boots, he looked like a very old John Wayne. "Is there something particular you're looking for?"

"Irises," I said. "Do you have any?"

He sighed once, a mournful sound. "All my irises just died," he said. "Can you believe it? I had a bunch of them, and they must've gotten some kind of blight. They just conked over on me." He snapped his fingers. "Overnight. Boom."

Boom. Just like that, my hopes were dashed. "Okay," I said, hoping I sounded nonchalant. "No big deal."

"You could go to Cosmos," the man said. "It's an hour or so down route Ninety-Two, but I'm sure they'd have some." He rolled his eyes. "They have *everything.* Thank God they're not any closer to Fairfield, or they'd run me out of business."

"All right," I said. "We'll try that. Thank you."

"Irises?" Dominic asked as we got back in the car.

"Irises," I repeated. "They have three petals on the outside that you can see. But inside . . ." I paused, cupping my hands and then opening my fingers one at a time. "Inside, there are three more. And then inside that, three more again."

"A hidden trinity," Dominic whispered.

I nodded, trying to hide my disappointment. "You'll have to go to that Cosmos place to get one, though. I can't go with—"

"Hon?" John Wayne emerged from the store, waving a bouquet over his head. "I just found this wedding bouquet." He thrust it through the window at me, wiggling it under my nose. "It was for a wedding that was canceled at the last minute. Just yesterday, in fact. Groom got into a car accident or something." He pointed at the bouquet. "But look. Right in the middle there."

I gazed at the flowers, a gorgeous blend of white and pink peonies, orange rosebuds, lily of the valley, and lemon verbena leaves. There, off to one side, was a single purple iris, the petals so delicate as to seem transparent, each one curved inward, hiding the treasure inside.

"You want it?" John Wayne pushed it at me again, his eyes wide with excitement.

"Yeah, we want it!" Dominic reached for his wallet. "How much?"

"Oh, keep it," John Wayne said. "Please. It's already been paid for anyway, the poor bastards." He gave us a little wave. "Glad I could help. You take care now."

"Thank you!" I called, leaning out the window as Dominic backed out of the parking lot. "Thank you so much!"

He gave us another wave, lifting a short arm over his head and wiggling his fingers. I sank back into the seat, studying the intricate flower again. It was perfect. I'd never thought of it in such terms before, but it was exactly what we needed. A perfect, hidden trinity. "Wow," I breathed. "Well, you've got everything you need now."

Dominic's hands tensed on the wheel. "You've got to come back and do this with me, Marin. Please." He looked at me for so long that I reached for the dashboard, afraid he might swerve into traffic. "Please," he said again. "I can't do it by myself. I know I'm a guy and I'm supposed to be all tough and shit, but I've never been so scared in my life. I can't do this without you."

I bit my lip, looking out the window. "I just told my father that I was going to the gift shop at the hospital. I've already been gone way too long, and I still have hell to pay for sneaking out last night. I can't. Seriously. I have to get back."

"Tonight, then." His chin was quivering. "We'll do it tonight. Can you get away? Can you tell him something?"

I leaned my head back against the seat. This was never going to end.

Until it did.

"You've come so far with me already. Please don't leave me now."

I didn't have to look at him to know that I would say yes, but I did anyway, just to let my eyes sweep over the angles of his face, the wide plane of his cheekbones, the small slope of his chin.

Don't leave me now.

He'd just said that. To me.

It would be one of the biggest risks I'd ever taken in my

life, one I still couldn't be sure I was ready to take. But did you ever know? Was there ever a moment when the answer came? Whap! Just like that?

"All right," I said.

"All right?" He reached over and took my hand. "Really?"

I nodded. I didn't want to say anything more out loud. My throat hurt, two parallel threads of pain making their way up along the inside of it.

He squeezed my hand and then brought it to his lips, pressing them against it.

It was for him, I thought later, that I would go.

For him, and no one else.

Twenty-One

There was no scene later on that night with Dad, no situation that required another lie so that I could sneak out to Dominic's. It was almost too easy. He was going to stay overnight at the hospital, but since only one visitor was allowed to sleep in Nan's room now that she'd been moved out of the ICU, I had to go home. He drove me, draping the inside of his wrist over the steering wheel the way he always did and throwing me sidelong glances. He looked guilty, as if he felt bad for having to leave me alone.

"I know you're exhausted," he said. "You haven't slept in almost twenty-four hours. Probably even longer. Just go right to bed, okay?"

"I will." I got out of the car and moved toward the steps of the house.

"Rinny?" He was leaning out his window.

My heart twisted, hearing him use the nickname he'd given me when I was little, a word he hardly ever used anymore. "Yeah?"

"Promise me you'll just go to sleep. Okay?"

I nodded, already trying to justify the gesture. Once it was over, I'd never lie again. After tonight, I was done. "Okay," I said. "Kiss Nan for me."

He waved goodbye and spun out of the driveway, the truck disappearing in a cloud of dust down the road.

My phone buzzed.

It was Dominic. *Pick you up at eleven?*

I looked at my watch. Six-thirty. Maybe I'd be able to get some sleep after all. My knees sagged, thinking of it.

I took my phone out. *See you then.*

The moon was barely visible when Dominic pulled the Jeep into the driveway of his house later that night, the night so dark as to appear vacated. A bitter taste pooled along the edges of my tongue as we got out of the car and shut our doors. Neither of us had said a word on the drive over; I wondered if Dominic was trying to reserve all his mental energy for what lay ahead the way I was. He'd said this afternoon that things were worse—five hundred times worse—than yesterday. And yesterday had been a nightmare. Demon or no demon, I couldn't imagine what awaited us upstairs now.

I didn't have to wait long. We were in the foyer for less

than five seconds when a screaming sounded from upstairs. Loud thumping noises followed, a series of raps that shook the walls and made the crystal chandelier shiver. Dominic winced and then reached into a small hall closet. He withdrew a cloth bag and then held it out to me.

"Is this the . . ." I swallowed. This was real. What we were about to do was moments away from happening. Words were getting harder and harder to form.

Dominic nodded. "The box with the bird in it and the iris. I have two candles in there, too, just like it says, and a pillow for her head."

Another scream, louder than the first, reverberated down the hallway and then pealed off in the distance.

"Who's with her?" I asked, shouldering the bag.

"My mother," he said. "And the night nurse."

"Your mother?" I pulled back. "I thought she was leaving."

"She didn't want to. Not after Cassie cut herself so badly last night."

Well. That was something.

"Okay. But how're we going to get past them?"

"Cassie's been calling for you again," Dominic said. "Incessantly. Just like in the hospital. My mother knows I'm bringing you over."

Once again, we climbed the beautiful marble staircase and made our way to the third floor. Another ruckus sounded, the crash of glass breaking, a dreadful shrieking that made my toes curl inside my sneakers.

"Listen," Dominic said over his shoulder, "when we get in there, we just have to do what we need to do, no matter who's around. But we have to hurry, okay? I'm really worried that we're running out of time."

"Out of time?" I repeated. "What do you mean?"

"She's so weak." He grabbed my hand. "You'll see."

I nodded, gripping his fingers. The screams intensified as we crept closer to Cassie's room. They were no longer human; now there was a hungry, murderous quality to them, a raging tenor that made the inside of my mouth turn cold.

Mrs. Jackson emerged from the room as we approached, slamming the door behind her as if something might be following her. She paused for a moment, pressing her forehead against the smooth wood, and didn't move. Even from behind, I could make out the orange ball in her stomach. It was as large as a grapefruit now, twice the size it had been yesterday.

"Mom."

She turned at the sound of Dominic's voice, staring at the two of us with glazed eyes. "It's not her in there," she said, one hand still clutching the knob. "I don't know who it is, but it's not my Cassie. It's not her fault, the things she's saying. . . ." Her voice began to rise, bordering on the edge of hysteria. "We have specialists coming. The best in the world. They'll fix it, what's wrong with her. They'll fix it." She clutched at me suddenly, her fingers grabbing handfuls of my shirt. "And you, Marin! You'll go in and see if you can comfort her? Try to calm her down, even for just a little while?"

Dominic moved quickly as his mother's knees gave way and caught her with both hands as she sank to the floor.

"Sarah." Mr. Jackson appeared from around the corner, moving in next to his wife and son. "All right, honey. I've got you. All right."

We watched them disappear down the steps, Mrs. Jackson sobbing against her husband's chest. Even with all of the mistakes they'd made as parents, neither of them deserved this. Not in a million years.

"I'm sorry," Dominic said. "I should have told you I told them you were coming."

"It's all right," I answered, watching as Dominic pulled something out of his pocket.

"What's that?"

He held up a small crucifix for me to see. It was as delicate as a twig and strung on a silver chain. The emaciated figure of Jesus was draped on the front, the letters *INRI* engraved in a crude plaque above his head. "My mom gave it to me a long time ago, right before my confirmation."

"Dominic, you're not a priest. And the book didn't say anything about using a crucifix."

"I know." He wrapped the chain around his fingers like a pair of brass knuckles, until only the crucifix protruded between them. "But it can't hurt."

For a moment, I realized how foolish he sounded, how foolish both of us were, pretending, hoping that we could actually dispel some kind of venomous spirit from inside a girl, according to the directions inside a book of witchcraft. And then in the next moment, behind the closed door, I could hear the strange grunting sounds coming from within, a litany of curses uttered in sudden, menacing spurts. We had to try. We just had to.

"You ready?" Dominic's skin was the color of Silly Putty; his lips were tinged a pale purple. His Adam's apple strained against the muscles in his neck, as if trying to release itself. I nodded and reached out, clutching one of his belt loops with my first two fingers just as I had before. My breathing had already shifted, and my legs felt numb. I fought back the urge to pee and held my breath as Dominic opened the heavy wooden door.

For a moment, I wondered if we were in the same room as we had been in before. Then I realized that it was the same room, except that everything inside it, but for a narrow mattress in one corner, was gone. A green Navajo-print blanket was tossed to one side of the mattress and parts of the white carpet had been torn up, curling back at the edges like gigantic pieces of peeled paint. But it was the temperature that was different, a subzero feel to the air that turned my breath visible, as if I had stepped outside on a winter's day. The hair on my arms prickled, and my teeth started to chatter.

Cassie lay motionless, grunting, in the middle of the mattress. Her arms and legs had been tied to either side, the rope double-knotted at both ends. An unusually tall woman dressed in white pants and a white tunic stood over her. Her lower lip jutted out and a large blue mass sat nestled inside her jawbone like an overripe tangerine. Cassie stirred as the door opened, the sounds now like a heavy, wounded animal, and turned her head toward me. Her eyes were the same oblong shape as yesterday, the pupils narrowed and cylindrical as she fastened a hateful gaze in my direction.

"Get out, bitch." It was a hiss, a spitting of words.

I stared at the chunks of hair that had been pulled out from the sides of her head, the bare, bloodied patches along the outside of her skull. Her face, a swollen map of open wounds, was now nearly unrecognizable, the figure-eight carving oozing fresh blood. Inside her brain, the blackness swirled, a slithering rope of tar, gliding in and among the crevices with a deliberateness that conveyed an ownership, an undeniable right.

"Oh my God," Dominic whispered. "How much more of this can she take?"

"You're Marin?" The tall woman in the corner glanced at me. I nodded. "Mrs. Jackson said you were coming, that you needed privacy." She dropped her arms as she strode toward us, crossing the room in five or six steps. "I'll be right outside if you need me." The door made a soft clicking sound behind her.

"Cassie?" Dominic's voice was too loud. His fingers gripped the crucifix. "We just want to sit next to you, okay?"

A hideous grin emerged across Cassie's face at her brother's words. "Yes," she rasped. "Come over. Closer."

We moved slowly toward the mattress, sinking down next to the girl as we got within arm's reach. I slid the bag off my shoulder with shaking hands and pushed it toward Dominic. "See if you can get the bird in her left hand," I whispered. "I'll try to give her the iris."

He leaned over his sister, prying her stiff fingers apart so he could put the tiny animal in her hand. Cassie closed her fingers around it, and Dominic looked over his shoulder, nodding for me to do my part. I crouched down, inches away from her other hand, when Cassie lurched suddenly, throwing the dead bird across the room. It hit the wall with a dull thud and then slid down to the floor in a tiny heap. She arched her back, emitting a howl of impossible magnitude. It was not human, not even animalistic. This time, it was something unknowable, completely foreign to human senses. "Don't touch me!" she screeched. "Don't you ever touch me!"

I dropped the iris and lurched, falling back against my hands.

"No, Marin!" Dominic stumbled, too, but he composed himself, reaching out to me with a trembling hand. His lips were blue. "Please. Please. We have to try again."

I crawled toward him, retrieving the iris, and held it close to my chest.

"You're afraid," Dominic challenged his sister. He had gone back over to retrieve the bird; inside his other hand, the crucifix was trembling. "You're just scared."

A dim cackling sounded from the back of Cassie's

throat, a noise even more terrifying than the screams. "You should talk," she hissed. "Still crying at night for Mommy and Daddy who go so far away all the time. I hear you in there, curled up in your bed. Crying and crying, like a little boy."

Dominic paused at her words, his body stiffening. He did not look at me.

Cassie's body began to shake, first slowly, as if she was twitching, then with more force until she looked like a rag doll being throttled at the neck, her head jerking from side to side, her legs flopping like dying fish. Her eyes rolled back in their sockets and did not return. She was still again, the shuddering movements quelled without warning.

And then, a new sound: "I want to see the other one in the room." It was an old woman's voice, raspy around the edges with a deep, gravelly center, and I noted with horror that it was directed at me. "The other one," she hissed. "Where is she?"

Cassie sat up, her arms straining against the ropes, and hurled a vicious gaze in my direction. Her head jerked tight, as if locking in position, and she opened her mouth once more. "Here I am, little girl. Take a good look."

As if on cue, Cassie flung herself back down against the mattress. In the next second, her T-shirt flew up, displaying the skin along her stomach, flayed and torn, clawed as if by talons from the inside out. Red glowed everywhere, gobs of it, dripping, leaking, smearing every last bit of surface where her skin had been, a gutted animal left to die.

"Marin!" Dominic's face was white with horror. "Come on. We've got to go to her! Right now. We've got to do this, even if we have to sit on her hands to do it!"

Cassie lifted her head again, regarding us with hateful eyes. She growled and lunged, a chained tiger snapping at a piece of dangling meat. "Get away from me, you piece of shit! No one comes near me unless I say so! Get out!"

I stood frozen to the spot, too frightened to move, but Cassie's words seemed to energize Dominic, and he grabbed my hand, dragging me toward her. I stood there panting, and then dropped to my knees, trying in vain to wedge the fragile flower inside her hand. But Cassie crushed it under her fingers, smashing it into the rug until there was nothing left but bits of stamen and yellow pollen. The petals lay to one side, bruised and broken, remnants of what they once had been. She threw her head back and arched her spine. Her toes were rigid; the veins along her arms stood out like cords. Somehow, the ropes around them held fast.

"Go to hell!" she screamed. "Both of you!" She raised her head, widened her voided eyes. Abruptly, the crucifix flew out of Dominic's hand and smashed against the wall. I screamed and flinched, covering my face with both arms.

Cassie's head jerked in my direction, and another low, cackling laugh emerged from her throat. "You. Who do you think *you* are?" She hissed her words, hate leaking from every syllable. "You think you can come into my presence with your so-called gift? Do you have any idea where your pathetic ability comes from? That the only reason you can see me at all is because I recognize myself in you?"

"Don't listen, Marin!" Dominic was yelling, but he sounded far away, as if he were deep underwater. "She's just trying to scare you! Don't listen!"

The low, terrible laugh rose again from inside the girl's throat. "Do you want to see *your* pain?" she mocked. "LOOK!"

Once more, Cassie fell back flat against the mattress. For a moment, her body was completely still. Then, slowly, her head tilted back until the only thing visible was the ridge of her throat pressing like a gigantic cord against her skin. Her mouth opened mechanically, as if someone were pulling the top and bottom apart at the hinges. A faint gagging noise sounded from the back of it, and her tongue lolled to one side, limp as a piece of meat. And then, impossibly, the head of a snake appeared from inside the hole of her mouth. Its skin was the color of burnished coal, and it was as thick around as one of Cassie's arms. It flicked its pink tongue as the rest of it emerged, liquid-like, from inside her throat, between her lips.

A hoarse shout came from Dominic as the reptile appeared. But he composed himself in the next moment, retrieving the crucifix again, standing with his feet apart as the snake slithered down the front of Cassie's stomach. The ritual from the green book was forgotten; he was working only from instinct now. "Get back!" he said. "Go back to where you came from!"

The snake raised its head at Dominic's words, almost as if it was listening, and then turned in my direction. Its pink tongue flicked in and out of its mouth, tasting something in the air, and its eyes were dark slits. It moved across the room fluidly, thick coils undulating, as if slipping through oil. Behind it, the terrible cackling laugh sounded again from Cassie's mouth. "Look at me now! *Look* at me, and watch me destroy you!"

I was shaking so hard that it felt as though my entire body had been converted into a single vibrating nerve. Somewhere from very far away, I could hear Dominic's voice. "Don't listen, Marin! Don't look!"

"Where do you think your precious mother is now?" Cassie's cackling voice charged at me. "She's where all hopeless souls go, where they are cast down after despairing and turning their back on the world!" The pink tongue flicked. The black tail slithered across the floor, moving the snake closer. "But she left you something behind to remember her by, didn't she? A gift from me. A blessing from hell!"

NO!

It was the answer no one else had been able to give, the one that had been there all along, staring me in the face. My gift, my blessing, was no such thing at all. It was a malevolent force, something seared within me as a result of abandoning Mom, of leaving her to die, as malicious a thing as the snake still crawling toward me, hissing and spitting and moving closer with every second.

"Yes," the voice hissed. "It's the truth, isn't it, Marin? *Isn't* it?"

At the sound of my name, I started up from the corner as if someone had pulled me by the hair and raced toward the door. I clutched the icy doorknob and struggled to open it. It didn't budge, didn't even turn. A crushing sensation from the inside out enveloped me, and I struggled for air.

I could hear my voice being shouted somewhere in the background—"Marin! Marin, wait!"—but the doorknob loosened, and I was out, pushing past the night nurse, racing down the hallway, stumbling down the stairs, hanging frantically to the railing even as my feet gave out beneath me, even as I swayed and clutched and then fell down the last three steps.

Another voice sounded, a man's this time, calling my name, but it was so faint that I was sure I was imagining it. The front door was directly ahead.

Fifty feet.

Thirty.

Ten.

"Marin!" The male voice again. Dominic, maybe? Mr. Jackson? No matter. The knob turned in my hands, the heavy front door opening to the darkness outside. I cringed under the sudden brightness of the porch light and raced down the long, serpentine driveway, which would lead me to the street, which would lead me home. Which would lead me . . . where?

"Marin! Marin!"

I did not hear the car coming around the bend of the driveway, did not see the headlights carving a path directly opposite me; there was only the terrible sound of brakes screeching against pavement, the insidious crunch of metal as something collided into my right arm. And then I was airborne, suspended against the inky darkness as if caught in a photograph, pinned against the sky until my body crashed back down to the ground, a pile of bones and muscle, breath and blood.

For a split second, I caught sight of the moon, hanging like a faint thumbnail there in the sky, watching.

Waiting.

And then, nothing.

Twenty-Two

I woke to a searing pain in my right arm, a column of fire that traveled from my elbow all the way up to my shoulder. The snake! It had bitten me, crawled inside my mouth. Now it was writhing inside my belly, slithering up through my arm, its pink tongue flicking, spitting, engulfing me with its horrifying presence, strangling the life out of my bones, my lungs. I screamed, clutching at the strange white sheet covering me, and flailed at the silver railings on either side of the bed. "Get it out! Get it off me!"

Someone moved to the side of the bed and grabbed at my hands. "Marin." It was Dominic. "Marin, listen to me. Nothing's there."

"No! It's there! I can feel it! It's right there! Get it out! Get it out, before it bites me! Before it kills me!"

"Marin, stop!" Dominic's voice shook. "You're not in

Cassie's room anymore. You're in the hospital. You had an accident." He cleared his throat as his voice broke. "You got hit by our gardener. . . . He was just leaving for the night, and he didn't see you in the dark. You're in the hospital. We're getting your father; he'll be here any second, okay?"

But I was hysterical. "Get it off! Get it out!"

Dominic stepped back as another figure with short hair and long, white arms emerged from somewhere in the room.

"I'm sorry," she said. "But you're going to have to leave now. We have to calm her down." The long hands pushed up the sleeve of my gown, tapped at a vein beneath my skin. A pricking sensation—the snake?—incited another scream, and I arched my back as it deepened, and then sank into oblivion once more.

I came to again, as if waking from a dream, and whimpered. My right arm was encased in plaster and my fingers poked out like sticks from one end, but the fiery pain had dulled. I moaned again, disoriented, and tried to open my eyes. They felt like leaden curtains, my eyeballs like orbs of fire.

Dad lunged from a chair in the corner, bending down over my face so that I could see him. "Here I am, Rinny. I'm right here. You're in the same hospital as Nan, just a few floors down. You broke your arm, honey, but it's all right. It's going to be all right."

I struggled to sit up, winced against a new pain that

shot through my collarbone, the length of my arm. My eyes were blurry; a crust around them pulled at my eyelashes. I rubbed them with my good hand, blinked a few times. Stared down at the strange blue shape shimmering beneath the bandages around my forearm. *My* pain. For the very first time, I was looking at pain inside my own body. Why had I thought it might look brighter inside me than it did in other people? Or larger, for some reason? It was neither, just another blue shape—this one thin and long, like a rectangle—hovering just below the surface of my skin. I moved my arm stiffly to the right to see what might happen, but the shape did not change. To the left. Nothing.

"Don't move it right now," Dad said. "Just rest."

I looked up, tried to shuffle through the thoughts in my head, which were flung like so many playing cards on the floor. "What happened?"

"I need to ask you the same question." His voice was soft, but I could hear the restraint behind it. "Dominic Jackson met me here after the hospital called and said the two of you were at his place. He said you got spooked and ran out of the house, and that's when a car hit you. You broke your arm in two different places."

It was starting to come back, but slowly, a fishing line reeled in through murky water. Running down the steps. Someone calling my name. The room. The snake.

The snake!

I sat up with a start, ignoring the shooting pain in my

arm. As if by reflex, my breath reverted again to a series of shallow pants. My eyes swept the room, scanning the floor, the corners, under the meal table, the television. I yanked at my sheets, tore back the blanket covering my legs, and then curled my feet up under me. But there was no sign of it.

"Marin?" Dad looked bewildered. "Honey, what is it? What are you doing? What's wrong?"

"The snake!"

His eyes skittered across the floor as he took a step back. "There's no snake, Marin. Is that . . ." He looked stricken. "Is that what you saw? They had a snake? At their house?"

I nodded, sobbing, reaching for him. "It came out of her. Out from inside Cassie. I saw it! It was right there, moving toward me, getting closer and closer. She . . . it . . . told me that that was what my pain looked like, that that was what I had inside me." I sobbed, helpless, overcome again with the horrifying memory. "I have evil inside me, Dad. That's why I can see the things I see. It's evil. It's from hell."

He grabbed me around the shoulders, leaned in an inch from my face. His eyes were as wide as quarters, his voice tight and clipped. "You listen to me, Marin. I don't care what you saw or heard in that room, but there is nothing evil about you. There is nothing evil *inside* you. *Nothing,* do you hear me?" His voice shook, but it was as strong as I had ever heard it.

I pushed against his shirt with my good arm, refusing to hear him. "But that's what it *said*! And it's the only thing that makes sense anymore! In the room that day, when she invited me over. Oh, Dad, she tricked me. She was doing something awful, some kind of ritual that involved contacting dead spirits. I never told anyone, because I didn't think anyone would believe me. But it . . . she . . . must have recognized the evil inside me. She told me! She saw it! And then she showed me!"

His face paled at my words, his fingers releasing themselves slowly around my wrist. *"Spirits?"* he repeated. "You were contacting spirits?"

"*I* wasn't! She was! I was just trying to get out of there! But she left me, she locked the door. . . ." My voice crumpled into sobs again.

"Oh, Marin." He pulled me to him, let me sob against his shirt. "Oh my God."

"I'm evil, Dad." My chest heaved and shook.

"You are not evil." He sat back, cupped my face in his hands. "Listen to me. *Listen* to me! I know"—he paused, his voice shaking—"I know in my *soul* that the ability you were given is not evil."

"You can't say that!" I turned my head, trying to dislodge his grasp. "You don't know!"

"I *do* know."

"How?" I stared at him, desperate in a way that I had never been before. He had to give me an answer this time. He had to.

"You want to know how I know?" He let go of me and paced the room, raking a hand through his hair. "For an entire year now, Marin, I've watched you walk around with your eyes down, hidden behind your sunglasses, refusing to look people in the eye. I've tried to put myself in your shoes, tried to imagine what it must be like to have to do such a thing just to preserve your sanity. But the other night in the hospital, while we were sitting there with Nan, I watched you take off your sunglasses and look at her." He tried to smile, but it came out as a grimace. "For a minute, I thought maybe some kind of laser beam was going to shoot from your eyes. Your gaze was so intense, so full of everything you feel for her." His eyes rimmed with tears. "I may not have had much of a reaction the next day, when the doctor told us about her recovery, but that's only because I wasn't that surprised. Even if you hadn't had this ability, Marin, the love you felt for your grandmother that night would have worked a miracle. It would have changed her forever."

My breathing sounded far away, and for a moment, I could not be sure it even belonged to me. "You really think I healed Nan?" I whispered.

"I think God healed Nan," Dad said. "Through you."

It was as if something inside just shattered, and then somehow restored itself, all in one moment. I sank into the pillows and closed my eyes.

It was too much.

It was still too much.

And even if it was true, I had no idea how to bring myself to believe it.

"It can't . . . ," I started.

Dad sat down on the edge of the bed again, taking my hand in his. "Why can't it?" he asked. "Why not?"

"Because it doesn't make sense!" I cried. "It doesn't . . . It's not me! It's not who I am!"

"Do you know who you are?" Dad's gaze was steady, his jaw set tight. "Do you, Rinny?"

I inhaled sharply, not letting go of his hand. The truth was simple. Awful. I had no idea who I was. But I didn't want to tell him that. I didn't even want to admit it to myself.

"It's okay," Dad said. His voice was tender. He reached out, cupping my cheek against his palm. "It's okay, baby. I'm here." I closed my eyes. "I'm here."

Somehow, I slept. When I woke again, it was dark. The room smelled different, like salt and grease. I tried to sit, keeping my arm close to my stomach, and startled as Dad stood up from the corner. "Oh!" I said. "You scared me."

"I'm sorry." He held out a white paper sleeve of fries. "I went to Burger King. Got some food. You hungry at all?"

I took a fry. It was hot and soft and salty. I took another. And then one more.

Dad reached into the bag, pulling out various items. He unwrapped a burger and put it on a napkin, tipped over another sleeve of fries, inserted a straw into a plastic cup. "Here, I got you a chocolate shake too. Extra thick, no whipped cream. Eat up."

I picked up the burger, took a little bite, pulled on the straw inside the shake. Even my teeth felt sore. "How's Nan?" I asked.

He smiled. "I just checked on her a little while ago. She was sitting up. Eating pudding. They had to practically tie her down so she wouldn't get out of bed and come find you."

I smiled at the thought of Nan elbowing a nurse, getting loud with a doctor. It wasn't often, but sometimes Nan could get ornery with people who told her she couldn't do certain things. Especially when it came to her family. "I'll get out of here soon, won't I?" I said. "We can go down and see her?"

"Absolutely. And then she'll be home in a few more days and things can start getting back to normal."

Normal? What was normal? I wasn't sure if I knew what that was anymore. Dad grabbed his drink and sat down on the edge of his chair. For a moment he slurped on his straw, watching the floor. Then he set the cup down, balanced his elbows on top of his knees. "You know, I've been thinking about what we talked about yesterday," he said.

What had we talked about yesterday? I couldn't remember.

"About Mom," he prodded. "And God. About how He could have helped her, made her think differently before she went and did what she did?"

I nodded, looking down at my hamburger bun.

"The truth is . . ." He hesitated. "Well, you were right.

About me not having an answer for any of it. I didn't have one. And I'm sorry for that. But I don't think anyone does, Rinny. That's just the way it is. Life is full of questions that don't have answers. I have a ton of them."

"Like what?" My voice was a whisper.

He looked at me with shiny eyes. "Like why someone I loved so much would choose to leave without even saying goodbye. Like why I couldn't help her, why I couldn't be enough to lift some of her sadness. Like why you can see pain in people." He swallowed with difficulty. "I don't have answers for any of those questions, Marin. But, you know, I've also started to think that if I can accept that, try to come to terms with the fact that an answer just doesn't exist, I can sort of come to peace with it too."

He took a breath, studied his intertwined fingers. "You remember that day when you came and told Nan and me about your eyes?"

I nodded.

"I didn't know what to tell you or not to tell you. Half of me was scared to death, thinking you had come down with some kind of terminal illness, and the other half was pissed off because I thought you were just making it up, trying to get attention or something." He clenched his jaw. "I don't know if I've ever felt so hopeless. So inept as a father. As a man. Again."

I could feel the tears coming, and I made no move to stop them.

"I couldn't sleep for weeks after you told us, just kept

tossing and turning, thinking about you and your eyes, and then all of a sudden, right out of the blue, I remembered something your mother told me once." He hung his head, his lips wobbling the way they did when he sometimes fought back tears. "It was during one of her episodes, when she would withdraw and shut me out, and I kept trying, trying to get through to her, to help her out. But things just kept getting worse, and I kept getting angrier and angrier. We got into a big fight, and I ended up screaming, 'What do you want me to *do*?' And she raised her head off the top of her knees—she was sitting there in the window, with her head pressed down on her knees—and she said, 'Just love me. Please. Just keep loving me.' "

His mouth trembled as he stared at me from across the room. "That's what I remembered that night, lying there, thinking about you. And that's when I realized that I had to make a decision. I could either love you the way you were—no matter how weird or strange that might be—or I could shut you out." He took a deep breath. "I fell asleep, thinking about it. And when I woke up the next morning, I realized that I had turned a corner. I'd made the choice to hold on to something again, even if I wasn't one hundred percent sure of it. I think in that moment I decided to find a road somewhere between denial and despair. I'm not saying I became some kind of saint afterward." He shook his head, made a little snorting sound through his nose. "All the arguing we've been doing has proved that. But it helped. A little. It did. It still does." He moved forward, taking my hand in his. "The point is that I had to make the choice. And it made all the difference. You could try to do the same thing with me, Marin. If you want."

"I can't."

"Why?" His hold tightened. "Why can't you?"

"Because I don't deserve to." My voice welled with tears.

"You do deserve to!"

"I don't! I *left* her, Dad! I left Mom. Even after you asked me not to." I leaned forward, speaking with a ferocity that I did not know I possessed. But there was nothing left to lose now. "And I wanted to leave. I *wanted* to. I couldn't stand being around her anymore. All her moods and the sleeping and . . ." I could feel myself unraveling, a thread loosened from the skein. Any moment, the whole thing would give and collapse to the floor, a pile of loose ends. "I just didn't care anymore. I didn't. And so I left. And now she's dead."

"Marin. *I* left her that day." Dad's voice was cracking. "*I* left. And do you want to know why? Because I felt the same way. I was sick of it too. I was worn down by her sickness, of not being able to help her, and I gave up. I rationalized it all the way to work that day, too, telling myself that you were there, that things would be fine. But the truth was, I had no right to put you in that kind of situation. I was the adult. I did it because I was weak, because I was selfish. Because I was tired."

Could I believe him? Had he been carrying this around too? Something so similar, all this time?

"We're human, Marin. Which means that sometimes we fail the people we love the most. But Mom's death wasn't your fault. Do you understand me? It wasn't your fault. It wasn't ever your fault." I clung to him, the weight of something deep lifting, a boulder shifting. "The other truth here, Marin, is that Mom failed herself. Not you. Not me. Not God. She decided to give up. That was her choice."

I cried with him for a long time then, not because I was afraid or ashamed or even angry, but because for the first time in a very, very long time, it felt as though something inside of me was starting to open.

And maybe even breathe again.

"Now you listen to me," Dad said after I had stopped, drying my tears on the edge of his sleeve, blowing my nose into a tissue on the bedside table. "It's over now, okay?"

I rubbed my eyes with my free hand. "What's over?"

"The whole thing with Cassie. With Dominic. That whole family. It's over for you. Do you understand? You're not to go back there. Ever. You're finished with it. Finished." He shoved his hands deep inside his pockets. "I told that kid the same thing, too, in no uncertain terms."

"You mean Dominic?"

"Yes. Dominic."

"You weren't . . ." I winced. "You weren't like, really rude to him or anything, were you?"

"No." Dad stood up. "I just told him that if I saw him anywhere around you again, I'd break his neck."

"Dad!"

He smiled. "I was polite," he assured me. "But he got the idea. Believe me."

I let my head fall back against the pillow and emitted a deep sigh. I wondered how Dominic was doing, *what* he was doing. It wasn't his fault that the exorcism had gone so terribly awry. What would he do, now that the buried heart and hidden trinity hadn't worked? What *could* he do? There were no other options left. We had to tell Father William to get someone. An expert, just as he'd promised he would. It would take a while for everything to start falling into place, months, maybe, for the bishop to be petitioned and a real exorcist assigned to the case. Still, it was the only way. There was nothing left.

I cringed, imagining the look Dad must have given Dominic in the hospital, the uncertain way he'd probably reached up to pull on his earlobe.

"Marin." Dad's voice was a warning. "I mean it."

"I know." I looked at him. "I know. All right."

Twenty-Three

I was in bed at home the next morning when the doorbell rang. The hospital had discharged me the night before with a prescription for painkillers and strict instructions to rest. Nan had seconded the order from her hospital bed, making me promise that I would stay in my bed for the day, getting up only to use the bathroom. I smiled, thinking of her. She looked good when we'd gone up to see her, the color back in her cheeks, her eyes bright again. She'd gripped my hand when I stood by her bedside, her eyes roving over my cast, but I assured her that I was okay. Which I kind of was, somehow. Or at least I wasn't as panicked as I had been the day before. Something had shifted a little after the talk between Dad and me. If I still wasn't sure about all of the things he had said, some of it had resonated. Some of it had helped.

It was early, especially for a Saturday, not even eight

o'clock yet. Outside, the morning was full of new light, the sun already low in the sky. I could hear Dad going down the hall, muttering to himself. There was no telling what he might say or do if it was Dominic out there on the porch. My stomach twisted, thinking about it.

"Hey, Lucy!" He sounded pleased, but my stomach plummeted at the name. I'd treated my friend so poorly, doing everything I could to avoid her over the last few days, and now I would have to answer for it. Well, I deserved to. It was time to pay the piper. "Yeah, yeah, she's here," Dad said. "Come on in."

I sat up against the pillow, my upper body movements still clumsy from the cast, and crossed my legs. My heart thumped under my pajama shirt, and my palms were sweaty. "Hey," I said when Lucy appeared in the doorway.

She hung back for a moment, as if frightened. She was wearing a red T-shirt with a picture of the Grinch on the front and an old pair of faded jeans. Her hair had been pulled back into a half-ponytail, the ends loose and wavy along her shoulders. The red disk in her tooth looked like a flattened raspberry, and the yellow blob in her stomach was twice the size it had been. "You're okay?" she whispered. Her big eyes filled with tears.

"Yeah." My own eyes filled. "I'm okay."

Lucy moved toward the bed in a sudden rush. Her pretty face was squished up, the soft skin along her neck mottled with pink blotches. "Oh, Marin, I was so scared. I haven't heard back from you in like two days, and then my mom told me last night that she heard that you'd gotten hit by a car right outside the Jacksons' place, and . . ." Her eyes widened. "Your phone must've blown up from all the texts I kept sending you, but I never heard back, and I . . ." She paused, gulping for air. "God, I didn't know what to think."

"I did get hit by a car." I motioned my head toward the cast. "But I only broke my arm. And with everything that happened, I have no idea where my phone went. It could still be in the middle of the street, for all I know." I patted the side of the bed, and Lucy sat down on the edge of it. "You didn't have to come," I said. "I really am okay."

"Didn't have to *come*?" Lucy's eyes widened. "What, are you kidding me? I ran to the *hospital* last night, but they said it was too late for visitors, so I waited as long as I could this morning—my mom kept saying don't go over too early, don't crowd her, blah, blah, blah—but I seriously couldn't wait another second. I just left and walked over. I had to come, Marin. You're my friend." Her voice wobbled. "I mean, that's what friends do."

I shook my head, my nose prickling with tears. "Oh, Luce, I'm sorry. I haven't been a good friend to you at all."

Lucy sniffled. "You've had . . . a lot going on."

"No." I hesitated. "Well, yeah. I have. But I haven't been honest with you, either. There's something about me that I've never told you. Something big."

Lucy bit her lip. "You're sick?"

"No." I let the truth come out slowly, haltingly, the way

it had with Dominic. I watched as the expression on Lucy's face slid from disbelief into confusion and then wonderment. A long moment passed after I finished, and I twisted a section of the bedsheet, waiting for her response.

"Wow," Lucy breathed finally.

"Yeah." I coiled the sheet into a rope, pulled it tight around my finger. "Wow."

"I mean like, oh my God."

I shrugged.

"Can you see anything inside *me*?"

"Uh-huh."

"Like what?"

"Well"—I pointed to Lucy's mouth—"there's a red shape inside your tooth."

"My tooth?" Lucy brought her hand up to the edge of her face, tongued the inside of her mouth.

"It's probably just a cavity. I see them all the time in people." I grinned a little. "But you probably should brush your teeth a little bit more. Especially considering all the candy you eat. Oh, and you have a little yellow glob in your stomach too. I just started noticing that one a few weeks ago. It kind of looks like a Jell-O square." Lucy was still staring at me. I dropped my head, traced an invisible line across the top of my sheets. "I know it sounds crazy. It *is* crazy. Do you think I'm a freak?"

"No," Lucy answered. "I think you're amazing."

"Yeah. Amazingly *weird*."

"Well, it's a little weird," Lucy conceded. "Definitely

different. But different doesn't have to be a bad thing. It's just . . ."

"Weird."

"No.

"Yes."

"No." The annoyance in Lucy's voice startled me. "Think about it, Marin. For some reason, you're getting the chance to see things in a way that I never will, not in a million years. You're literally looking at things through a lens that none of us will ever get the chance to see *once*, let alone the way you have. Holy cow, if you ever wanted to go into medicine, you'd be able to help people the way no doctor could ever dream of doing!" She gasped, thinking of it. "How could that make you a freak? It makes you special, really. Incredibly, amazingly special." She shrugged, a flush of pink rising along the skin of her neck. "I kind of just want to give you a big hug right now, you're so special."

We both laughed.

"I'm sorry I lied," I said. "I just . . . I didn't know how to tell you."

Lucy nodded. "It's okay. I . . . I . . . ," she stammered, tugging at the bottom of her hair. "I lied to you, too, actually."

"About what?"

"I've been throwing up." Lucy's neck turned crimson.

"You mean on purpose?"

"Yeah." She pulled at the skin on her wrist. "I've been doing it for a while now. Which is probably why you can see the yellow thing inside my stomach. It hurts all the time, but it's getting harder and harder for me to stop."

"Oh, Luce." I took her hand again.

"I know." Lucy nodded.

"You can't do that."

"It's so stupid. But I love candy. I love food. And I don't want to get fat." Her eyes filled with tears. "I want to look like my mom, you know? She's so perfect."

"Your mom's not perfect."

"She's close enough. I heard some jerk on the bus the other day call her a MILF. My *mom*! A MILF." She closed her eyes. "It's disgusting, but you know. They think she's beautiful."

"You're beautiful," I said.

"Yeah. On the inside, right? On the outside, I look like a first-class midget with crazy hair and a sugar addiction."

I almost laughed at the absurdity of Lucy's statement. It was incredible how many things people believed about themselves and how untrue most of them were. Including me. "You're definitely small," I said. "But I also think you're one of the prettiest girls in school. And not just on the inside." I paused. "You're like an angel with a broken wing."

Lucy's face softened, her whole face giving way with gratitude, and right then and there, I knew that we were going to make it. That she was one of the good ones. And that I was going to hold on to her with both hands.

"You can call me," I said. "You know, when you get

nervous and think you should throw up. And I'll remind you of all the reasons why you shouldn't. We can go for a walk or something. Or just hang out and watch movies in your room." I paused. "You wouldn't throw up in front of me, would you?"

"No!" Lucy looked horrified.

"Well, okay, then." I put a hand on my friend's knee. "You in?"

"I'm in," she whispered. "Thanks, Marin."

"You got it. Now can you do me a favor?"

"Yeah, of course. Anything."

"Can we talk about something else? Anything else?"

Lucy laughed once, a burst of relief from the middle of her chest. *"Well,"* she said after a minute, "did you get my text about the Prom Bomb?"

"No." I leaned forward. "Did Randy say yes?"

"Oh, Randy." She waved her hand. "I couldn't ask him after what you told me about the nose picking. I really couldn't. I went up to him and everything, and then I just turned around. All I could think about was his finger up his nose. I mean, *seriously.*"

"So you're not going?"

"No, I am! When I went up to talk to Randy, his best friend Pete was there. You know Pete Lorusso? And he followed me after I turned around and asked me right there if I had a date yet for the prom!"

I couldn't help but laugh. She was so excited. I was happy for her. I really was.

"And then last night, he called and told me that he'd rented a stretch limo! Just for the two of us!" Her eyes were bright with excitement. "Oh, Marin, you have to go to the prom! Just ask someone. Anyone! We could double-date. It would be so much fun."

"It'd be great." I struggled to make my voice sound light. "I could sit in a corner in my sunglasses and a big poufy dress and point out all the pain in everyone's bodies."

Lucy's shoulders sagged, remembering. "You could charge people," she said, grinning. "Ten dollars for anything you see in the shoulders and up, twenty for anything below the waist."

"Fifty for a full-body scan." I laughed, but it was a hollow sound, wisping away into the corners, the last of it ringing in my ears.

Lucy reached out and rubbed my good arm. "Things are going to work out with all this. I know they will."

"Yeah." I uncrossed my legs, anxious to move, and got up off the bed. "Hey, you up for a walk?"

"A walk?" Lucy looked alarmed. "Aren't you supposed to rest?"

"We'll go slow," I said. "I need some fresh air. Come on."

"Just to the water and back, Marin!" Dad called as we slipped out the front door. "Fifteen minutes, tops. Then I want you back in bed."

"Okay!" I said.

Lucy slipped her arm through my good one and fell into step beside me. "He's worried about you," she said.

"Yeah." I smiled a little. "He does that sometimes."

The air had softened a little overnight; the sharp edge to it replaced now with a muted balminess. Birds twittered and swooped overhead, their aerial acrobatics a welcome distraction for the moment, and green was everywhere. I thought about the crested rhizome again, with roots now, buried in Dad's garden. Now that spring had arrived, who knew what could happen?

Lucy was talking about what kind of dress she wanted—definitely something pink, maybe with a few sparkles in the front—when a Jeep rounded the corner at the other end. Swirls of dust spun out from beneath the tires, and it veered from one side of the road to the other, as if starting to lose control.

"Move over," Lucy said, pulling at my arm. "This guy thinks he's at the Indy Five Hundred or something."

But I already knew who it was. I glanced over my shoulder, scanning the house for any sign of Dad, but he was nowhere to be seen.

"Marin." Lucy tugged at me. "Come on. Move over."

The Jeep braked so suddenly that the wheels spun, spitting bits of rock and dirt in our direction. Lucy's fingers tightened around my arm, but I did not move as Dominic got out on the driver's side and came toward us. His eyes were luminously large, the circles beneath them dark as shale. "Marin!" His shoulders sagged. "You're home. You're okay?"

I nodded. "I'm all right."

He slid a hand through his hair. "They wouldn't let me into the hospital last night, and after your dad made me leave, I couldn't find any information about how you were doing." He shook his head, then glanced at Lucy, who was looking first at me and then back at him, trying to put the pieces together. "Our gardener's been having a heart attack. You know, the one who hit you. He's been up all—"

"It wasn't his fault," I interrupted. "He couldn't have seen me. It was so dark."

Dominic's face eased an inch. "Yeah. All right. God, as long as you're okay."

I hesitated, but only for a moment. "How's Cassie?"

His response was interrupted by a shout from behind us. "Get out of here! Now! Get the hell away from her!" Dad had burst out of the front door; he was running toward us, waving his arms over his head.

Dominic's face blanched. He took a step back and then another. "She's dying, Marin." He held my gaze, and glanced back at Dad. "She won't make it through tonight. Her blood pressure is already sixty over eighty and it keeps dropping. The emergency nurses are there, and my parents called Father William. He's on his way."

My heart surged. "To do an exorcism?"

"No." Dominic shook his head. "To deliver last rites."

"An exorcism?" Lucy's fingers clutched at my arm.

"You leave her alone!" Dad was fifty feet away, his voice loud and raspy. "I mean it! What did I tell you in the hospital? She's been through enough! Get out of here!"

"Marin." Dominic spoke quickly, his words streaming out of his mouth. "I've been up all night, thinking. There's a reason why the iris and the bird didn't work. They weren't the right things. The book said a *single being,* remember?" He took another step back as Dad got closer and raised his voice. "A single being with a fractured heart, a hidden trinity." His voice choked as he lifted his arm. "My wrist doesn't hurt anymore. The pain inside it is gone. Don't you see? It's you, Marin. *You're* the buried heart. The hidden trinity. Your gift—seeing, holding, healing. All three. In one being. It's you, Marin."

"Get out of here!" Dad's nostrils flared as he stopped in front of the Jeep. He pointed a finger across the hood of the car. "I'm not kidding. I'll call the goddamned police right now if you don't leave."

"Okay." Dominic lifted his hands up next to his ears and took a few steps backward. "I'm leaving. I'm leaving." The blue shape inside his wrist was gone. There was nothing there but skin and bones, clean tendon and muscle. I thought back to all the times we'd held hands, each one gingerly, quickly, as if the other might pull away. Had it been enough to heal him?

"Now." Dad was breathing through his mouth, panting like a dog.

Dominic got in the car. Looked at me through the thick pane of glass. Slammed his door shut.

"Let's go, Marin." Dad's voice was terrible.

"No." I stepped forward. "I have to help, Dad. I have to. She's dying."

"Wait, Cassie's *dying*?" Lucy's voice went up a notch.

"You don't have to do anything." Dad shook his head, breathing hard. "You don't owe anything to that girl. The last time you went near her, you almost got killed. Now get in the house. I'm telling you, Marin, if I have to carry you . . ."

It had all led to this moment, I realized, the long, slow agony of it, the terrible dance of doubt. It was time now to take a stand. To make a decision between despair and denial. It was time, as Dominic had said once, to try and trust the thing inside and go with it. See what happened.

I grabbed Dad's hand. "You told me last night that you thought this thing inside me was good. That I was good. That it might even have been God working through me. Now it's my turn to try to believe that, Dad. It's the only thing left. I have to try." I took a breath. "I can't let her die, Dad. I can't."

He clenched his fists as I opened the passenger door and grit his teeth as Dominic leaned over to help me inside and shut the door. Through the window, I could see the lemon-yellow orbs in his cheeks, both of them getting smaller and smaller in the rearview mirror as Dominic turned the car around and sped away. Lucy stood next to Dad, the top of her dark head a few inches shy of the middle of his chest, her mouth in the shape of a little O.

The Jeep gunned its way down the road, cresting the small hill.

And then they were gone.

Twenty-Four

"The snake," I said, remembering again as Dominic careened down the hill. I gripped the edge of the seat. "Oh God, Dominic, I can't see that thing again."

"Listen to me." Dominic sat up straighter, taking my hand in his. "I was up all night, reading about exorcisms. The stuff the priests have to do . . ." He paused, shaking his head.

"What do you mean?"

"They have to wait." Dominic's tone was ominous. "I mean, really, really wait."

"I don't understand."

"They have to wait for the real demon to come out. For him to manifest."

"What do you mean, the *real* demon?" I repeated. "You're telling me that snake wasn't it?"

"No." Dominic shook his head. "There's all this other stuff that demons do to try to throw the priest off during an exorcism. All the weird voices, the eye rolling, the laughing and jerking the body around. It can even appear as other things, like the snake we saw. They do all that to try to scare the priest off. But it's not real."

"You can't tell me that snake wasn't real. It was moving, Dominic! It was spitting at me with its tongue!"

"It wasn't. I mean, it was, but I'm telling you, it was just a mirage, a smoke screen. Demons are actually really stubborn about staying quiet. They hate being found out more than anything; their discovery is actually the first sign of defeat. If they could spend the rest of a human being's life hidden inside them, just to torment them, they would be ecstatic. It would be considered a win on their part, a complete taking over of a human soul."

A silent, thundering moment passed.

"I know the whole thing sounds surreal," he went on. "And trust me, if I hadn't already seen the things I've seen with my own eyes, if it wasn't happening to my own sister, inside my own home, I wouldn't believe it either."

"All right, so what happens?" I asked. "I mean, after the real demon manifests?"

"Well, then the actual battle begins. The priest has to try to get it to leave the person's body. They use all sorts of different prayers taken from a book called *The Rite*. There's prayers for luring the demon to speak, and prayers for getting it to leave the body. But leaving is the last thing the demon wants to do. So it will torment the priest and say all different kinds of things to get him to break." Dominic's knuckles turned white against the steering wheel. "The thing is, by that point, it's the actual demon doing all the talking. Which means that everything that is said is a lie."

"A lie?"

"Yeah." Dominic made a sharp right onto Greenbriar Lane. Two more miles and we would turn onto the paved road in front of his house. "It's the devil speaking, Marin. The devil is all about lies. I mean, one of his nicknames is the Prince of Lies. He'll say or do whatever he needs to say to get the exorcist to doubt himself and give up."

"Like about my mother," I said. "About my gift being evil."

"Yes," Dominic said. "Exactly. But the exorcist knows not to listen. He just keeps at it and at it, no matter what. Until it leaves again." He shifted in his seat, glancing in the rearview mirror. "It's not always as easy as that, of course. Some exorcisms can take weeks or even months. And some never work."

"So a demon can just stay in the person?" I asked. "Forever?"

"Or until the person goes insane. Or kills themselves. But that's the only thing the demon wanted in the first place."

I could not be sure if the wave of nausea that swept over me then was due to the sudden swerving of Dominic's car or the words that had just been spoken. Either way,

I clapped my hand over my mouth and brought my head down between my knees.

"Marin?" Dominic reached out and touched me on the back. "You okay?"

I didn't answer. A nameless fury was surging inside, an urgency that coursed through me like blood. Why were *we* doing all this? Where were the adults? Why weren't they taking over, assuming charge of things the way they were supposed to be doing? Or were we really the only ones with the answers? The only ones who knew, when all was said and done, what to do here?

"I really think that with Father William in the room," Dominic said, "and you believing in what you have, that we have a chance."

I sat back up, smoothed my palms over my cheeks.

"I told you the pain in my wrist is gone." He lifted his hand, twisted it from side to side as if to demonstrate. "That can't be an accident. Think of all the times you've held my hand, Marin. All the times I've held yours." He flushed. "I mean, it hasn't been a *lot*, but it's been enough, I guess."

He believed me.

He believed in me.

It couldn't be so hard for me to do the same, could it?

"Father William's going to be there?" I struggled to buckle my seat belt with my free hand, a ridiculous thing, since we were less than a half mile from his house, but it was the only thing I could think of to do, maybe even the last protective gesture I would make for myself. And yet maybe, if Father William was going to be present . . .

"Yeah. My mom called him this morning." Dominic leaned over, clicking the buckle into place for me. "I told them they had to, that there were no other options left. They were totally against it at first, but when I told them the whole story . . ." He looked at me, waiting.

"Tell me they laughed." My voice was fierce. Dangerous.

"No." He sounded awestruck, as if he still didn't believe it. "They didn't laugh at all."

I felt my shoulders loosen. "Do they believe she's possessed now?"

"I don't know what they believe. But they called Father William. It actually took a while to convince him to come. He kept saying he wasn't an exorcist, that there was no way he could do anything. But then my mother got on the phone. She was crying. She told him Cassie was dying, that at the very least, he could come be with her, even deliver last rites if he had to." He rubbed his cheek. "I guess it worked. He's on his way."

The priest was on his way.

And now so was I.

Mr. Jackson met Dominic and me at the top of the stairs, his relief palpable as he caught sight of my casted arm. "Oh, Marin. Thank God you're okay. I was going to drive to the house today . . ." He coughed, his fingers tightening over his mouth. "I'm so sorry. For all we've put you through."

The moment was interrupted by a loud crashing sound above. I yelped and then pressed my good hand over my mouth, staring wide-eyed at the ceiling. Small pieces of plaster fluttered down like dusty snowflakes, coating the green rug. Another crash, louder than the first. This time, a picture hanging in the foyer slid off the wall, the glass smashing into a thousand pieces. The sound of a scream ricocheted through the walls, and the banister winding its way along the staircase trembled.

"Come on." Dominic pulled me toward the stairs. Mr. Jackson's face twisted in anguish as we moved past him, but he did not say anything.

Dominic held my hand as we ascended the steps, and he did not drop it when we caught sight of Father William standing just outside the door. The priest limped over, his eyes sweeping over my cast. "You're all right?" he asked.

"Just a broken arm." I squeezed his hand. "You came."

"I don't . . ." His face was ashen. "I don't know what I can do."

"Have you seen her?"

He nodded. "She's in terrible shape."

"She's possessed," I said tightly. "Like I told you. You have to help her, Father. You have to."

"There's no way we can know if she's actually possessed, Marin." The priest searched my face. "I told you, that's up to a professional to determine."

"You don't have to believe us," I said. "Maybe it won't matter. Maybe just having you in there will help."

"I'm here to deliver last rites, Marin. I told you before, I'm not an exorcist."

"You can still help her, Father," I said, gripping his hands. "You can still try."

"Why aren't you listening to me?" An incredulous expression passed over his face. "It's not possible."

"Anything's possible," I said. My brain was moving a mile a minute. "Think about the doctors who told you you'd never walk again after you broke your neck. What would have happened if you'd listened to them?"

Father William gazed at me silently.

"You believed in yourself. You wanted to walk again. And you did, despite what everyone else around you was saying. I know you haven't been trained as an exorcist. But you're a Catholic priest, which is one of the strongest weapons we have right now in this house. You've got to believe that you can help."

"Marin." He took a step toward me, as if getting ready to shake me by the shoulders, but I warded him off, taking a step in the opposite direction.

"Just *try*!" I almost screamed. "Why can't you just go in and try? That girl in there is almost dead and you're going to stand here and argue about not having the right credentials? Please, Father! I'm telling you—"

"Did you bring the book, Father?" Dominic interrupted, putting a hand on my shoulder. "My mother said you were going to bring the prayer book you need to do an exorcism. Do you want me to get it for you? Do you have it here?"

"In the car," Father William said hoarsely. "Inside a black bag on the front seat."

"I'll be right back." Dominic raced toward the steps, bounding down them two at a time before disappearing through the front door.

Father William held my gaze for a long, silent moment, and for the first time, I could see the fear in his eyes. His lips were dry and cracked, and when he ran a tongue over them, the tip of it shook. I reached for his free hand and took it.

"I've only read about exorcism rituals," he whispered. "I've never actually done one. It might not work."

"I know. But we have to try."

"We?" He shifted his cane, leaning heavily against it. "You can't come in there with me, Marin."

"She has to be in there." Dominic burst out from the top of the stairs again, panting heavily. "Cassie knows Marin can see the demon inside her. She believes Marin can help it leave." He glanced at me. "And I think she can too."

If Father William understood that Dominic knew about my eyes, he gave no indication of it. "It could be dangerous," he said instead. "If the demon manifests . . ." His face paled a bit, as if the reality of the situation had finally dawned on him. He reached inside the black bag, pulled out a purple stole, and draped it around his neck, patting the ends in place against his chest. "You musn't listen to anything it says." His voice was different now, a man preparing for battle. "You know everything the devil or his minions say is a lie. Everything."

"I know."

"Stay behind me." Father William took a small booklet out of the bag Dominic had given him. The title on the cover read *The Rite*. "I'll be saying a lot of prayers from this book and moving around, holding a crucifix."

"Cassie needs to see her," Dominic argued. "Marin has to look at her or touch her."

"Fine." From inside the bag, the priest plucked a small plastic bottle of water with a picture of a crucifix on the front. "Just try to stay out of the way. I don't want to trip over you or worse, have you trip over me." He unscrewed the top of the bottle, flicking a few drops of the water on me and then against his own face. "Holy water," he said, recapping it once more.

"It helps?" Dominic asked.

"Everything blessed by God helps," Father William said. He looked at Dominic as if seeing him for the first time. "*You* haven't seen the demon, have you?"

"Me?" Dominic looked startled. "No. God, no."

"Fine." Father William nodded once. "Then you'll have to wait downstairs. We'll come get you when we're done."

"But I've—" Dominic protested.

"Absolutely not." The priest held up his hand. "Marin and me only. Or I don't go in."

Dominic and I exchanged a glance.

"It's okay," I said, taking his hand. "I'm in good company."

"I'll be right outside," he said, squeezing my fingers. "Right here. The whole time."

I nodded.

"Okay, then?" Father William asked.

I squared my shoulders and took off my sunglasses. "Yes."

It was time.

If Cassie's room was cold before, now it was achingly so, the frigid air knifelike inside my lungs as I drew a breath. I could feel the tiny hairs inside my nose freezing, and the tips of my fingers began to feel numb. But it was impossible to focus on my discomfort when I saw Cassie across the room. She was still tied to the mattress, still dressed in the same clothes, but everything else about the girl I had once known had vanished. Her neck was elongated and swollen, like something out of *E.T.* The skin on her face was stretched taut, a hide pulled over a board and scraped raw, and her eyes bulged from their sockets, as if something from the inside was pushing on them.

Even more terrifying was the blackness inside, which engulfed everything, from the top of her head to her feet. A low, wheezing sound drifted from her lips, like something was literally sucking the life out of her. Despite her physical agony, a horrifying sneer was plastered across her lips, and her tongue moved suggestively in and out of her mouth. Worst of all were the noises: grunts and groans that emerged from behind her gasping mouth, interspersed with odd cackles and hysterical laughter. It was no longer Cassie Jackson in that room. I knew the demon had taken over completely. It had manifested.

Father William approached the girl cautiously, limping, a rosary entwined in his right hand, a wooden crucifix in his left. He had left his cane by the door. "Hello, Cassie," he said.

"Cassie doesn't live here anymore," the demon hissed. "She's decided to . . . go elsewhere." She tittered hideously, as if letting us in on a horrifying secret.

"Where has she gone?" Father William's voice shook.

"Farther down." Cassie's lips curled back. "Where it's warmer."

Father William was already reciting a prayer of some kind, and he stood over Cassie, pressing one end of the purple stole against her forehead.

"In nomine Patris et Filii, et Spiritus Sancti."

In the name of the Father, and of the Son, and the Holy Spirit.

The exorcism had begun.

A litany of prayers poured from Father William's mouth as he read from the black book. He knelt next to Cassie, still pressing the ends of his purple stole against her forehead. His voice shook. *"God, creator and defender of the human race, look down on this your servant whom you formed in your own image and now call to be a partaker in your glory . . ."*

Cassie rolled and writhed under his touch, desperate to get away from the purple and white silk garments. Her body gyrated, first to the right, and then to the left. Tennis-ball-sized shapes appeared along the sides of her neck and then the tops of her arms with such speed that it looked as though the entire length of skin might split beneath them. Suddenly, her screams turned to pitiful cries, a horrible, mournful noise that leaked out of her. "It burns!" she wailed. "Please. Take it off! You're hurting me!"

Father William removed the stole from her forehead and placed it against the right side of Cassie's neck, directly over one of the horrible shapes. Beads of sweat appeared along his hairline, and his eyes were as wide as bottle caps. *"Hear, Holy Father, the groaning of your supplicant Church: do not suffer your daughter to be possessed by the father of lies. . . ."*

He spoke with effort, and I could hear the strain in his voice, the thick pull of fear from somewhere deep inside. For some reason, the red shapes glowering at the base of his spine seemed to be getting larger by the minute. Taking a step forward, he shook holy water onto Cassie's feet and then her face, reciting a prayer to Saint Michael.

"Nooooooo!" the demon screamed. "Stop it! Stop it!" Cassie threw her head back and arched her spine. Her toes were rigid. "The one you pray to is not with you!" she hissed in a strangely metallic-sounding voice. "No one is with you, Priest. You are alone. Deserted."

Father William stiffened at the demon's words. His whispered prayers got louder as he continued to recite the rosary, but his words shook audibly.

"Father!" I said, trying to make myself heard over the demon's words. "Don't listen!"

He nodded blindly, his lips still moving over the silent words of his prayers. He turned back to Cassie, squaring his shoulders as if to brace himself. The red orbs inside his back were twice the size they had previously been, and the back of his shirt was damp with perspiration. He held the crucifix over her upturned face and bellowed out a plea:

"Hear God, lover of human salvation, the prayer of your apostles Peter and William and of all the saints, who by your face emerged as victors over the Evil one: free this, your servant, from every foreign power and keep her safe. . . ."

"Shut up!" the throated voice inside Cassie commanded. "Your words are useless! You are completely powerless over me! There is nothing you can do! *Nothing!*"

Father William reached out with his right hand and pressed it against the middle of Cassie's chest. He was fumbling, stammering, trying to get more words out, glancing at the book and then back at the girl. The lifted crucifix made a strange shadow along the shredded skin of her face, and the swollen shapes along her neck were ringed with pink marks. Suddenly, she jerked her head out from under the priest's hand and then turned, clutching at her throat, moving toward him, her mouth opening and then closing like a gutted fish. A new voice emerged from her mouth, childlike, desperate. "Oh, Booey! Booey!"

Father William's face paled as Cassie clawed at the knees of his pants, burying her face against his legs. "Booey, help me! I can't breathe! Please, Booey!"

Father William took a step back, his mouth ajar, the rosary in his hand forgotten. He looked stunned. Lost.

"Don't listen to it!" I grabbed Father William by the wrist.

But it was clear that he could not hear or see anything except the innocent voice coming out of Cassie. "Booey, please!"

He fell to his knees, a bone cracking beneath the skin, his face gray. "Boooooooey!" the demon wailed again in the child's voice. "I can't breathe! Booey, help me! It's so dark! Please!"

Father William staggered to his feet.

And then he turned and stumbled from the room.

I followed, the sound of the vile cackling behind me as I slammed the door. Dominic was on the floor, knocked down by Father William's abrupt exit, and he leapt to his feet as he saw me, reaching for me with both arms.

"What happened?" he asked, clutching at me.

"I don't know." I twisted out of his hold, moving toward the priest, who was at the other end of the hall, both hands covering his face.

"Father." I stayed a few feet behind, not wanting to frighten him. "What's wrong?"

He sank to the floor at the question, as if it had undone him, one hand still covering his face.

I slid down next to him, inches away. "Is it because of Booey?"

His head lurched up so quickly that I reared back. I stared at the sorrow swimming there in his eyes, the absence of hope.

I knew that look.

I did.

"Who's Booey?" I asked.

He set his jaw with deliberation, even as the tears streamed down his face. "I'm Booey," he said. "Booey was my nickname growing up, the only way my little brother could pronounce Billy. That day in the pool, when he was calling for me . . ." He broke off, his eyes searching something in the distance. "The demon knew. It knew."

"Knew what?" My voice was quivering.

"That I pushed him." The priest's voice surged with fury. "That I let myself get so overcome at his little annoyances, his bugging me all the time, that I pushed him in."

"But then you dove in," I protested. "You told me you went in and got him. You saved him."

"Not without hesitating first." The sadness in the priest's eyes was liquid-heavy, the crest of an impending tidal wave. "Not without letting him flounder for a few seconds. He called for me, and I turned my back. I let him suffer." He buried his face in his hands. "I let him suffer, alone in that water. I let him drown."

"But then you turned around again." I grabbed the priest's hand. "You turned around, and you dove in and pulled him out."

He shook his head, not hearing me, a million miles away. "And I broke my neck. I was unconscious. It was too late."

I thought about what I had admitted to Dad about leaving Mom, about not caring anymore. It was the same thing that Father William had done, the same walking away, turning his back, even just for a moment.

And yet.

A ferocity filled me then, and I squared my shoulders under the weight of it, lifted my chin. "Father, please. We make mistakes. And that's all. It doesn't mean we're evil. It just means we're human."

He shook his head as I talked, resigned to his defeat.

"We're still good people, Father." I grabbed his shoulder, shaking it hard. "We are. But you have to believe it. You have to let the rest of that stuff go and make the decision to believe that you're still good." I rubbed my fingers over his gnarled knuckles. "You told me the other day at the hospital that you made the decision to do your rehab like you'd never done anything before. With a real commitment, remember? You said you had things to do. Places to see." I was crying now, talking for both of us. "That's still true. You still have things to do, places to see. But you won't be able to do them unless you make the choice again to believe in yourself. To believe in your own goodness. Because I'm pretty sure after all this time, that that's what God is. The goodness in us. That's his gift to us. Our blessing."

He lifted his head, tried to fix his gaze upon my face. He seemed to be trembling under the weight of my words, steadying himself with one hand against the wall.

"I don't know if I can go back in there again," he whispered. "I don't know if I have it in me."

"You do have it in you." I stood up, pulling him to his feet. "I can see it. Let's go in there together. You can lean on me when it gets too hard, and I'll do the same."

He hesitated, deliberating my words.

And then he nodded, once, and pulled himself back up.

The priest took his place next to the bed again, the sweat wiped from his brow, the purple stole around his shoulders, the rosary entwined in his right hand. Just as before, he gripped the crucifix in his left hand, holding it now like a sword. A rip stood out in the knee of his pants, and his shirt hung loose and untucked over his belt, but his voice sounded different. Stronger.

"I command you, vile spirit, in the name of Jesus Christ, to leave this daughter of God and go back from whence you came!"

Cassie lolled her head to one side, cackling insidiously. "But I *like* it here!" The demon's voice was a mocking falsetto. "It's so warm! And she smells so sweet!" The voice changed again, deepening into a throated growl. "You will never make me leave. She's mine now! All mine! And I will live in her forever!"

Father William wiped the sweat from his brow and readjusted his hold on the crucifix. He looked startled as I knelt down next to him, but when he turned back to Cassie, his voice was louder. He addressed her again, the determination behind it unmistakable, a new vigor in his tone.

"I cast you out, unclean spirit, along with every satanic power of the enemy, every specter from hell, and all your fell companions; in the name of our Lord Jesus Christ."

At the words, Cassie arched her back and shrieked. I reached out with my good hand and held on to Father William's belt loop as he continued to chant the prayers from *The Rite.*

Cassie's fists clenched under the words. She shouted obscenities over the litany, and the pupils in her eyes disappeared once more. A groan sounded again, a deep, guttural sound, like metal tearing from the inside out. Her head tossed from side to side. She made a sudden jerking movement with her arms. Her biceps bulged, and a vein in her forehead strained as the ropes around her wrists loosened and then split.

Before I could tell what happened, Cassie leapt from the mattress, knocking Father William to the floor. He landed with a sickening thud, crying out in pain as the crucifix fell and skittered to one side. The force of the blow knocked me in the other direction, opposite the priest. My casted arm made a dull knocking sound against the floor as it hit, and I curled it up against me, struggling back to my feet. Before I could blink, Cassie had ripped the rosary out of Father William's other hand and roped it around his neck. Foam curled and spit from the corners of her mouth, and her tongue flicked in and out as she yanked tight along his throat and pulled. "You're nothing, Priest! She's mine now! *Mine!*"

Father William's arms flailed. His lips began to turn blue, and I could see the crystal edges of the rosary cutting into his neck. I lunged for Cassie, grabbing her around the waist with one hand. But my injured arm made the movement a futile one, and Cassie didn't budge. She moved up farther along Father William's neck instead, tightening the rosary even more, her neck bulging with exertion. Father William's eyes protruded from their sockets; his hands clawed the floor.

"Dominic!" I screamed. "Dominic!"

He burst in all at once and rushed over to the priest, struggling to dislodge his sister's grip on him. But it was as if Cassie had turned to stone. Dominic pulled and strained, to no avail. Father William was making wild gasping noises, his legs banging like heavy logs on the floor. I could see a trickle of blood leaking out from beneath one side of the rosary, and his Adam's apple stuck out of the middle of his neck like a walnut.

"It's me you want!" The words came out of my mouth before I had a chance to think about them. "It's *me* you want!" I said, louder this time. "Not him. Me!"

Even from behind, I could see the muscles loosen in Cassie's arms. With a whip of her head, she glared at me over her shoulder. Beneath her, Father William still thrashed, desperate for air. I did not move, did not even blink. The repugnant grin reappeared on Cassie's face, a thin widening of the lips that stretched from ear to ear. A throaty giggle came out of her mouth as she let go of the rosary and slid in my direction.

Father William inhaled once, hoarsely, as if coming up from the depths of the ocean. Dominic rushed toward him, cradling his head in both hands.

I took a step back as Cassie crawled toward me on all fours. Her hair—what was left of it—stuck to the sides of her bloodied face, and her nails made a scraping sound against the floor. This demon was going to try to kill me right here, right now. I backed up into the corner. One step. And then another. Cassie matched my movements, right down to the pauses in between them. There was nowhere for me to go. I was trapped.

A voice sounded behind her then, so strong, so forceful that I screamed, not recognizing it, unsure of where it was even coming from.

"I adjure you, ancient serpent, by the judge of the living and the dead, by your Creator, by the Creator of the whole universe, by Him who has the power to consign you to hell, to depart forthwith in fear, along with your savage minions, from this servant of God!"

It was Father William, up on his feet again, holding *The*

Rite in one shaky hand, the crucifix in the other. Cassie stopped crawling, regarding him with a mixture of contempt and amusement, but Father William did not move, except to raise the crucifix in his left hand. He looked back down at the black book and began again. His face was set like stone, the words pouring from his mouth in a torrent.

Cassie shrank back at the holy words, regarding the priest with wary eyes. Inside, the black snake slipped effortlessly through her arms, her chest cavity, down among her bowels, flicking its pink tongue, silent as silk.

"It is the power of *Christ* that compels you!" Father William said.

Cassie brought her hands up to her ears and screamed. Her fingertips had begun to turn blue again and the skin around her lips was a deep violet color.

"The power of *Christ*!" he roared.

"No!" Cassie backed up into the corner behind the mattress, cowering and whimpering.

Father William stepped toward her. His breath came out of his mouth in tiny white bursts, and he walked without the aid of his cane. *"It is God Himself who commands you, the majestic Christ who commands you!"*

"Stop!" Cassie curled up inside herself, hiding her face between her knees, clutching at her ankles. "I beg you, stop!"

"God the Father commands you; God the Son commands you; God the Holy Spirit commands you. The mystery of the Cross commands you."

With every mention of God, Cassie's body recoiled, as

if a whip were striking her skin. She thrashed and flailed, screamed and pleaded, her voice growing weaker and weaker. "No more! No more! Stop! Please!"

The snake slithered and recoiled, once and then again. It was working. Somehow, somewhere, Father William had found the strength not only to confront the demon, but also to expel it. He believed again. He did.

"The faith of the holy apostles Peter and Paul and of all the saints commands you. The blood of the martyrs commands you. The continence of the confessors commands you. The saving mysteries of our Christian faith commands you!"

Cassie had stopped flailing. She lifted her head from between her knees and let her legs settle indolently in front of her. Another eerie giggle came out of her mouth, softly at first, and then getting louder, until it became a hideous-sounding scoff. *"Gotcha!"* She laughed again, a raucous, evil noise that came from deep inside her chest. "Made you think you had it in you, Father, didn't I?"

Father William took a step back, scanned the book again, frantic. *"Depart then, transgressor!"* His voice trembled around the edges. *"Depart, seducer, full of lies and cunning, foe of virtue, persecutor of the innocent."*

I could hear the fear again, thick as syrup, as he continued to struggle. I moved closer to him, stretching out my good hand and resting it firmly on the priest's shoulder. He glanced at me, his eyes full of terror, and then nodded. His jaw seemed to clench itself, and the skin along his forehead was slick with sweat.

Cassie seemed to pause at this show of unanimity. She raised her legs again and shrank back into the wall, as if caged, her eyes gleaming with suspicion. I took another step forward. Cassie's hooded eyes followed me. I took another one, moving in front of the girl. What was I doing? I didn't know. But it was time. I had to try.

Behind me, the priest continued his litany. Cassie was no longer concerned with him. She stared at me instead, the hate seeping in and around the bones behind her eyes. "You faithless bitch!" she hissed. "Don't you look at me!"

I moved in closer.

"Look past the evil!" Father William's voice rang out behind me. "Look for the good, Marin. Look for God!"

And right then, I understood.

Here, now, was the time to choose the good.

To *see* the good. Despite the horror and the blackness, despite everything else that insisted otherwise.

Stepping forward, I threw my arms around the girl, holding her with both arms, the good and the bad one, and clutched her to me. Her skin was like ice, the tips of her fingers black again. Cassie gasped for breath, writhing under my touch. I gripped harder, pressing her against my chest, burying my face against her horrible, icy form. A strange, rotting smell drifted from her pores, and a wheezing sound came out of her mouth. Every cell in her body, every bone, muscle, vein, every inch of her was suffocating, dying.

My body started to shake as Cassie arched away from me and began to scream, a hoarse sound, devoid of air.

I held on tighter.

I believe you are bigger than the evil I see.

I believe you are good.

I do. I believe.

Behind me, the priest's words got louder as he recited more prayers, the volume turned up, a torrential litany of salvation and deliverance. *"I adjure you, profligate dragon, in the name of the spotless Lamb, who has trodden down the asp and the basilisk, and overcome the lion and the dragon, to depart from this child, to depart from the Church of God!"*

I believe that what is inside me is stronger than you.

I retreated slightly as Cassie grew limp under my hold. Oh my God. Was she dead? I stared as her head fell back between her shoulders and a pinhole of light appeared right in the center of the bowl of blackness inside her skull. It was so small that I almost missed it—until in the next second it expanded a fraction of an inch more. It swelled and then faded a third time as the priest intoned his prayers: *"Tremble now, serpent, and flee!"*

I kept my eyes fastened on it and held Cassie tighter.

You are in there. You are.

I can see. I can touch. I can heal.

"Be gone to hell, from whence you came!"

I know who I am.

Cassie contorted once, twice, her muscles relinquishing all their strength as she slipped out of my hold. We fell to the floor in a single, jarring movement. I righted myself quickly, but Cassie's limbs twitched spastically, her legs and arms jerking with such violence that I screamed, sure the girl's body was going to split in half, terrified that the real end was near. And then, with a final, howling shriek, Cassie clasped both sides of her face with her hands and lay still.

No one moved. I was not sure if anyone in the room was even breathing. Cassie remained motionless, her arms ribboned with blood, one of them flung over the top of her head, her chest rising and falling in violent tandem. Another pungent smell, something like vomit and excrement, filled the room, but the cold began to dissipate, the iciness leaking out like a stream in the wall.

"What—" Dominic whispered.

But Father William only raised his hand, signaling him to wait.

After an interminable amount of time, Cassie opened her eyes. With difficulty, she raised her face and stared out at us. The horrifying mask had left; her eyes were back to their usual roundness. The skin along her arms and face was still raw, but there were no more bulging shapes pocking it, no more tightness along the bones. She opened her mouth to speak, but nothing came out.

"Cassie?" Father William whispered.

She blinked. "Why am I on the floor?" Her voice was soft. A stranger in her own body. "What happened?"

Father William rushed over to a satchel in the corner and took something out. When he returned, he was holding a round, silver object. It looked like an old-fashioned stopwatch, complete with a link chain. He pressed a tiny button on one side, and the top sprang open. "Cassie," he said. "Kneel and receive the Body of Christ."

It had to be a test of sorts, what he was doing. If the demon was still inside her, Cassie would not be able to receive Holy Communion, would not perhaps even be able to continue being in the same room as the Host. But the demon had fooled us before, just moments earlier. What if this was the same kind of thing? I pressed my fingers to my lips and waited, holding my breath.

Father William got down next to the girl and helped raise her to a kneeling position. She looked confused and uncertain, glancing around the room fearfully, as if she were on some strange planet. I stared, straining until my eyes smarted, but I could glimpse nothing of the previous blackness anywhere inside her. There was the purple glob along her tongue, exactly where it had been before, and the small red cuts along her arms. The cut on her cheek glowed a soft rose color under her skin, but that was all. Nothing else. Nothing black.

"The body of Christ," Father William said. He held up the tiny white wafer in front of Cassie, and paused as she regarded it with both eyes.

She opened her mouth and closed her eyes as Father William placed the Host on her tongue. And when she swallowed, the small group of us closed around her, our arms fencing her in, and let her weep.

Twenty-Five

Every once in a while, I let myself go back and think about all of it again. Sometimes it doesn't feel real, as if it was just one long, terrible dream; other times, I have to fight to keep breathing as the pictures come flooding back. Afterward, as the memories subside, I get the distinct feeling of having been snatched back from the lip of hell, of someone pulling me back just as I was about to fall.

And sometimes, I think I know exactly who that someone was.

My eyes have stayed the same. I still see the shapes and colors of pain inside people, and maybe I always will. A new therapist I've been seeing, a middle-aged lady named

Cindy, who actually believes that I can see pain, seems to think it might have developed as a kind of reaction to Mom's suicide. She says there's proof that things like that have actually happened to people. Apparently some kind of sixth sense develops after certain kinds of trauma, the brain's way of trying to make sense out of incomprehensible situations. And she says that it might even go away, a little at a time, as I keep learning how to deal with Mom's suicide and how to move forward.

Sometimes I wonder if and when that time will come. I still think about Mom. A lot. I hope she's not too disappointed in me that I never got to see her pain, or that if I had, I probably wouldn't have known what to do with it. I hope she forgives me. I hope she knows that I've forgiven her, even though she didn't say goodbye. Dad and Cindy have told me at least a hundred times over that things weren't my fault, but I still feel guilty. I can't help it. She was my mother. And I failed her. Little by little, though, I'm starting to come to terms with that, which is what Cindy says I have to do, even though I'm not too sure what that even means. I guess in the long run, I just hope I can learn to let it go. Because holding on to it—especially for this long—hurts too much.

Sometimes I let myself imagine that it was Mom who extended my blessing to me somehow, a kind of final communication between us that we missed doing while she was alive. Not the way the demon suggested, of course, but the opposite, born out of a love so strong that when I looked hard enough, I could see it.

Feel it.

And for right now at least, that's a part I know I never want to let go of.

Twenty-Six

A few weeks later, I rode my bike to Lucy's house to help her get ready for prom. We were in her room; Lucy was giddy with excitement. She whirled around the perimeter of the bed in a pink dress that looked like a cupcake with sprinkles, a sweet, powdery scent drifting out from her hair. She had on heels, in which she did not navigate very well, and her hair had been professionally done that morning, complete with baby's breath and miniature pink roses.

"How late do you think you'll be out?" I was sprawled across the bed in jeans and a T-shirt, eating spoonfuls of peanut butter cookie batter right out of the bowl.

"I don't know." Lucy leaned into the mirror for the hundredth time, adjusting a loose sprig of baby's breath above her ear. "My mom says I have to be home by eleven, but everyone's going to Lizzie Sweitzer's house to watch movies after, and then to Ted's Diner for breakfast, so I don't think that's going to happen." She turned around, squeezing her hands together. The yellow dot in her stomach was almost completely gone, the red blob in her mouth healed after a trip to the dentist. "You know this is absolutely the first and last prom I'm going to without you, don't you?"

"What are you talking about?"

"Oh, Marin, come on! I know you said it was too late this year, but now you don't have an excuse. You're coming next year, and that's the end of it."

"Lucy, no one even considered *asking* me to prom this year. What makes you think it's going to change next year?" There was Dominic, of course, but I hadn't seen or heard from him in weeks, not since that last day with Cassie and Father William. There had been a single text that night, a "How are you?" to which I'd answered "Okay," and then nothing.

Nothing at all.

"Because you're different now." She turned back to the mirror, unperturbed. "Better different, I mean. You lost the sunglasses, for one thing. And you look at people now. You hold your head up. People won't be so afraid to approach you." She winked. "It'll happen. You'll see."

I rolled my eyes, scooping out another blob of cookie dough with my finger. It was true about the glasses; I'd stopped wearing them for the most part after Cassie's ordeal, since nothing I saw anymore could come close to what I'd seen during those days. I kept them in my purse, at the ready in case of really big crowds, like school assemblies and going to the mall. Places like that were still overwhelming, requiring some kind of barrier. Without my sunglasses, though, I was even plainer-looking with my boyishly short hair and forgettable features. Lucy might have had big plans, but I wasn't holding my breath.

The doorbell rang. Lucy's hands froze above her hair. "He's here? *Already?* It's only five-thirty. I told him not to come until six!"

As if on cue, Mrs. Cooper knocked on the bedroom door.

"Don't come in!" Lucy yelped. "I'm not ready!"

"Oh, come on!" Mrs. Cooper said on the other side of the door. "I'm dying to see how gorgeous you look! Plus, your date has the most unbelievably beautiful flowers I've ever seen. I'm totally jealous."

Lucy rolled her eyes and stood up. "I'm almost ready. Tell him I'll be right there!"

"Don't keep me waiting!" Mrs. Cooper's voice bubbled down the hall. "I'm getting the camera!"

"Okay." Lucy turned to face me and squared her shoulders. "Final once-over. How do I look?"

I got up off the bed and stood in front of her. "You look beautiful," I said, arranging a wayward curl along her shoulder. "Really. Like a princess."

Lucy flushed, and then pressed my hand. "Thanks," she whispered.

I followed her out of her room and down the hall, wincing at the loud clacking sound her high heels made against the hardwood floors. She looked a little like a stork, lifting her knees too high so as not to fall over, but I didn't say anything.

Tomorrow night, Dad and I were going to get some new tulip bulbs from Lowe's, maybe a handful of iris ones, too, and plant them in the garden, but I wasn't sure how I was going to spend the rest of tonight. It was Saturday, though. Maybe Nan would want to go to the movies.

Lucy stopped walking so suddenly at the bottom of the stairs that I bumped into her, almost knocking her off her feet.

"Dominic?" she asked.

She said the name so quietly I almost missed it, until I looked up and saw him standing there in the doorway. He was dressed in khaki shorts and a green button-down shirt. His hair had been brushed and parted, his skin scrubbed pink. In his arms was a beautiful bouquet of flowers, peonies and roses, hydrangea and clematis, little purple budded ones and the pink kind, too, the stems wrapped tightly with silk ribbon. But I only had eyes for the iris, a single white one in the middle, like a moon.

I took a step around Lucy and swallowed, as if that might dislodge the ball blocking the words inside my throat. It didn't work.

"Hey, Marin." His voice was soft. "Your dad told me you were here. I hope you don't mind."

I shook my head, blinking. He had to be here to talk some more about Cassie. Maybe thank me again, although he would have to be stupid not to think that the hundred and two times he'd done it that night hadn't sufficed. But then, maybe that was what the flowers were for. To thank me. Again. In a different way. His sister was better; his family was back to stay. Yes, that was it. Flowers. To thank me.

"I was . . . wondering if you would go to the prom with me," he said. "Not at the school or anything. It's too late for all that. There's a place in the park, though . . . under the willow trees. Next to the tennis courts? You know, where we were supposed to go that day and never ended up. We could sit and talk, just chill. Maybe have our own prom there. Sort of." He looked embarrassed, mortified even, as if this might have been a good idea when he first thought of it, but now, said aloud, it sounded like the stupidest thing in the world. He coughed. "Um . . . anyway, it was just an idea. It was—"

"I'd love to." I stepped forward so as not to lose my nerve. "It sounds perfect."

Lucy squeezed my arm and I stopped, remembering. Her date hadn't arrived yet, and there were supposed to be pictures, ones that Lucy wanted me in too. I'd planned to wave as she left in the stretch limo, watch as the black corner of it disappeared around the block, text her throughout the night to see how things were going. "Have the best time," she said, throwing her arms around me.

I squeezed my friend with both arms. "You too."

"Call me tomorrow!" Lucy said as I stepped out onto the porch. "We'll compare notes!"

I smiled as the door shut behind us, staring at the flowers as we made our way down the sidewalk.

"You like them?" Dominic asked.

"I do," I said. "They're beautiful."

"I didn't know what kind to get. There's so many different types out there. I was a little nervous."

I smiled. "They're perfect. Really."

"I'm so sorry I haven't called or texted." He slid his fingers around mine, coughed a little. "It kind of took me a while to"—he shook his head, scrambling for the right words—"process everything, I guess. Longer than I thought it would."

I nodded. I understood. I was still processing it.

"How are you?" he asked. "I mean, really."

"I'm all right." His skin was warm; his fingers held mine along the curve of his palm, but not so loose they would slip. "What about you?"

"Okay." He nodded, as if thinking. "I slept through the night last night. First time in a while. All the way through, without any nightmares."

I nodded. It had taken more of a toll on him than I'd let myself realize.

"Cassie's doing better too. It took some time, but she's really coming around."

"I'm so glad."

He squeezed my hand. "We're going on a family vacation. All of us. This summer."

"Really?" I smiled. "That's great."

"It is sort of great." He gripped my hand, stopped walking. "I'm sorry again I didn't call, Marin. Please don't think it's because I wasn't thinking of you, because I thought of you every single minute that I wasn't thinking of . . . of everything else. The truth is, I was afraid that if I saw you again before I had a chance to get over everything, I'd never be able to stop associating you with that night." He paused, rubbing his thumb over the edge of my hand. "And then I realized that I didn't ever want to stop associating you with that night. That because of it, you gave me my sister back."

My heart swelled, looking up at him. He seemed older somehow, a different look behind his eyes. I wondered if I did too.

"I've missed you so much, Marin."

"Me too."

He dropped my hand and brought his fingers up alongside my face. "Do you know how long I've wanted to kiss you?"

"How long?"

He smiled, brushing his lips against my forehead. "Guess."

"As long as I've wanted to kiss you?"

His mouth moved down, hovering against my cheek. "Probably longer."

Our noses bumped. "I doubt it."

It's like magic, I thought as his lips closed over mine.

But better.

Acknowledgments

First thanks goes to my agent Jessica Regel, who encourages me to write whatever moves me next, and then pushes me to finish it. I couldn't do it without you. Thank you also to the luminous Jennifer Arena at Random House, who read the original manuscript at its roughest and still somehow saw the potential. This story could not have been shaped into its final form without the brilliant advice of Laura Biagi. You're amazing. Thanks, too, to Chelsea Eberly, who helped me fine-tune the final drafts and breathe new life into some of the more intricate strands of the manuscript, as well as the entire staff at Random House who helped bring my book to the shelves. You guys are so good at what you do, and I am grateful to be a part of it.

None of my books get written without the necessary time to write them. As a mother and teacher, this kind of time can be especially difficult to find and navigate. Thank you to all the people who altered their own schedules so that I could do exactly this, including the ones who cheered me on from the sidelines, especially Paul Galante, Sarah Galante, Sophia Galante, Joseph Galante, Gina Marsicano, Roland Merullo, Kemi McShane, Conor Tougher, Chelsea Martelle, Nancy Sanderson, Herbert Plummer, Terry Plummer, and Judy Plummer.

Family, all.

I am blessed to know each and every one of you.

About the Author

CECILIA GALANTE is the author of several young adult and middle-grade books, although *Be Not Afraid* is her first YA horror novel. A graduate of Goddard College, she is an English teacher and lives with her husband and children in Pennsylvania. Visit her online at ceciliagalante.com.